"Why don't I tuck you to bed?"

N...

refused to let it show...

him wanted to gauge her reaction, to know now she'd respond to his question. He'd been drawn to her from the beginning, and that connection urged him to test the waters.

"Bed is good," she said, without giving away whether or not she'd thought anything more of his question than an innocent query.

Nathan walked her to her bed and peeled away the blankets. She looked at the bed and then to him, the sleep gone from her eyes. Her eyes flicked with fiery provocation and heat tore through him.

"Where will you sleep tonight?" Autumn asked, taking another step and closing the distance between them.

An invitation? Was he imagining the flash in her eyes? Did she want his honest answer? "Here. With you." A bold statement.

A long, heated moment passed between them. She looked from him to the bed, to the couch, and back to him.

She grabbed his shirt and pulled him to her, fusing her mouth...

CAPTURING THE HUNTSMAN

BY
C.J. MILLER

Published in Great Britain 2015
by Mills & Boon, an imprint of Harlequin (UK) Limited,
Eton House, 18-24 Paradise Road, Richmond, Surrey, TW9 1SR

© 2015 C.J. Miller

ISBN: 978-0-263-91538-9

18-0515

Harlequin (UK) Limited's policy is to use papers that are natural, renewable and recyclable products and made from wood grown in sustainable forests. The logging and manufacturing processes conform to the legal environmental regulations of the country of origin.

Printed and bound in Spain
by CPI, Barcelona

C.J. Miller loves to hear from her readers and can be contacted through her website, www.cj-miller.com. She lives in Maryland with her husband, son and daughter. C.J. believes in first loves, second chances and happily-ever-after.

To my brother Brian. Always prepared, whether with a quick quip or a plan of action to save the day. The level head to my over-emotion and the rock when I'm floundering. Love you, Bri.

Chapter 1

Clearing leaves from the paths around the Trail's Edge campground leading to the Appalachian Trail was a full-time job. As luck and financial misfortune had it, Autumn Reed had plenty of free time. She hadn't rented a cabin in weeks, not since the news broke that a serial killer was stalking female hikers on the trail. She fit the general description of his victims, which made it that much more disturbing.

She'd procrastinated starting the task all day and with the sun setting low and casting shadows, she wished she had come out earlier. The trail after dusk was pitch-black, and she knew better than to be alone on the trail after dark.

Autumn called to her dog, Thor, feeling better with him at her side. He outweighed her by twenty pounds and his build was enough to intimidate anyone who had the idea she would make a good victim. He was the one constant in her life. She could always count on Thor.

Thor looked back at her from thirty feet ahead, but he didn't heel. The wind blew, rustling dry leaves in a symphony she usually found pleasant, but now she feared would mask footsteps. She turned in a circle, looking around her. She and Thor were alone.

She called to Thor again. It wasn't like him to disobey, but if he had caught sight of a squirrel or rabbit, he might be thinking about giving chase.

"Thor, heel." She spoke sharply to make sure he knew she wasn't playing around.

Thor ignored her. His attention was focused on the woods, his back arched and his legs locked. The hair on the back of her neck stood on end. What had Thor seen? Was it a hiker? The trail had been empty for weeks. Maybe it was a bear. Though it was rare for them to wander this far down the mountain, a bear would pose more danger to Thor than he'd realize. One swipe of a bear claw would send Thor sprawling.

She called to her dog again, her feet sliding in the mud as she jogged toward him, scanning the tree line for a bear. "What's gotten into you?" She reached his side and heard a low growl in his throat. Despite his size, Thor wasn't an aggressive dog. What was wrong?

She followed his line of vision into the woods, peering through the gray and brown tree trunks, wondering what had Thor so riled.

The view hit Autumn hard, knocking the wind from her lungs. Suspended from a hickory tree and swinging slightly in the wind was a figure wrapped in ivy vines. Were those dirty hiking boots? Were those wooden arrows? Why did it smell like charred wood? The scent was heavy in the air.

Horror washed over her and she gasped in air, doubling over and emptying the contents of her stomach on the ground in front of her.

As quickly as horror had struck, so did fear. Grabbing Thor's collar, she dragged him toward her cabin. She stumbled, the heel of her boot once again getting caught in the mud. Scrambling to her feet, she didn't let go of Thor's collar. She needed to call for help, but she needed to be somewhere safe.

Entering her log cabin and bolting the door shut behind her, she reached for the satellite phone on the counter. She dialed 9-1-1 with shaking fingers.

Calming the fear that pulled her vocal cords tight, she managed to choke out a few words. "I need help. I just found a dead body."

Nathan Bradshaw caught the call from his police scanner. A body had been found near the Appalachian Trail at a campground called the Trail's Edge. A woman had called it in to police. A witness? Besides not having an arsenal of resources at his fingertips, the lack of a witness had been one of the most difficult parts of the case. No one had lived to provide a description of the serial killer stalking the trail, and if anyone had seen anything, the person wasn't coming forward with information.

A quick internet search revealed the address of the Trail's Edge campground, and Nathan plugged

the location in to his GPS. The body wasn't as close
to the trail as the other victims, most of whom had
been found in the backcountry, farther away from
civilization. A break in the killer's pattern or an un-
related murder?

The only way to find out was to be on the scene.

Nathan had been tracking the Huntsman for weeks,
from Boling Springs, Pennsylvania, to Smithsburg,
Maryland. The killer was consistent, which made it
more infuriating that no one had caught him. Nathan
was growing better at predicting his movements, and
it was a matter of time before he got inside the killer's
head and caught him.

Nathan needed to find justice for his sister. His
mother, his former brother-in-law, his niece and his
nephew were counting on him to catch Colleen's
killer.

Nathan arrived on the scene in thirty minutes amid
a flurry of activity. FBI agents were combing the area,
shouting commands at the park rangers who'd been
called to assist. The local police were on the scene,
as well. Nathan scanned for a familiar face, irritation
flickering when he spotted special agent-in-charge
Roger Ford talking to a tall, slender woman. Nothing about her said law enforcement or park ranger.
She had to be the witness.

Roger Ford, Nathan's former brother-in-law and
the current lead investigator on the case, wanted nothing more than for Nathan to disappear. Ford was a
good agent, but he was by the book. By the book
wouldn't catch the killer. But Nathan had no bounds
to what he was willing to do.

Ford had ten years more than Nathan on the job and he was using his considerable weight and connections to shut Nathan out. Punishment for what had happened between Nathan and Ford's sister, or maybe Ford didn't believe Nathan could be objective, but either way, Nathan had made a promise and he wasn't backing down.

Nathan knew the exact moment Ford spotted him. Their eyes connected across the distance, hostility plain on Ford's face. Nathan gave Ford credit for blatant honesty. They'd never gotten along and Ford hadn't pretended otherwise. The woman Ford was speaking with turned, as well, looking over her shoulder in Nathan's direction.

Nathan hadn't seen her before, but his gut reaction was strong and swift. Even at this distance, he could see she was beautiful. She was nearly as tall as Ford, her body lithe, her brown hair pulled into a ponytail and her arms crossed over her chest. She wore khaki pants and a blue-and-gray windbreaker, a style he had seen on several hikers he had spoken with during the course of the investigation.

Approaching Ford was a bad idea, but Nathan needed to speak to the witness. More than finding out what she knew, he wanted to talk to her. The impulse was so strong, he hadn't realized he'd left his observation spot until he was standing next to her, facing Ford. She smelled of the outdoors, like fresh pine and earth.

"What are you doing here? I told you to stay away from my crime scenes," Ford said, annoyance clear in his voice. "You're worse than the press."

"You know why I'm here," Nathan said. When the FBI had refused to assign Nathan to the case, citing he couldn't be objective because he was too close to one of the victims, Nathan had taken a leave of absence from the Bureau to investigate on his own time. The killer had proved to be smart and had avoided the FBI's traps. If they wanted the killer in custody, they'd need to work outside the box. The red tape of the FBI didn't allow anything outside the box.

Nathan introduced himself. "Special Agent Nathan Bradshaw."

"Stop misleading the witness. You're not working this case," Ford said.

Curiosity gleamed in the brunette's eyes. She ignored Ford and extended her hand. "Autumn Reed. This is my campground. I am the person who found the body." Her voice quavered and he shook her hand. It was trembling.

Ford gritted his teeth. "Why don't you either enjoy your vacation or go back to work on another case instead of impeding my work on this one?"

Abandoning this case wasn't an option for him. Colleen's killer deserved to pay, and Nathan would see that she and his family had justice. "You know I can't walk away from this one."

Ford's face didn't relax even a fraction of an inch. He believed it was most important to follow protocol, and Nathan on the scene flew in the face of the rules.

"If you won't walk away, I can force you to stay away. Don't make a nuisance of yourself," Ford said.

Nathan tucked his hands into the pockets of his pants. "I don't plan to be a nuisance. I plan to catch a killer."

Autumn rubbed her temples, a massive headache throbbing. Fifteen minutes after she had made the emergency call, park rangers, CSI and local police had converged on her land. The FBI had arrived later.

The most recent arrival was a man who had taken post next to her. His serious expression and deep-set eyes drew her to him. Whatever his reason for being on the scene, Autumn was glad he was. Though he hadn't cracked a smile, an air of strength and bravery surrounded him. Her instincts about people were usually pretty good, and her instincts told her Nathan Bradshaw was a good friend to have.

He was handsome, almost too handsome. She felt a little guilty for thinking about his looks under the circumstances, but it was hard not to notice. His dark hair was cropped close to his head in a look she liked. Broad shoulders tapered to a lean waist, and the tailored cut of his black wool coat suggested wealth and style. Not the best jacket for hiking, but it looked great on him.

Special Agent Ford continued to talk about the investigation. "The sheriff mentioned you live here with your brother. Where is he?"

The mention of her brother chilled Autumn to the core. She believed what she had seen in the woods to be the work of the Huntsman. No one had outright said it, but she knew it. Her concern for her brother increased tenfold. "Blaine is hiking the trail. I haven't heard from him in a few weeks."

"The sheriff tells me your brother has been in trouble around here," Ford said.

The sheriff of their town, also known as her former fiancé and Blaine's ex–best friend. What had he told them about her and Blaine? "My brother has been hiking for months. I haven't heard from him in weeks." Not since the news had reported on the murders along the trail, which had amplified her anxiety. Though her brother was a gentle man, if he knew anything about the murders, he would keep his mouth shut.

"Is that unusual?" Ford asked.

Blaine was a free spirit and Autumn worried it would get him killed. "Not unusual for Blaine. I've been concerned about him. He could be in danger." The skitter of fear never seemed to go away completely. Until Blaine was home, she would worry about him.

"A male doesn't match the profile. Our killer targets women."

Another tremor of fear traced up and down her body. She could become one of the victims.

"Why don't you give her a few minutes? You can see she's taking this in. We've invaded her home and her land," Nathan Bradshaw said.

Gratitude for Nathan surged inside her.

Special Agent Ford snorted. "*We* are not doing anything. You'll return to your hotel room and forget we've found another victim. In the morning, check out and go home."

Nathan didn't move. Autumn had watched animals circle each other over territory. This was about the same.

"I know this situation is difficult." The warmth in Nathan's tone surprised her. It was the first time someone had expressed empathy for what she had been through tonight. The coldness in her chest lifted slightly.

"I control this crime scene. You need to leave. We can't have anyone compromising evidence," Ford said.

Autumn looked between the two men. "Do I have to leave, as well?" She hadn't considered the possibility the FBI would want her to vacate the premises until they finished their search. Where would she go? She had friends in town, but since her father's funeral, she had been keeping to herself. What could she do with Thor if she had to leave?

Ford moved closer to her. "Your cabin isn't part of the crime scene."

Crime scene. Her home, the place where she had always felt the safest, had become a crime scene. She wished her brother was home to help her. For that matter, she wished her father was there. Anyone to take away some of the loneliness and emptiness, emotions that were amplified by her fears. They had once been happy at the Trail's Edge. They'd talked about their home being like a resort and their jobs nothing like work. Those memories were only a few years old, but they felt dim and distant.

"Are the cabins part of the crime scene?" Nathan asked.

Anger gleamed in Ford's eyes. "Not at this time." The words were punctuated with irritation.

Nathan retreated a step and faced Autumn. "What

do you think about renting one of these cabins to me for a few days?"

Autumn swallowed hard, trying to think of a diplomatic way to handle this situation. She needed the income from renting one of the vacant cabins, but she didn't want to place herself on the wrong side of Special Agent Ford. He could make life difficult for her—such as by insisting she leave the Trail's Edge for an extended period or leaking to the press that a murder had occurred at her campground. If the threat of the Huntsman didn't frighten away business, a murder on the premises surely would. Her business may not recover, and then what would she do? Her options were limited.

"I have a few empty cabins for rent," Autumn said slowly. "But if Special Agent Ford and his team need a place to stay, I think it's fair to offer them first dibs." There. She hadn't lied to Nathan and she had given Ford priority, even if something about him rubbed her the wrong way.

"We're staying at a motel in town," Ford said, jutting his jaw. "Our mobile unit won't make it up these paths. But that shouldn't matter. We don't consider this location a hot zone."

Regardless of what the FBI thought, how would she ever feel safe again with the overarching sense of violation and terror that had clung to her since the moment she and Thor had seen the body? "How can you know he won't return?"

Special Agent Ford lifted his brow as if her question amused him. "We know his profile. We know how he behaves. Now, if you don't mind, I have some questions I'd like to ask in private."

"I'm more comfortable with Nathan staying with me." Where had that come from? The words had popped out of her mouth before she could censor them. She didn't know who looked more surprised—Nathan or Ford. If he was planning to question her about Blaine, she wanted someone else in the room as a buffer. She would become defensive about her brother, and her irritation with Sheriff Daniel would shine through.

"Let me stay. You know I'll ask her the same questions you're planning to," Nathan said.

Ford set his jaw. He looked between her and Nathan.

After a few moments of hesitation, he let out his breath sharply. "Ms. Reed, tell me what you were doing before you found the body."

Nathan moved closer to her, and the air around her heated. His stance was protective, almost as if he wanted to shield her from this unpleasant conversation.

Autumn answered Ford's question, trying to give helpful details, but not sure what was important. Images of the victim flashed in her mind, but not clear enough to form a complete picture.

Living in this area, she was friendly with many of the trail's frequent hikers. Was the victim someone she knew? Autumn had read every article she could find online about the killer and his victims, and as yet, each victim had been identified. All females, but it made her anxious to think about Blaine on the trail.

She would have recognized tonight's victim if he was her brother, right? She wanted someone to reassure her the victim wasn't Blaine. "Do you know who the victim is?" Autumn asked.

Ford shook his head. "We don't expect to make that information available until we've gotten positive identification and notified the victim's family."

The FBI agents weren't allowing her near the crime scene, and fear fogged her brain. Could the victim be her brother?

"Do you routinely walk your dog on this path?" Ford asked.

Autumn struggled to clear her mind and focus. Routinely? No. Frequently? Sure. "Sometimes. I don't really—"

He lobbed another question at her before she could finish her thought. "Have you read or heard the news reports about the dangers on the trail? Have you spoken with your brother about the Huntsman? Have you taken any precautions?" Ford asked.

Was he trying to catch her off guard? Did he think she had something to do with the murder? Ford studied her, his eyes burning into hers, as if the answers were hiding inside them. She needed a few minutes of quiet alone to compose herself and her thoughts. "I've read about the Huntsman and I've been more careful about going out at night. I keep my dog with me as added protection." He was a rescue dog and Autumn thought he might be part Labrador retriever. She didn't add that Thor was more friendly pup than fierce beast.

"Why did you take your dog to that location?" Ford asked.

His questions were starting to sound familiar. Was he asking the same question in a different way to trip her up? Autumn pressed her hand against her roiling stomach. "I don't know. I don't plan a route."

Ford stared at her. "And?"

Frustration pulled at the edges of her temper. "And nothing. I don't know what you want me to say."

Nathan moved his body partway in front of hers. "Ford, come on. She's had a rough night. She told you what she knows. If she thinks of anything else, she'll call. Let her get a good night's sleep and revisit this tomorrow."

Gratitude for this near stranger surged inside her. She needed a break to try to cope with the horror of the night.

Ford stiffened, his eyes narrowing slightly. "I'll call you tomorrow morning, Ms. Reed." Ford's gaze swerved to Nathan. "Go home. Stop forcing your way into my investigation."

Ford stalked away from them in the direction of the crime scene. Autumn relaxed, realizing she'd been fisting her hands and curling her toes in her shoes.

Autumn pulled the collar of her jacket up to block the wind that kicked up. "Mr. Bradshaw, if you want to follow me, I can register you."

"Please, call me Nathan." He set his hand on her lower back, steering her toward her lighted porch. Normally, she wouldn't have liked a man being so forward with her, but Nathan's hand through her jacket was warm and comforting. After what she had seen in the woods, she didn't want to be alone and she welcomed the connection.

When her brother had announced his plans to hike the trail, Autumn hadn't realized how unsettled she'd feel alone at the campground. It was the first time she had been alone for any length of time at the Trail's Edge, and without any campers, she felt even more lonely. The short distance to town didn't feel like a short distance in the middle of the night when it was utterly quiet and she was poignantly alone. And now, knowing someone had been murdered on her property sent a chilling sense of fear along her spine.

She forced herself to play hostess. "Nathan, welcome to the Trail's Edge. I wish you were visiting under happier circumstances. This is a great campground. The views are beautiful and it's usually peaceful and quiet."

He tossed her a half smile and her heartbeat quickened. "Believe me, I wish the same."

She opened the door to her cabin, and Thor rushed to greet her. She snagged his collar before he ran outside and caused a commotion. She hated to keep him penned in the house, but now wasn't the time to let him run around the campground. He would drive the investigation team crazy, and she didn't want him hurt.

Ford's words didn't comfort her. The Huntsman was still at large.

Suppressing a shiver of fear, Autumn stroked Thor's ears. "This is Thor. He was with me when we found the body. He found it first. Unfortunately, I don't think he will make a very good witness." She dragged Thor away from the door, and after Nathan stepped through, she shut and locked it behind them. The warmth of the room stung her face. She hadn't realized how cold it had gotten outside.

As soon as she registered Nathan into one of the cabins, she would turn up the pellet stove and curl up near the heat with a cup of hot chocolate. Though she doubted she would sleep tonight, perhaps she could rest in the warmth and comfort of her cabin.

"I'm sorry you have to go through this," Nathan said.

Autumn blinked, her eyes feeling gritty with exhaustion. She sat at the kitchen table, her registration sheet blank in front of her. "Why here? Why would he pick this campground of all places?" The Appalachian Trail was more than two thousand miles long. When she'd read about the case three weeks ago, she hadn't considered the killer would strike so close to her home. For so long, the Trail's Edge had been her sanctuary from the world.

Nathan took a seat kitty-corner from her. His nearness both calmed and excited her. "I haven't determined how he chooses an area or why he chooses the victims he does and what makes him move on to another location."

"Does that mean he could come back?" Autumn said. "Ford didn't seem to think so."

Nathan looked from her to her dog. "I don't think he's finished here. You described the smell of burning to Ford, but no fire. At every other scene, he has burned his victims' body. I think you and Thor interrupted the killer before he was finished with his routine."

Her stomach grew queasy and Autumn closed her eyes. "He was planning to burn her? That wasn't in the news."

"It's a detail the FBI has been keeping close to the chest."

What about Nathan? "Why are you working this case? Special Agent Ford indicated he didn't want your help."

Nathan's face darkened and a shadow crossed his eyes. "My twin sister was the killer's third victim. I'm doing this for her and our family." Grief underscored every word.

"Oh, Nathan. I'm sorry for your loss." Her words were a useless platitude. She remembered the article in the news about the third victim. The unnamed victim had been planning to go hiking with a friend, but when the friend became sick, she'd gone alone. A park ranger had found the body less than a quarter of a mile from the trail. It made sense now why the ranger had been drawn to the location. A fire along the trail was cause for concern.

"Thank you. Finding Colleen's killer is the only way I'll sleep easy at night," he said.

"You don't trust Ford to find her?"

"No."

No explanation.

With his intense dark eyes watching her, she found it hard to think, hard to put together rational thoughts. She'd never had this kind of reaction to a man. It had to be the stress from the night. Finding the body and the exhaustion catching up to her. Being lonely for too long. Missing her father and missing Blaine. She needed a friend, and at the moment, Nathan was the only one who fit the bill.

Nathan straightened his shoulders, as if pulling himself together. "I know you're tired, but I'd like to ask you a few more questions, if you're willing to answer them."

Autumn pulled her hair free of the elastic band holding it. She rubbed her fingers along her scalp, trying to massage away the headache that pulsed there. "Does that mean you're not planning to follow Ford's suggestion?" Seeing the raw emotion, she wondered if it was wise for Nathan to stay involved in the case. But how could she refuse to answer his questions knowing how much this meant to him and his family?

"Never considered walking away. Stopping him from killing again is too important."

Chapter 2

The Huntsman moved to an area and killed one or two victims every four to seven days. Seven victims in total, each a seasoned female hiker or camper spending time on the Appalachian Trail, each a model citizen by the accounts of her friends and family. Nathan didn't believe the killings were random, especially given the descriptions of the victims. They were carefully planned and executed, in the same manner that a lion stalked its prey, waiting for a vulnerable moment to attack.

Nathan had four days, maybe one week max, until another body turned up. If the killer was hunting in this area, Nathan needed to get one step ahead of him. He needed an expert in the region, someone to help him pinpoint hiker hangouts and popular camping spots. Though the trail had had few hikers in recent weeks, the Huntsman would find someone. "How much do you know about this area?" Nathan asked Autumn.

He had been working the case since Colleen had been killed and he'd found locals to be the most helpful. He wasn't the outdoors type, and this investigation required a lot of time on the trail. If Autumn could fill in the knowledge he was missing, Nathan would find the killer that much faster.

Autumn shifted in her seat, pushing her dark hair over her shoulders. "I've lived here all my life. I know the trail and the plants and animals, at least in this immediate area."

It was what he'd hoped to hear. "I'd like to hire you to help me."

Autumn inclined her head. "To help you how, exactly? My brush with his victim is as close as I plan to come to a killer."

Nathan leaned forward. "I need to know more about the trail in this area. I can tell you about the places where he strikes and you can tell me if anything near the Trail's Edge fits the description."

Autumn shook her head, her hair falling around her shoulders. "I'm sorry. I can't help you. I understand this is difficult for you." She touched her fingertips to her chest, momentarily distracting him and drawing his attention. "It's too dangerous for me to be involved."

Returning his gaze to her face, he tried to hide the eagerness in his voice. "Please, Autumn. My family is counting on me. I will protect you and keep you safe. I will stay until we know the killer has moved on."

He had given his mother his word. He had promised her that Colleen would have justice. He couldn't go home until he had seen his promise through.

Autumn searched his eyes. She was considering it. Weighing her options. The Huntsman was a dangerous man, and he was looking to add more victims to his list.

Nathan played his trump card. "Ford suspects your brother and I know how Ford operates. He wants someone to pin this on. Do you want that person to be your brother?"

Autumn leaned back in her chair and her eyes went wide. "My brother did not do this. I don't care what the sheriff said or what Ford thinks."

Though Nathan wasn't ready to say her brother was innocent, he wasn't jumping to the conclusion he was guilty, either. Nathan wasn't looking for a patsy. "Then work with me to prove it."

Autumn appeared dumbstruck for a moment. "I could show you a few places around here that are popular."

Relief rushed over him. "Thank you, Autumn. You're doing a brave thing."

Autumn set her elbows on the table and rubbed her forehead.

The urge to comfort her struck him and Nathan laid his hand over hers. Unexpected heat flared at the contact. Her eyes flew to his and he held her gaze for a long, loaded moment. He had noticed how beautiful she was. It wasn't relevant to the case, except that he'd need to remind himself to keep every interaction professional. He wasn't opposed to breaking the rules, but only when it benefited the investigation. A flirtation or an affair with Autumn Reed would be a distraction.

Nathan withdrew his hands before he was tempted to stroke her hand or her wrist with his thumbs. "I know you're worried about your brother. He'll be fine. The FBI has undercover agents spreading the word to hikers."

Autumn tucked her hands against her body. "My brother is impulsive at times. He doesn't always stay on the trail. He might not know how dangerous it is. The best I can hope is that Blaine won't cross paths with the killer."

What could he say to make her feel better? The odds were small of meeting the Huntsman, but as evident by his victims, not impossible. "The trail is hundreds of miles long. The chances of this man finding your brother are slim. Males have not been his target."

"A man? Are you sure the Huntsman is a man?" Autumn asked.

His work in psychological forensics told him they were dealing with a man, possibly ex-military, with a love of guns and an obsession with nature. "I can't say for sure until we find him, or her, but I have a basic profile. A man, mid to late fifties, may have had a regular job in society at one time, but now he keeps to himself. People who know him would describe him as a loner."

Autumn stood and walked to the stove. She set a teakettle on it and turned on the burner. "I don't want to be forced from my home, but I don't want to be foolish, either. Do you think it's safe to stay here? I might be able to stay with a friend in town for a few nights."

If she was away from the trail, she would be out of the killer's reach. Based on what he knew, the killer didn't leave the general vicinity of the Appalachian Trail. He was probably more comfortable where he had places to hide. "It's your decision if you want to leave." Nathan didn't want her to feel unsafe in her home, as if she had to run and hide.

Autumn took a deep breath and seemed to consider that. "How often does a serial killer break pattern?"

Nathan hedged. He hadn't expected the killer to leave a body this far from the trail in a nondiscreet location. "The Trail's Edge is the first campground where a body has been found."

Autumn shuddered. "In other words, he's broken his pattern or there isn't a pattern."

Both were possibilities. "Right."

Autumn swallowed hard. "I won't let him chase me away from my home. I won't go running scared. If he comes here, I'll be ready for him."

Autumn hated leaving the Trail's Edge. Even when she had errands, she made them quick. In the past decade, she could count on one hand the number of times she had spent the night away from her home. The slim possibility that the killer would return to his crime scene while the FBI was circling seemed too remote a reason for relocating, something that would put her even more off balance.

Her world had been flipped upside down by the killer. She'd lost reservations. Parents who'd enrolled their children in her after-school nature program had pulled them out. She lived with the constant fear of Blaine being in danger.

Her kettle of hot water whistled and she pulled out two mismatched mugs, one with a picture of a bear stamped across the front and the other with the Trail's Edge logo. Hot chocolate. Hot chocolate would calm her. "Can I get you a mug?" she asked and held up the box of hot chocolate.

"Thank you. That would be great."

Autumn fixed the two drinks and handed one to Nathan. She stirred her mug and then lifted it to her lips to take a sip.

Nathan did the same with the cup she'd made him. "Thanks for the hot chocolate. What would you say to allowing me to return the favor? I can take you into town for dinner."

Autumn almost spilled her mug. His question was a jolt to her system. Was Nathan asking her out? His interest was in tracking a killer. Was his request in that vein?

Nathan flashed a smile at her, one that reached to the corners of his eyes. It made his entire face change. The intensity disappeared, the harshness erased. He seemed more approachable and laid-back. She pressed her hands to her mug, keeping herself from reaching out and touching his jawline. Running her thumb over his lips to see if they felt as soft as they looked. Pressing her lips to his to taste him. Pushing her body up against his. One gorgeous smile and her imagination took flight. She was already reconsidering her stance on relationships—that is, that she wasn't ready to date after ending her engagement to Daniel.

Nathan set his mug on the table. "You can show me where the locals hang out on the weekends. We might catch some rumors about the murder that could prove useful."

Not a date and that was good, right? Why did she feel disappointed? In the space of a couple hours, her emotions had been slammed around inside her, leaving her off-kilter. Fear. Excitement. Lust. Confusion. "Going into town has nothing to do with the trail."

"You can point out the people who have stayed here and I can talk to them about what they've heard about the Huntsman. With the number of investigation vehicles here, rumors will run wild. People will want to talk to you about the murder and I can ask them what they know."

Autumn swallowed hard. She avoided going into town for a number of reasons. Among them was keeping away from gossip and crowds. Dealing with everyone knowing a body had been found at the Trail's Edge was overwhelming. She hadn't processed the events of the night and wasn't ready to discuss them in public. "I don't want to talk about the murder."

Nathan inclined his head. "I'll deflect the questions from you. You won't have to say anything."

But she'd have to hear it. The gossip. The slander. She was best staying at the Trail's Edge. "I'll take you to an available cabin and give you a list of places to eat in town. I'll give you directions and you can go on your own."

He shook his head. "I won't know whom to talk to

and insiders won't talk to an outsider like me. I need you with me, Autumn. You're honey to the bees." His voice was low and smooth, rolling off his tongue, utterly persuasive. It wasn't what he said; it was the smooth way he said it. He could have told her he wanted to go for a hike naked, and she'd strip out of her clothes and sprint toward the trail.

Perhaps she was making a big deal about nothing. She could go into town this once and get it over with, show the town she was fine after her broken engagement and a murder at the Trail's Edge. She'd face the gossip head-on, set the record straight and not let it blow out of control. "We can have dinner in town. A quick dinner." Of course, showing up in town with a handsome stranger would set off rounds of new gossip, but Autumn would hold her head high.

Nathan radiated an air of authority, and in combination with his good looks, he could talk his way into anything. Autumn didn't care for that. Daniel had been that way, charming and sweet. But he wasn't ready to settle down, a fact he'd hidden from her but not many others in town.

"I'll show you to your cabin." Autumn set her mug on the counter and grabbed the key to the cabin she'd rented him. The paperwork could wait. She'd put some distance between them before he talked her into doing something else.

She and Nathan trudged outside. The wind had picked up and the temperature had dropped. Many nights, Autumn had enjoyed sitting on her front porch rocker and drinking in the tranquility of her slice of heaven. But tonight, for the first time in years, she was afraid of the woods and of what she couldn't see. The perfect, soothing darkness was now a hiding place for a killer.

Autumn ignored the people milling around, tried not to think about the body and pretended Nathan was another guest renting a cabin. "Have you ever been camping before?" Autumn asked. If she were alone, she would have cut through the woods, but she made it her policy to teach guests to stay to the marked trails. Staying to the trails meant she and Thor could find them if they were lost, versus attempting to locate someone in the vast forest that lined the trail for miles on either side.

"This case has required I spend a good number of nights under the stars. But I'm not really the camping type."

Mother Nature was strong, swift and unforgiving. "I've marked the paths through camp. I recommend you stay on them whenever possible."

"Yes, ma'am," he said, sounding serious.

If he did as she asked, she wouldn't spend the night wandering in the dark looking for him. Desire edged at the fear inside her. Finding Nathan Bradshaw in the dark could have some interesting possibilities.

"I plan to have my trusty trail guide with me if I venture onto the trail," Nathan said.

She stopped and faced him, feeling uneasy about the idea of Nathan depending on her too strongly. "I said I would help you, but I'm not sure how much I'll be able to do. Don't get your hopes up." Set the bar low and be pleasantly surprised if things went well.

Nathan touched her upper arm and heat waves

shuddered down her body. "You've already helped more than you know, and I have confidence in your outdoor skills."

She gave him a wry grin and stepped away from him. "Usually people assume when it comes to the trail, I'm incapable and incompetent."

"Why's that?" Nathan asked.

Was he digging into her psyche or did he really not know? "I'm a woman, which many people assume means I don't know how to rough it or that I'll complain if I can't wash my hair. Also, I'm what my dad used to call 'scrawny.'" All her life she'd been waiting for curves that hadn't come. "I don't pack a lot of muscle but I've got endurance, and on the trail that can be important."

Autumn took the stairs to the front door of the cabin. She looked around and noticed that Roger Ford was watching them. Why was he opposed to Nathan working the case? Did he worry that Nathan would undercover something he couldn't?

"I don't think you're incompetent or incapable, but I do want you to be cautious." Nathan was standing close behind her, his breath hot on her neck. "I'll be watching over you, and I take that job seriously. I don't want anything bad to happen to you."

A warm shiver ran down her spine. She fumbled with the keys trying to make them work, her hands behaving as though disconnected from her brain. With Nathan standing behind her, she felt jittery and nervous in a very feminine, giddy way. "I will advise you to do the same."

His fingers reached and covered her hand, taking the keys from her. "Let me try."

The brushing of his hand against hers sent electric currents moving from the point of contact all the way to her toes. She released the keys and he unlocked the door quickly, pushing it open and stepping inside.

She could feel the heat radiating from his body, and she fought the impulse to lean close. Entirely inappropriate. Uncalled for. She had more control than this. Nathan would think she came on to every man who stayed here. She shoved her loneliness into a deep, dark place and slammed the door on it.

"Nice place," he said, no hint of sarcasm in his voice. "I've stayed in motels less inviting."

It had been Autumn's idea to remodel the cabins and outfit them with modern-day luxuries— coffeemakers, microwaves and quality linens and curtains to create a sense of home away from home. She did the cleaning and maintenance herself. Though the cabins were small, she'd arranged the furniture into a small eating area and a sitting area and placed a queen-size bed in the alcove opposite the fireplace. Two additional single beds folded out from furniture in the sitting area for children. The pellet stove in the middle of the room generated enough heat to keep the cabin toasty in the winter, and the shade from the trees kept it cool in the summer.

Autumn walked to the far end of the room where a double bay window gave an amazing daytime view of the forest. "This cabin is one of my favorites. It was the first one we remodeled." Autumn pulled closed the hunter green curtains that covered the windows.

Not being able to see into the woods made her feel as if someone was watching them. "In the morning, you'll probably catch a few deer wandering past. I've seen a few foxes at night, too. I think they have a den nearby. I'll bring you some fire starters and some logs." She turned, feeling the heat of Nathan's gaze at her back. He was watching her with those perceptive eyes, eyes she knew were taking in every detail.

She started the pellet stove. Though it was weak when first ignited, an hour from now, it would be throwing off a lot of heat.

"Don't put yourself out. I can gather wood if I need it." His voice had taken on a husky baritone, lower than it had been before. She felt the shift in the atmosphere, heat that crackled in the air.

Her skin felt achy and hungry to be touched. It had been six months, almost seven, since she'd had a date, too long since she'd gone out with a man. Her last date had been with Daniel, and by then their relationship had been circling the drain. She had found out he was cheating, and they'd been pretending they could move past it. That denial lasted about a week. "If you're running short on time and can't find dry wood, I have a woodshed twenty feet behind my cabin. You're welcome to take whatever you need. The pellet stove is pretty warm, but it can get cold in the morning. The bucket on the hearth has more fuel." She was rambling, a nervous habit, trying to deflect some of her feelings away from Nathan and fixate instead on the cabin.

He stopped a foot from her, sliding his hands into his trouser pockets, setting his attention on her. His gaze smoldered and a shower of sparks burst from her chest. Was she imagining the fire between them, or was this a reflection of her feelings for him?

He shifted and she caught a glimpse of the gun strapped to his side. His eyes blazed with passion, never leaving her face. This man was dangerous in more than one way.

She was hyperaware of the bed eight feet away, knowing the sheets would be cool and clean, and the feel of his body on top of hers heavenly. She drew in a deep breath, feeling as if there wasn't enough oxygen in it. She wouldn't let herself be stupid over a man again.

Nathan had warning signs she couldn't ignore. He had lost his sister, he was desperate for her help to find a killer and he was around for only a short time. They could keep their relationship firmly on professional ground for a week. When the killer moved on, so would Nathan.

Autumn needed to go outside and get some fresh air before she became light-headed. "Let me know if I can get you anything." She said it casually, but replaying the words in her mind, she wondered if he heard the unintended double entendre. *Anything*. Her in bed?

He caught her arm and heat sizzled in his touch. "Tomorrow evening, drinks and dinner at seven?"

She made the mistake of meeting his gaze. It was impossible to say no to him when his face filled with intensity and expectation. "Seven is fine, but I can't stay out late." She needed some boundaries between them and she wanted an excuse to end the night early.

He dropped her arm and stepped back. "I'll see you tomorrow."

With a final nod, Autumn fled outside.

The FBI and park rangers finished at the scene at 10:00 a.m. the morning after Autumn and her dog had found the body. The last vehicle to leave was the county coroner's van.

Nathan had slept restlessly. It wasn't just the noise. It wasn't just the gorgeous brunette sleeping in the cabin next door. He was closer than he'd ever been to catching the Huntsman. Excitement and determination sizzled in his veins. Nothing could get in his way. Not Roger Ford and not Nathan's attraction to Autumn Reed.

Nathan dragged a hand through his hair, rereading the page of case notes he'd written. Too little sleep and too much coffee had his nerves on edge, his concentration frayed. The words on the page were interrupted by thoughts of Autumn Reed. Of course the only witness on the case would be strikingly beautiful. Nathan enjoyed the company of a pretty woman, but in this situation, he would have preferred a bridge troll whom he found unbelievably unattractive and who wouldn't create any unnecessary distractions. He needed to focus on the case. He had enough factors playing against him.

Nathan turned to a fresh sheet of paper and jotted down a few notes about Autumn, her brother, Blaine, and the Trail's Edge. It was easier to record his observations of her while she was on his mind. Maybe if he wrote it down, he'd stop thinking about her.

He was sucked into his work, one detail leading to another, and when he looked at the clock, it was nearly six-thirty. He'd been reviewing the case since six in the morning, and after more than eleven hours of graphic descriptions, photos and notes, he needed a break.

Nathan showered and changed into clean clothes, figuring he'd treat his evening out with Autumn like a date to make it easier to blend with the residents of Smithsburg. Waltzing into a local hangout and announcing he was investigating a murder had a way of sealing lips and making people nervous. But taking a woman out for dinner had a way of inviting gossip, and if anyone had learned what had happened at the Trail's Edge, they'd be eager to talk about the case.

Which suited his motives perfectly.

At precisely 7:00 p.m., he knocked on Autumn's door. She opened it almost immediately, making him wonder if she'd been waiting for him, and if she had, why it sent a pulse of excitement through his body. He was doing this to find justice for his sister, not have an affair with a pretty outdoorswoman.

He let his eyes wander over Autumn. Her hair was loose around her shoulders and she wore a pair of black trousers and a green fitted top. It was a casual outfit, but it would catch the attention of every man in the restaurant.

A possessive streak tore through him and Nathan found himself disliking the idea of her flirting with someone else. He had suggested this outing as a means to gather information, purely professional.

Yet seeing her now, his interest roved south of professional, straight into the full burn of sexual interest.

He focused on their professional relationship. Autumn could point out people most likely to have heard rumors about the killer, or better, have useful information about the case. It didn't matter how she looked. His attraction shouldn't factor in to their relationship.

Realizing he was staring, he strove for indifference. "You look great," he said.

She touched the ends of her hair with her left hand. "Thank you. You look nice, too. Maybe a little too dressed up for the Wild Berry."

"I'm more comfortable in a suit than I am in hiking gear."

She shrugged and stepped onto the porch, pulling the door closed behind her. He tamped down the disappointment that she hadn't invited him inside. His primary intention was to find Colleen's killer. As Autumn moved past him, her shoulder brushed his chest and he caught the scent of pine and spice, a unique and yet distinctly feminine scent.

The drive down the mountain took twenty minutes and it was another five to the Wild Berry. Nathan parked next to a pickup truck with a rusted-out bumper and a red sedan with a plush monkey pressed to the back window. He took the keys from the ignition and turned to Autumn. "I'd prefer it if we pretended to be a couple."

Autumn fiddled with the strap of her handbag. "I don't think that's a good idea."

He set his hand on her upper arm and smiled at

her. If anyone saw them, he didn't want to blow his manufactured story. "I'm an outsider. If they think I'm with you, people will open up."

Autumn reached for the door handle. "If you think it will help. But I think you'll find most people are pretty blunt regardless of your relationship to me."

Nathan liked the idea of having an excuse to keep Autumn close. "It will help."

They climbed out of the truck and he circled it to stand next to her. He set his hand on her lower back and she jumped. She glanced over her shoulder at him, questions in her eyes. In response, he lowered his mouth close to her ear. "Just playing the part."

He guided her toward the entrance to the restaurant, and the sound of country music seeped through the door and covered windows into the parking lot. As he opened the door, the music grew five times louder, nearly deafening. Nathan scanned the restaurant and the patrons, a few who looked from their beers to Autumn and him, most who ignored them. After entering the bar, they found an open table near the window. He held Autumn's chair, waiting for her to sit.

The formality was intentional. Everyone in the room would recognize this was a date. Once Autumn took her seat, Nathan did the same.

A waitress with blond hair nearly to her waist tossed two menus on the table, and then set her hand on her hip, jutting it toward Nathan. "Hey, Autumn, who's your friend?"

Nathan caught a fleeting look of annoyance on Autumn's face.

"This is Nathan Bradshaw. Nathan, this is Francine."

Francine turned her attention to Nathan, letting her gaze linger on his face. "Nice to meet you. Can I get you a drink?"

"I'll have an iced tea," Autumn said, folding her hands on her lap, an edge in her voice.

What was the dynamic between Autumn and Francine? The waitress seemed friendly enough.

Francine looked at Autumn as if forgetting she was there. "Okay, sure thing. And for you?" Francine faced Nathan, giving him a smile he'd bet had earned her a good number of dinner dates.

"Same for me. Thanks."

Francine jammed her pad into the apron tied around her waist. "I hear you had some trouble up at the campground."

Autumn's eyes flashed with momentary panic.

"Not at the campground," Nathan said, keeping his voice low and calm.

Francine leaned in. "I heard you found a body in one of the cabins."

Autumn looked horrified, but Nathan chuckled, dismissing the lie. "Rumors can grow out of control quickly." He'd promised to run interference on rumors, and he would do just that.

Francine opened her mouth, but the look Nathan gave her had her clamping it shut. He wanted to stoke her curiosity without making Autumn uncomfortable or causing her problems at the Trail's Edge.

"We'll come over to the bar a little later to talk," Nathan said, looking across the table at Autumn.

Francine sighed. "I'll be right back with your drinks." She spun on her heel and strutted away from their table.

Nathan moved his chair closer to the table. Autumn's jaw was set and she glanced over in Francine's direction a few times.

"You two don't get along?" he asked.

Autumn shifted in her chair. "We went to high school together. She was the prom queen and I didn't go to prom. She's friendly when she wants to be." Autumn heavily accented the word *friendly.* "She's currently dating my ex."

Nathan caught something in her tone. Jealousy? Francine might be a good resource. Though she had come to their table and dug for information, she'd probably heard more rumors around town than he had. "Is your ex here?"

Autumn glanced around and then shook her head. "No. He's not."

Sensing she wasn't in the mood to talk about her former relationship, he changed the subject. "We'll give our waitress time to let the crowd know they might get a firsthand account of what happened at the Trail's Edge. Best way to drum up rumors about the killer and conversation about the trail."

Autumn studied his face, and he could see she didn't care for the idea of rumors flying. She blew out her breath. "I don't want everyone talking about me." Worry tinged the corners of her eyes.

"They won't be talking about you. They'll be talking about the Huntsman."

Autumn brought her hand to her forehead. "I have

a business to run. It's bad enough what's going on at the trail, but encouraging more rumors only fuels the fire."

"I don't want to cause trouble. I need information."

"I don't want the Trail's Edge or my family caught up in this disaster," Autumn said.

Protective of her family. Nathan filed that away in understanding her family dynamic. "You and Blaine are pretty close?"

Autumn shrugged. "We're all we have. It's been the two of us since my dad died a year ago."

Nathan had lived with his share of grief over the past year. The closeness of family was a concept that resonated well with him. "I'm sorry. That must make it doubly hard for you to be alone."

Autumn folded her hands in her lap and lowered her head. "I'm not totally alone. I have Thor." She let out a quiet burst of laughter. "You know, that sounds a little pathetic. But the truth is, I don't come into town much. I prefer being at the campground with Thor."

He heard something in her tone and he ran with it. "Why's that?"

Autumn looked away from him for a long moment. "I thought you were here to find out about the Huntsman, not about me." She lowered her voice. Not that their conversation could carry far over the noise of the music blaring through the speakers.

"I am. But before we get into that, I want to get to know you." He regretted the words if only because of the flare of mistrust in her eyes. What had happened to make her this suspicious of him? Some people had a problem with authority. Was it that he worked for the FBI? Was it men in general who bothered her?

She cleared her throat and glanced around. "You're only around for a short time. You shouldn't waste it getting to know me."

He shifted closer under the guise of hearing her better. He sensed being here was making her uncomfortable. "Do you want to leave? We can go somewhere else." It was the first time he was putting the case behind other priorities. At the moment, that priority was Autumn's well-being. He ignored the twinge of guilt. Nothing should come before justice for Colleen.

He laid his hand on her arm and she looked from it to him. Something lit in her eyes. Heat? Desire? Mistrust? Their eyes locked and held and pressure built in his groin. Under other conditions, he would act on that heat. He'd grab her, kiss her how a woman was meant to be kissed and let it lead somewhere smoking hot.

Autumn leaned away and, sensing her discomfort, he dropped his hand from her arm.

Francine appeared, setting their iced teas on the table. "Ready to order?"

Nathan hadn't looked at the menu, but he scanned it. "I'll have the cheesesteak with onions, mayo, tomatoes and fries on the side."

Autumn ordered a Reuben.

Francine jotted down the order. "Coming right up," she said, moving to another table and letting her hand brush over Nathan's shoulder as she collected the menus.

Autumn watched her leave. She straightened and pushed her hair over her shoulders. "She doesn't even care that we might be together. She intends to make it clear she could have you if she wanted you."

"That won't happen."

"She's dating Daniel now," Autumn said. She shrugged and drew her shoulders in as if making an attempt to take up less space.

"Daniel? The town sheriff? He's your ex?" Talk about adding another layer of complexity to the case.

"Yes."

"He pointed suspicion at Blaine," Nathan said, trying to get a sense of the subtleties.

"Yes. He and Blaine had a falling out."

Over her? "Why?"

She shrugged. "Nothing to do with the case."

She was making it clear personal questions were off-limits. He went another way. "I want to talk to anyone who loves to gossip." Deciphering the bull from the truth wasn't easy, but every now and then, he got lucky and caught a good lead.

Autumn glanced around the bar. "Loves to gossip? That's half the town. This is a small place. Not much exciting happens in Smithsburg and when it does, it's all anyone talks about."

Then everyone should have plenty to say about the murders. Hang out long enough, and after the last of the dinner crowd left, the drinking crowd would linger. Once the beer and wine had been flowing for a couple of hours, turning the subject of the barroom conversation to the murders would be easy. Francine might even do it for him.

A song he recognized with a slow, steady beat played from the speakers. "Why don't we dance?"

Autumn looked around. "What? Here?"

"No." Nathan pointed to the empty dance floor. "There."

She started to shake her head, but Nathan stood and took her hand, drawing her to her feet. "Come on, this will be fun."

"I don't see how this will help the case."

"It won't help the case. But you seem tense."

She pursed her lips. "Dancing will make me more tense."

"Give it a chance." Surprised she didn't refuse again, he led her to the dance floor, threading through the tables of people. He drew her into his arms, bonding her to him. She held herself rigidly against him.

"Relax," he whispered into her ear. "Everything is fine."

She relaxed, if only slightly, making it easier for him to move her around the small space. The wood floor was scuffed and worn. Autumn was the perfect height for dancing. If she laid her head down, it would rest in the crook of his neck. Her lips would be close to the part of his skin he loved to have kissed and her hair would be soft against him.

An image of Autumn naked in his bed sprang to mind. He could picture how their bodies would fit together, her long leanness and soft curves molding to his body. As quickly as the image surfaced, guilt snuffed it out. He had to stay focused on finding the Huntsman. With every moment that passed, they were closer to another kill.

She stepped on his toe and apologized. "Remember I mentioned I didn't go to prom? Lots of reasons for that."

Her breasts brushed against him and heat arrowed to his groin. "Doesn't mean we can't dance now."

"We're the only ones." She spoke through gritted teeth.

Didn't bother him to go against the grain. "Don't worry about what other people are doing. If it bothers you, close your eyes and I'll make sure we don't walk into anything."

She shut her eyes and he moved with her, holding her close. He inhaled, the scent of her hair like the outdoors, like pine, or juniper. Where that description came from, he couldn't recall, but it fit her. Juniper, fresh, clean and invigorating.

Nathan had thought he had a plan for tracking the Huntsman.

Nowhere in his plan did he factor in becoming attracted to Autumn Reed.

Autumn hated gossip and yet here she was, in the arms of a stranger, starting rumors. Her engagement to Daniel had ended six months before and even though he was already dating Francine, they were keeping it somewhat quiet. Daniel had jumped into bed with Francine the day after he and Autumn broke off their engagement. Or maybe Francine had been one of the women Daniel was seeing all along. She didn't want to know.

Autumn knew tongues would be wagging about her and the sexy stranger, yet she couldn't find the strength to pull away from Nathan. His sexual magnetism was a powerful lure, and she found herself agreeing to every word his silver tongue spoke. Though she didn't remember saying yes, she was out with him and she was dancing with him. Autumn didn't dance. She chopped wood. She cleared trails. She walked her dog.

The band of Nathan's arms around her back was strong as he held her, and it was too easy to sink against him. After what she'd been through in the past twenty-four hours, she needed this. He radiated confidence and it was easy to let him lead. With her head on his shoulder, she heard the sound of his heartbeat thundering in his chest, almost as loud as her own.

He brushed her hair behind her ear. "Our food's on the table."

The heat of his breath tickled her ear. She lifted her head. "What?"

"Francine brought our food."

Did he want to stop dancing? Had the song changed? She couldn't remember the song that was playing when they'd started. Nathan holding her was all that was on her mind. "We should eat."

She stepped away from him, her body instantly feeling colder. Refusing to let an awkward moment pass, she turned and walked to their table, feeling the burn of his eyes at her back.

"Autumn, what brings you to town?" A friendly, familiar voice. Hilde Sinclair lived close to the trail and maintained one of the trail shelters close to the Trail's Edge. She had been friendly with her parents when Autumn was young and she had been kind to

Autumn after her father passed away, sending over dinner a couple of times.

"Having dinner with a friend," Autumn said, nodding over her shoulder at Nathan.

Hilde smiled and waved. "I'll come by this week for a visit, okay?"

Autumn nodded and smiled. "Sure, that sounds good."

Moving to their table, she slid into her chair and examined her food. Nathan sat to her left and scooted his chair close to her. Why did he keep doing that? When they'd come into the restaurant, the chairs had been on opposite sides of the table and now they were inches apart.

The door to the lounge opened and Roger Ford stepped through. He scanned the crowd and sauntered to where she and Nathan were sitting.

"Looks like you two have gotten close."

His tone left no doubt that he didn't like what he was seeing. Why did he care so much? What was his grudge against Nathan?

"What do you want, Ford?" Nathan asked.

"I want you to leave town," Ford said.

"Not going to happen."

Ford slipped his thumbs through his belt. "You may have convinced Ms. Reed to help you, but does she realize who you are and what you've done?" The threat in his voice was strong, but Autumn wasn't following.

She glanced at Nathan. He looked unaffected. "She knows everything she needs to."

"About what?" Autumn asked, not liking the idea of being in the dark.

Ford grabbed a chair from an empty table and swung it around, joining their table. "Bradshaw and I go way back. You want to tell the story, or should I?"

Nathan gestured for Ford to continue. "You tell the story however you'd like."

"Bradshaw met my sister at a fund-raiser for our unit. Two years later, they're married and then he left her."

Nathan's face was unmoving, but his eyes conveyed his anger. "Are you done airing my dirty laundry?"

"Sure am." Ford stood. "Enjoy your meal." He walked away from the table and toward the bar, leaving a wake of curious stares in his path.

"You can ask me about it if you want to know," Nathan said.

Autumn didn't think it was her business. Nathan's ex-wife didn't factor into the investigation and opening the door to their personal lives wasn't something she wanted to do. For now, she was happy with that door staying firmly closed.

Autumn and Nathan drove past Lookout Point, a cliff drop-off with an amazing view of the Appalachian Mountains. High white peaks dived to lush valleys filled with evergreens and streams. Clouds dotted the sky, translucent puffs that turned dark before it rained. The Point was one of the reasons her grandfather had decided to build the Trail's Edge in this location. It looked different every time the seasons and weather changed, sometimes overcast, sometimes deep green and alive, sometimes white and icy with snow. Every scene was as beautiful as the one before.

Nathan turned into the Trail's Edge campground, their headlights the only illumination. She'd meant to leave an outside light on at her cabin. She had locked Thor inside. Usually, she preferred to let him wander outside, but she couldn't risk it with a killer loose.

He parked in front of her cabin and faced her. His dark eyes glimmered in the dim lighting. "Thanks for coming with me tonight. I didn't mean to keep you out so late." He glanced at the clock on the dash as he rolled down the sleeves of his shirt. He reached for his jacket on the backseat. The actions struck her as distinctly masculine. She couldn't recall either her father or her brother wearing a suit to more than a funeral. Nathan wore his suit as if it was made for him. How could something as simple as a man in a suit send a rush of steamy sensation down her body? Usually, suits and ties weren't her thing. She liked men how she liked to live her life: outdoors, simple and one with nature.

Sitting in the truck with him, she was unsure what to do. Bolt for the front door, waving good-night over her shoulder? Hug him and then flee? "I have some chores to do around the campground. I need to feed Thor and take him for a walk. He's been cooped up all evening." Why was she rambling?

"Let me come with you," Nathan said.

Autumn unbuckled her seat belt and they climbed out of the car. The fresh air felt good against her neck. The lounge had been too stuffy and hot. "You

don't have to do that. I can handle it." At the same
time, walking alone at dark on the campground post-
incident didn't feel safe.

Nathan followed her up the steps to her front door.
"I want to."

She was hyperaware of him behind her, the heat
of his body a contrast to the cold night air. Thor was
waiting and bounded to her when she opened the
door. He went to his dog bowl, waiting expectantly
for her to fill it. "I'm not looking forward to taking
another walk. Thor might find something, or someone, else."

"I promise I will keep you and Thor safe."

Why did his words feel so good? No man could
promise to keep her safe. The best he could offer is
that he'd try.

Autumn patted Thor's head. "Sorry dinner is late
tonight." She retrieved the dog food from the pantry
and Thor barely waited for the bowl to be full before
he dug in.

"He was hungry," Nathan said.

"He's always hungry," she said. "I buy more
pounds of dog food in a week than I do human food."

Nathan settled at her kitchen table. "While we wait
for him to finish, do you have any maps lying around?
I want a bird's-eye view of the area."

"I have the ones I give to campers," Autumn said,
walking to her desk drawer and grabbing one. She
handed it to Nathan and he opened it, spreading it out
on the kitchen table.

He traced his finger along the trails around the
Trail's Edge. What was he thinking about? The mur-

ders? "Tell me about places in this area where locals go that aren't well-known."

Autumn sat kitty-corner to him and peered over the map. She had it memorized, having given out so many in her lifetime and having walked the paths many times. From the time she was a child, she and Blaine had explored the forest surrounding the trail and had found a number of places well off the beaten path with great views or great hiking. "We have plenty of places like that. Unmarked trails and places for private picnics or parties."

"What about places more difficult to get to? Places where it takes more than a brisk walk to access?"

Autumn let her eyes wander over the map, picturing the places in the area that matched his description. "I can think of a few places. I can mark the general area on the map if you would like, maybe write down a few landmarks that might help you find them."

She took a pencil and put a star over those locations. Nathan leaned in closer. Her heartbeat escalated and she focused her attention on the map. If she turned her head, her lips would be close to his. Kissing distance.

"Some of these places aren't near any trails," Nathan said.

Autumn nodded. "I'm an experienced hiker and I know my way around. Most hikers don't see these places."

"I guess it's a good thing I have you to guide me."

Being in a position where she was alone with Nathan for hours, possibly days, made her equal parts anxious and excited. She was already thinking about how it would feel to kiss him and have his strong arms around her. That was dangerous. She wasn't ready to jump into an affair, regardless of how brief.

Ford's words at the lounge came to mind. Why had Nathan left his wife? It shouldn't factor in, but Autumn wondered if Nathan was a man who could be trusted. He wanted to find his sister's killer and seemed willing to do anything to accomplish that goal. Anything, including lying to her? Pretending to be interested in her? Thor's wet nose nudged her hand, giving her a chance to escape the conversation. "He's ready for his walk." Thor didn't have the same apprehension she did about walking through the campground.

Autumn grabbed the leash off the back of the door and attached it to Thor's collar. Normally, she would let him run loose, especially when not many guests were staying in the cabins, but she was feeling protective of him.

Autumn took out a flashlight from her closet. When she was eight years old, she'd been lost in the woods after dark and had been terrified she wouldn't be found. She'd done exactly as Blaine and her father had taught her, stood still and blew her emergency whistle. When they'd found her, she was shivering from terror and cold. She'd been careful since then about venturing out on the trail after dark without the proper equipment.

She'd take a short walk around the Trail's Edge property and make it up to Thor tomorrow morning with an extra long jog along the trail.

Ten minutes later, Thor was meandering in front of

them, dodging from side to side along the path, stopping to sniff the trees and bushes. As they walked, their feet crunched the leaves that had fallen to the ground.

"It's so quiet," she said, thinking about the chaos that had reigned the night before.

"Peaceful," Nathan said.

Autumn hoped that the Huntsman had moved on, farther down the trail, maybe lost himself in the woods or decided to give up looking for victims with the winter weather coming. "I wonder if the FBI has found the identity of the last victim," Autumn said.

"We might have to wait for the press release on that information. Ford isn't eager to loop me into the case," Nathan said.

"I sensed something between you two that first night and again tonight," Autumn said.

"Ford and I worked together years ago. He follows the rules to the letter and I prefer to consider the spirit of the law and do what's necessary to get the job done," Nathan said. "And since I was married to his sister for a brief time, he holds that against me, too."

Autumn stepped up her pace as Thor dragged her faster. He seemed bent on going to the location where the body had been found. The trees around the area had been roped off with yellow caution tape, but that wouldn't stop Thor. She pulled back on the leash, trying to dissuade Thor from moving in that direction. He didn't heed her, and since she rarely kept him on the leash, it wasn't unexpected.

Autumn turned the flashlight to the path ahead of them. "Thor wants to see the location of the body."

"Let him. We'll keep him off the scene, but I wouldn't mind having a look. Unless you want to return to the cabin and I'll take Thor myself." He watched her carefully. He was worried about her, and that warmed her. It had been too long since someone had cared about her.

Autumn didn't want to be alone. Not out here. Not at her cabin. Something inside her, intuition or caution, warned her to stay near Nathan. "You won't see much in the dark," Autumn said. The flashlight provided only a limited view.

"It might help you sleep to see you have nothing to worry about. The FBI cleaned the area and any evidence was photographed, bagged and collected."

Maybe seeing that tree, even in the dark, would begin to scrub the image of a body hanging from it out of her mind.

Allowing Thor to lead the way, Autumn pulled him to a stop near the yellow tape surrounding the crime scene. The wind blew, shaking more leaves from the treetops. Autumn let her flashlight pan over the scene, starting high, giving herself a view of the tree without someone hanging from a branch.

A crunching of leaves had her swinging the flashlight lower. A movement near the trunk of the tree caught her eye. She moved the flashlight to see more, frustrated that the narrow beam illuminated so little at this distance. It didn't help that she was shaking and Thor was twisted for her to let him off his leash.

A shadow, looking very much like a man, was lurking near the base of the tree. If the light hadn't given them away to the intruder, then Thor's barking did. Nathan snatched the flashlight from her hand and pinned it on a figure moving away from the tree. The intruder ducked beneath the crime-scene tape on the side opposite them, running between trees, barely a shadow and impossible to track.

Nathan drew his gun and it made a clicking sound. Was he planning to shoot at the figure? "Stop!" he shouted.

The intruder ignored him, almost becoming a ghost and disappearing. Nathan vanished as he gave chase, the bobbing of the flashlight through the woods eerie and unsettling. And growing dimmer. Nathan was gone. It would have been safer for them to run or call for help. Fear and panic tightened her stomach. Autumn reached for Thor, drawing him against her, her shaking vibrating the both of them. She hugged him to her.

She was alone in the woods in the dark. Nathan was chasing a madman. Could she find her way to her cabin and call for assistance?

The campground that she had called home now felt threatening. The dark felt ominous, the cold chilling, and the trees and brush were places for a murderer to hide.

The Huntsman had returned to the scene. Perhaps he was looking for another victim, perhaps he wanted to relive the killing and hanging or perhaps he was hoping to finish his ritual by starting a fire. It could be a teenager on a dare or the media snooping around, but his gut told him the killer was close.

He had to find and stop him. As Nathan chased the

figure, it grew more difficult to see. The trees were close together, providing too many places to hide. Nathan stopped and shone his light around the area.

It was still and quiet.

Autumn! He'd left her and Thor alone. The Huntsman could have circled back to attack her. It hadn't escaped Nathan's notice that she fit the profile for the Huntsman's victims.

How far had he run? How long had he been gone?

Nathan whirled, calling to Autumn.

His sister's face flashed into his mind. Colleen had died at this madman's hands. He wouldn't let him hurt another woman he cared about.

Nathan pushed his body to move faster as his brain tripped over that thought. He cared about Autumn. He'd known her a short time, but he'd had an undeniable connection with her.

"Autumn!"

Thor barked in response. Nathan was desperate to hear Autumn's voice. Was he too late? Had he made a critical error leaving her alone? His gun felt heavy in his hand. It did no good to shoot in the dark, but he would shoot to kill if Autumn was in danger.

When he yelled her name again, this time she responded. He moved in the direction of her voice.

When she came into view, relief rushed over him. She was squatting on the ground with her arms around Thor.

He pulled her into his arms and hugged her. Thor growled as if chastising him for his mistake.

"Are you okay?" he asked into her hair.

"Except for being left in the woods alone in the

dark after being scared by a psycho, I'm fine," Autumn said. "Was it the Huntsman? Did you see him?"

He hadn't seen enough of his face to provide any more details of the man they were pursuing. The glimpse he'd gotten had been quick. "I think it was the Huntsman."

"We should call Ford," Autumn said.

A crackling of a branch. An animal? Or the Huntsman stalking them? "Let me take you back to your cabin," Nathan said. He didn't want to alarm her further, but in their current position they were easy targets.

It was dark in an unfamiliar place, he had Autumn and Thor to protect and they were on the Huntsman's hunting ground. He hated to admit it, but Nathan knew when he was outmatched.

Nathan took Autumn's keys from her clammy palm and opened the door to her cabin. She walked inside, her face frozen in horror, her body tensed and her hands shaking. He guided her to the couch in the living room.

"Sit down. Let me fix you something to drink."

She nodded numbly and he retrieved a glass of water, setting it in her hand. She took a few small sips.

"I'll call Ford." As much as he hated to involve the FBI, they had equipment and crime-scene investigators who could lock down the scene and look for footprints and evidence. If it was the Huntsman, he might have left evidence behind, having been startled at the appearance of Autumn and Nathan.

Nathan pulled a throw blanket off the back of the

couch and wrapped it around Autumn's shoulders. He took the lighter from the mantel and lit one of the starter logs she had set in the hearth. After the fire had spread the length of the log, he laid a few pieces of wood around it, hoping it generated some warmth.

"You know how to start a fire," she said quietly. She kicked off her shoes and they hit the floor with matching thuds.

"I took a class on it in FBI school."

"Really?" she asked.

He sat next to her on the couch and slid an arm around her shoulders, pulling her against his body. He intended the gesture to offer comfort, but it had the unintended side effect of feeling good. Too good. "Nah, it's something I picked up." Nathan pulled out his satellite phone and dialed Roger Ford. Ford answered on the first ring. After explaining the situation, Nathan disconnected the call without waiting for Ford to bark commands at him.

Thor trotted over and sat next to the growing blaze, soaking in the heat. Autumn shifted next to Nathan on the couch, drawing her knees to her chest and leaning in to him.

After a time, the cabin grew warmer and her tremors faded.

The sharp knock on the door had Autumn jumping to her feet. Nathan caught her before she raced for the door. "Let's be cautious, okay?"

Autumn nodded her agreement. Nathan peered through the peephole, and seeing a park ranger on the porch, he opened the door.

The man stepped inside, pulling off his hat revealing bleached blond hair. His goatee was dark and neatly trimmed. "I received a call from Special Agent Roger Ford to check in and see if everyone is okay."

Autumn slipped past him and hugged the man. "Ben, thanks for coming out so late. I'm sorry you were pulled into this."

Nathan watched the interaction, unsure of the relationship between the two. They seemed close. Were they friends? Something more? Earlier that night when he'd suggested they pretend to be a couple, she hadn't mentioned she was otherwise involved with someone.

Nathan shoved aside his jealous line of thinking. It didn't matter what relationship Autumn and Ben had. It was irrelevant to the case, and justice for Colleen was all that mattered.

Nathan stepped back, allowing Ben farther inside.

Ben threaded the brim of his hat through his fingers. "I have a couple more guys coming to the scene and the FBI should be here soon. If the media hears about this, I'll try to keep them off your backs."

Nathan lifted a brow. "You think the media already knows about this?" If they did, how?

Ben shrugged. "If the sheriff and the Feds turn on their flashers and start piling up the mountain, someone is bound to notice. There's nothing up here but the Trail's Edge, and that will have people curious."

Small towns. Nearly every place Nathan had been in the past few months had been near a small town where the residents kept watch for their own.

Autumn wouldn't like reporters poking around. Would this bring a fresh wave of rumors crashing down on her, giving her more reasons to isolate herself at the campground? Though she hadn't mentioned the reasons why, she seemed to want to isolate herself at the Trail's Edge. Being away from it made her nervous. Was it social anxiety or something more?

Ten minutes later, another car pulled in to the campground. Nathan watched from the front window. "Your rangers are here."

"That's my cue. Let's lock this place down for the Feds," Ben said.

Ben stepped away from Autumn and joined the other rangers, leaving Nathan and Autumn alone.

"Will you stay with me? At least for now?" Autumn asked.

Nathan slipped his arm around Autumn's shoulders. He wanted to be outside, listening to whatever he could gather from Ford. "I'll stay with you." It would be at least thirty minutes before Ford arrived. He couldn't put Autumn's needs above Colleen's.

Nathan steered her to the couch and sat down, pulling her feet onto his lap. He rubbed her feet, trying to force her to relax. "You're safe here."

"Ford didn't think he would come back," Autumn said.

If the intruder had been the Huntsman, it could be another break in his pattern. More erratic behavior, which ultimately meant more dangerous behavior. Or perhaps they were filling in the missing details of their profile. "He has never killed on two separate occasions in the same location."

Autumn rubbed her temples. "That's not comforting."

He agreed with her statement, but didn't add to her lost sense of security. "We have no reason to think he returned to the Trail's Edge to harm anyone."

Autumn shot him a look. "How do you do this?"

"Do what?"

"Stay calm. Have a job hunting killers," Autumn said.

His sister had asked him the same types of questions. Colleen had been a dental hygienist. She'd built her life around her two kids, and she'd thought Nathan would have the same fate and not spend his days looking for murderers. His devotion to his job had ended his marriage. His ex-wife couldn't understand what he did and why it was important. He couldn't talk to her about the horrors he saw, and it had slowly destroyed communication between them. "I can't let the Huntsman kill anyone else."

Autumn seemed eager to talk, so Nathan listened as Autumn spoke about the Trail's Edge. Nervous chatter, but it seemed to be calming her.

The Feds arrived with sirens screaming and lights flashing. They weren't concerned about keeping their presence under wraps.

Autumn drew the blanket closer around her.

"Are you cold?" he asked.

"A little. It's getting better." She reached out her hand and laid it on his.

The casual touch evoked an immediate physical response. Desire turned into the hot blaze of arousal. It wasn't the time or the place, yet his body had its own ideas about what was important now. Spending the evening with her, touching her, being alone with her had set anticipation to a slow simmer.

Nathan drew his hand away. He couldn't allow this heat between them to roar out of control.

Autumn leaned toward him. "Do you think he's still here? Watching me?" She came to her feet, dropped the blanket and walked to every window in the cabin. She checked the latches and pulled closed the curtains, overlapping them so no one could see inside.

"This place will be swarming with Feds in a few hours. Unless the Huntsman wants to be caught, he's gone." How long or how far gone, Nathan couldn't predict.

A knock at the door had Nathan rising to his feet. "I'll get it."

He pulled open the door and came face-to-face with Roger Ford, and from his expression, he was angry.

Ford let out a string of curses. "I knew having you involved would bring trouble."

Nathan set his feet apart and refused to step back or allow Ford inside. "How does my being here control what the killer does? Is this the thanks I get for calling you first?"

Ford swore again and rubbed a tired hand over his face. "You're too close to the case. You need to step back and let us handle this. Tell me what you know and then take a break."

Nathan had heard the same line so many times, he expected it from every Fed he talked to about this case. "I'm not interfering with the investigation."

Ford set his jaw. "I don't need to tell you that I'll have to speak with you and Ms. Reed individually about what you saw and heard."

Nathan shrugged. "I'll be happy to tell you what happened tonight. You can speak to Autumn, as well. Why don't you talk to her first? It's late, and she's had a tough day."

Ford cocked his head. "A tough day? We're trying to solve a murder here. Get over having a tough day."

Autumn set her hand on Nathan's back, coming up behind him so quietly, he didn't have time to prepare. His body reacted—strongly—to her touch. "I can talk now. Or later. It's not like I'll be able to sleep anytime soon."

Ford looked between her and Nathan. "Fine. Let's talk now. Do you mind talking outside?"

"Not at all." Autumn stepped onto the porch and followed Ford down the cabin steps. Too far away to hear what they were saying, Nathan watched them. Autumn's arms were folded over her chest and she kept glancing over her shoulder at the spotlights the Feds were setting up around the area. Her face was solemn, her fear obvious. The scene was similar to the night before, and he wondered if she was experiencing flashbacks.

Ford leaned toward her, listening and nodding, asking a few questions.

After about ten minutes, Ford walked Autumn to the foot of the stairs and inclined his head toward Nathan. "Let's go."

Nathan followed Ford to the same place where he'd spoken to Autumn. Nathan related the details of their night, starting from when they'd left the Wild Berry and what they had seen in the woods. He could feel the heat of Autumn's gaze on him and knew she was watching, waiting.

"What's your relationship with her?" Ford asked.

Nathan didn't have a relationship with her, outside the professional one they were developing. "I'm renting a cabin from her."

Ford narrowed his eyes as if he didn't believe Nathan. "I saw you two together. You're doing more than renting a cabin."

"We're working together."

"So now you bring a civilian onto the case?"

"She's lending her outdoor experience."

Ford pointed a finger at Nathan. "Don't get in my way."

He didn't remind Ford again that he had called him first to let him know about the intruder. Nathan's priority wasn't to be top dog on the case. Colleen deserved to have her killer brought to justice however that needed to happen. "I don't plan on it."

Ford rocked back on his heels. "You know, you should get back to work and get assigned to a case. You're a good investigator, and the distraction would be healthy for you."

"I wouldn't be assigned to this case," Nathan said, knowing Ford's fake flattery was an attempt to get Nathan to back down. Men who were more manipulative and influential than Ford had tried to talk Nathan out of pursuing this case. But Nathan was dedicated. He wasn't stopping his pursuit of the Huntsman.

"You'd be assigned to a case where you can do some good," Ford said.

"I'm planning to do some good here."

Ford shook his head. "You're being a fool. I have real work to do. Stay away from my crime scene." Ford stalked away.

Nathan didn't argue. Poking around the scene wouldn't get him more information. The footprints might provide some indication of stature, but Nathan could look at those after the FBI finished processing the scene.

Autumn appeared next to him. "How'd it go? Does he know anything more? Did he tell you anything about the scene?"

He hated disappointing her. "They're working the scene now. I'm sure they're looking for the killer. Ford won't share information. We're on our own."

Autumn looked from him to the crime scene. "I don't understand any of this. Why would the killer come back? What does he want?"

An interesting piece of the puzzle that would form the killer's psyche. "Maybe he left something behind? Something significant to him? Maybe he didn't finish the job and wants to complete his ritual." Or did he return to confirm the body had been found and taken down? "Why do hikers hang packages from trees?" Nathan asked, thinking again about the body in the tree.

Autumn shivered. "Like food and such?"

Nathan nodded.

"I leave a few packages along the trail with emergency supplies and I string them in the trees to keep animals from getting to them. If anyone is hiking the trail and comes up short, they are welcome to it. It's an unwritten rule on the trail." She paused. "Do you think there's a connection between emergency supplies and how the killer places his victims?"

"Not sure yet," Nathan said, putting the information on file.

Autumn rubbed her arms and he wished he could sweep her against him and assure her she was safe. The need to hold her, touch her hummed in his veins. Being alone with her was utter temptation. The temptation to reassure, console and to claim.

"What are you thinking?" she asked.

He wasn't about to admit he'd been picturing carrying her into her cabin, stripping her naked and having her. "About the case."

"You looked pretty intense."

"It's an intense situation." Not just the murder. Her. Being with her. It wasn't the right time to think about kissing her and holding her. His reaction to crime scenes had always been strong and visceral, and though he wasn't proud of it, the need to blow off steam with some physical exercise—like sex—was enticing.

"I don't understand why someone would do this," she said.

Nathan forced himself to concentrate on her words and not her mouth. Her lips, pink and inviting. "Maybe he can't control the urge."

He stepped closer and Autumn took a step away. Had he been foolish to believe he could keep her safe? The killer had struck once and possibly returned to the scene, and Nathan's gut told him he wasn't finished.

In previous cases he'd worked, Nathan had had a partner, a team and trained professionals to bounce ideas off. This was the first case where he was on his own. The urgency to keep Autumn as his trail guide, and partner, escalated. Without the FBI's resources at his disposal, he needed another advantage. He needed Autumn.

But was he drawing her into an investigation that would get her killed?

Chapter 3

Autumn's stomach knotted when Daniel's cruiser pulled onto the campground. His arrival had an ominous feel to it. They hadn't spoken since their breakup.

Daniel climbed out of his car and strode directly toward her. He had grown his beard out again and it was the same color as his dark hair. Though not tall, he spent a lot of time in the gym and at the gun range and was in good shape. Autumn didn't want a confrontation, but she had no way to avoid him. Dread and anxiety swept over her, making her more tired than she already was.

Daniel looked between Autumn and Nathan. "Why does it seem like every time there's trouble, a Reed is involved?"

Autumn wouldn't let Daniel bait her. "The Huntsman is in this area. We're one of the closest camping areas to the Trail. Do the math."

Daniel narrowed his eyes. "Where's your brother?"

Did she have to answer him? This wasn't his case. He was in his uniform, but Autumn had seen him use his position as sheriff for his own purposes in the past. "I don't know."

"How convenient."

Autumn held back the angry words that came to mind. "If you'll excuse me, I've had a long night."

Daniel reached for her, but Nathan was faster. He stepped between them before Daniel could catch her arm. "She said she was leaving," Nathan said.

Daniel straightened, trying to put himself eye level with Nathan. "Who are you? Autumn's keeper?"

"I'm a friend," Nathan said.

Daniel looked between Autumn and Nathan and snickered. "Whatever. People who get close to the Reed family never seem to fare well. Good luck."

Daniel turned and walked away, leaving Autumn feeling as if she had a hot poker burning a hole in her gut. How could Daniel talk to her that way? Alluding to the trouble her family had gone through was low, even for Daniel.

Autumn and Nathan went into her cabin and closed the door. The places where she felt safe were growing smaller. What was next, someone bursting into her home and causing problems here, too?

After several hours in her cabin, nervous energy ticked in her veins. She was going stir-crazy. The FBI and park rangers were still scouring the woods. The fireplace was blowing hot air, and Autumn grabbed a blanket off the back of the couch and threw it over her legs.

The FBI wouldn't find the man she and Nathan had seen at the crime scene. He was long gone, which meant he was still hunting, watching and waiting to strike.

"What will we do now? Wait for them to leave and then look around ourselves?" Autumn asked. With Daniel on the scene whispering in Ford's ear, he'd repeat his theory that Blaine was guilty, keeping her brother at the forefront of Ford's suspect list.

Nathan reclined and let his head fall back onto the couch. "We might see tracks in the morning. But the FBI will probably stay, too, or return when the sun comes up."

Special Agent Ford wouldn't share information with them. They'd have to find evidence themselves, evidence to prove Blaine was not the Huntsman. "We need the information they've found at the scene."

Nathan nodded his agreement. "I haven't figured out how to acquire that yet."

"I might have a way."

Nathan lifted his head and his eyes swerved to hers. "Oh?"

"I have a friend at the coroner's office. A friend who loves to gossip. We could find out what she knows." Her willingness to pry into this case took her aback. She didn't have any business involving herself with the coroner or the victim. But knowing the identity of the dead woman would remove that trifling doubt in her mind that the victim was someone she knew. Unlike Roger Ford and Daniel, she could review the information without the bias of assuming her brother was involved.

"If you have a contact, we should explore that option," Nathan said. "Why would she risk her job?"

Aside from being a gossip, Natalie was a casual friend. She'd enjoy the attention and would want to tell someone what she knew about the case. As the case grew more popular in the media, Natalie would become more eager to take a position near the spotlight. "She might enjoy talking to a cute FBI agent."

"You want me to flirt with her?" Nathan asked.

"Sure, why not?" Autumn asked, already not liking the idea.

"People saw us together tonight at the lounge. She might not buy it that I'm walking in with you and then flirting with her."

Autumn shrugged. "Tell her the truth. Tell her I'm helping you with the case."

Nathan leaned forward. "Is that what we're doing? Just working the case?"

For a long, loaded moment, Autumn considered admitting she felt the attraction between them, but something held her back. "Yes. Aren't we?"

His unbearably gorgeous face almost had her handing over the truth. But before she did, Nathan set his hands on his knees and pushed himself to his feet. "I'll head back to my cabin. I want to make some notes about the case. I'll make a few calls and see if I can learn something."

"You're leaving?" She clambered to her feet, her hand shooting out on its own accord and gripping the front of his jacket.

He glanced at her hand holding on to him. "Is that a problem?"

Panic surged inside her. She didn't want to be alone. Thor was good company, but she needed someone tonight. A person. A man. Someone to make her feel safe, and Nathan fit the bill. "Maybe you could stay. I don't want to be by myself tonight."

He took a deep breath as if weighing his choices. His eyes darted from her to Thor and back again. "I'll stay."

Relief rushed over her, followed by a flare of panic. It was a small cabin. Where would Nathan sleep? Autumn scanned the room. She had limited options. "You can take the bed and I'll crash on the couch."

"I can't kick you out of your bed, and I don't mind the couch. It's probably nicer than some of the places I've slept recently."

She looked at him from head to toe. He was too broad across the shoulders to fit on the cushions and his legs would hang over the ends. "I don't think you'll be comfortable."

He rolled his shoulders. "The couch is fine. I'll run to my cabin and grab a few things. I'll be back in a minute."

Autumn watched him leave, then locked and bolted the door behind him. Even though the park rangers and FBI were trolling the scene, their lights bright against the dark of night, and their voices carrying across the air, she wasn't taking chances.

She grabbed a set of fresh linens from her closet and wrapped the sheets over the couch cushions, adding a few blankets at the end. She put out fresh tow-els in the bathroom. Would he need anything else?

Was she being silly about this? What difference would it make if he slept here or twenty yards away in his cabin? She didn't have an answer she could verbalize, but she felt safer to have Nathan in the room with her.

Daniel jogged to Nathan as he walked to his cabin. "She's a real piece of work, isn't she?" he asked.

Nathan glanced at the sheriff. He wasn't in the mood to get in the middle of someone else's broken relationship. "What do you want, Sheriff?"

"I think you need to know who you're getting in-volved with."

Autumn had made it clear their relationship was professional. Despite the overarching sense of attrac-tion, she wasn't ready for anything else. He consid-ered her boundaries good. They would keep him in line and focused on what was most important: find-ing the man who had killed Colleen.

"She's working the case with me. I don't need to know anything except that she's good outdoors."

Daniel regarded him carefully. "You know about her brother, right? And her uncle?"

"She's mentioned her brother." Several times.

"He isn't quite right in the head. He's dangerous. He takes after his uncle."

"What's wrong with his uncle?" Nathan hated that he was getting baited into a conversation about Autumn's personal life. She had indicated it was off-limits. It felt like a betrayal to indulge in what amounted to gossip with Daniel.

"He was a crazy old man. Would go off alone in the woods for days at a time. Come back smelling like garbage and telling wild stories about bears and wolves. When he went off to war, he came back even crazier. Loved his guns and knives. Went off in the woods one day and never came back. Worst part was that Blaine adored his uncle. Thought his gun collection was great."

An interesting family dynamic, but having a nut in the family didn't mean Blaine was the Huntsman. "Thanks for the warning. If Blaine comes back to the cabins, I'll be careful."

"Sleep with one eye open, man," Daniel said.

His comments had Nathan wondering about Daniel. "Why are you telling me this? I thought you and Blaine were friends."

"We were. But he's too out there for me. When the murders started along the trail, I thought right away of Blaine."

"Did you tell Autumn?"

"No way. She doesn't listen to me. Our relationship ended badly and when it comes to her family, she has on blinders."

"I'll keep it in mind," Nathan said. Autumn had been evasive about her family. Was she knowingly hiding something about her brother?

Nathan knocked on the door to Autumn's cabin, announcing his presence. "Autumn, it's me."

She unbolted the door and pulled it open. He

stepped in carrying his duffle and a thick brief-case filled with folders and papers. "I won't keep you up if I do some work, will I?" He wouldn't let Daniel's words get to him, but he was a fellow law-enforcement officer. Daniel could be bitter about his relationship with Autumn or he could have good instincts and something was off about the Reed family.

"It won't bother me."

"Cute pajamas," he said, nodding at the green nightclothes she had clutched in her hand.

She glanced at the pajamas and frowned.

"Did I say something to upset you?" he asked, touching her chin lightly and tilting her head up. He would get inside her head. He would find out if she was holding back something about her brother, even if she was subconsciously trying to protect him.

"Are you teasing me? I imagine most of your sleepovers involve women in designer pajamas."

He laughed. "I don't have sleepovers with women often. I'm married to the job. And when I do, I rarely take notes on her pajamas." But since she'd brought it up, now he was thinking about what pajamas he'd like to see her wear. She had a knack for distracting him.

That quickly, he'd forgotten about trying to ferret out more information about her brother.

An hour later, Nathan was stretched out on her couch, the sheets and blanket Autumn had given him tucked around his waist. He was sandwiched between the fireplace and the pellet stove, the heat in the room nearly unbearable.

It wasn't just the heat. It was her.

Nathan rolled from his side to his back. His arms didn't fit on the couch and it was difficult to find a comfortable position when he couldn't fully extend his legs. He'd slept in worse—a car's passenger seat on a stakeout, motels better suited for mice than people and, in the past few months, on the cold ground without appropriate gear.

This was much better. At least he was somewhere clean and protected from the elements, wrapped in a sheet that felt great against his skin.

He heard the bathroom door open and the light switch flick off. Autumn crept across the cabin, her feet making the floor creak, and she appeared, her face hovering above his, her hair falling around her shoulders. "Are you still awake?"

Since his eyes were open, the question didn't require an answer. "Waiting for you."

She knelt on the floor next to the couch, tugging her robe tighter around her. If anything, it made the garment less modest, outlining her lithe figure. "I keep seeing it in my head."

Nathan rolled onto his side and pushed himself up to sit. "Don't. It's over. The intruder is gone." He hesitated to tell her he wouldn't be back. He'd been wrong about that once before. Time alone must have let her thoughts drift to the scene, both when the victim had been hanging from the tree and to the man they'd seen lurking near it. Nathan understood the difficulty. Sometimes, weeks after a crime, horrible images replayed in his mind without warning.

He reached for her hands, to offer comfort from the terror he saw in her. Her hand was warm and soft in his and the shadows from the fireplace cast light across her face. She shifted, the robe parting near the top to reveal a shirt beneath. He'd gotten a preview before she'd put her sleepwear on and now he wanted to see more. The shirt was thin. Maybe one of those tank tops with the straps that fell over a woman's shoulder in invitation. An invitation he wouldn't decline.

Stop.

He needed to find Colleen's killer. He had promised his family he would do this. Besides that, Autumn was his partner, someone who would help him solve the case. She had also found one of the Huntsman's victims. He couldn't have a relationship with her—it would muddy the water, make them lose concentration. Nathan had questions about her family, and getting involved with anyone close to the case was a mistake.

Before he could pull his hand away, Autumn laid her head on their joined fingers, her hair falling across his arm.

The fire crackled in the air, sparks dancing inside the hearth.

"I don't feel like it's over. The killer won't stop," Autumn said.

The Huntsman wouldn't stop looking for victims until he was caught. All the more reason to focus and work as fast as possible before the body count rose.

His skin burned hotter with every instant she was pressed against his hand. She shifted closer, bringing their bodies within inches. He fisted the blanket against his body, keeping her from seeing how badly he burned for her.

"I need someone to hold me," she said. "Just for a few minutes."

Her words decimated the last thread of control Nathan had clamped over his libido. His arms slipped around her waist, pulling her to him, her chest pressed to his. Her robe opened farther, revealing he'd been right about the top's thin straps. Longing, hot and intense, rocked him, mixing with the scorching need to taste her.

She licked her lips, bringing his attention from her eyes to her mouth. Her perfectly shaped mouth, lips slightly parted. He didn't know who closed the space between them, but in the next instant his mouth was pressed to hers, her lips searing his.

The kiss was hungry, needy, her tongue outlining his lower lip, demanding a response. He returned the kiss with equal fervor, his tongue parrying with hers, his kisses slow and thorough, and his pulse kicking up a notch in response.

Her lips were soft and pliant, her hands planted on his shoulders, her nails digging in, holding him close.

The kiss was rooted in the need for comfort, the need to scrub away the horrible night with a few moments of closeness and warmth. He understood that need too well. But the kiss, gentle and soft, took on a life of its own. He tasted her hunger, her loneliness and her sadness.

He broke the kiss, studying her face. "Tell me what's on your mind." Because it was more than him and when they were kissing, he didn't want to share her.

"I was thinking about what Ford said about your wife," she said.

He jolted. "You want to talk about my ex now?" The mention of her was ice water on his libido.

"Ford mentioned you abandoned her."

"He was right."

Autumn drew away. "Why?"

"We weren't right for each other. She was needy and I wasn't ready to take a step back from my career. The more we fought about it, the more I drew away. I knew it wouldn't work, so I left her."

Autumn came to her feet and crossed her arms. "I see."

Her voice reeked of censure. "Do you? Relationships have complexities we can't fully explain."

She narrowed her eyes. "Meaning what?"

"Tell me more about your brother and your uncle."

She inhaled sharply. "Why are you asking about Blaine and my uncle?"

Now he felt guilty. He hadn't meant to use what Daniel had told him against her, but he was feeling as if the gloves were off. "Is your brother involved in what's happening on the trail?"

Her head jerked back. "Get out of my cabin."

He didn't want to start a war with her. He wasn't the enemy. "Why are you avoiding the question?"

She fisted her hands at her sides. "Get out. Get out now."

This raw anger on the heels of that kiss proved they had something between them, something big that neither of them was ready to explore. A fight extinguished the possibility of this ever being more.

Autumn's legs moved slower as they neared the crime scene, her psyche wanting her to turn away, logic assuring her that the space had been cleaned and any trace of death removed.

Thor bounded ahead and when she heard Nathan's voice, she considered going on a different path to avoid him. But he'd already spotted Thor.

"Good morning," he said, breaking the ice.

"Hi." She was angry he had dug into her personal life and implied Blaine was involved with the Huntsman, but after a night of terrible sleep mulling over what had happened, she was starting to think she'd overreacted. Why was she so defensive about her family? She could defend Blaine because he wasn't involved and that didn't mean she needed to get angry.

He spoke before she could. "I'm sorry. I crossed a line. I shouldn't have implied Blaine was involved in the case."

An unexpected peace offering. "Talking about my family regarding this case is off-limits, okay?" Autumn said.

"Okay," he said in agreement.

She glanced at the oak tree, needing to look at the space, needing to see it in the light of day, to dim some of the memories.

The sight jolted her senses. After seeing that spot again and again in her mind, it was empty. No person and no animals were near the tree. Nothing hung from the branches. Besides the tree branches and trampled ground, the evidence of what had occurred was gone. In a few weeks, the area would again be littered with leaves, erasing the incident from the forest entirely.

Only her memories of that night would remain.

"I'm planning to look around on the trail today," she said. She should have told him she was quitting, but that would make Blaine look guilty and it would leave her alone.

"I'll tag along, if that's okay," Nathan said.

She nodded. At least he was wearing hiking boots and the right clothes. No suits today. The red flannel shirt and hiking pants looked too good on him. Most hikers she knew wore clothes that were a little frayed with worn knees and at least a grass stain or two. He brought a refined look to outdoor clothing.

The weather on the trail could be volatile, anything from hail the size of golf balls to fluttering snowflakes lightly falling from the clouds. The sky was darkening to the east and the morning was overcast, a low fog hanging on the ground, making it hard to see into the distance. "We'll have a storm roll through by midday. The weather can be unpredictable. We need to be back to the campground before the weather turns rough."

Autumn didn't need a map. She knew the paths surrounding the Trail's Edge. She considered bringing Thor with them, but he'd been behaving skittishly and she didn't know if he'd follow her commands if something happened, such as tracking the shadowy figure to his hiding place.

After returning Thor to her cabin with a hefty

sense of guilt for leaving him inside again, she set out from her cabin with Nathan.

The past forty-eight hours had contained two amazingly polar incidents, equally poignant, evoking completely different reactions. The violence and terror of finding a victim in the woods and the heated excitement of Nathan's kiss.

She wouldn't spend the day obsessing about the kiss, but hiking the trail had the disadvantage of giving her an abundance of time to think. Usually, it was something she liked best about the trail. Today, she wished for something to occupy her.

She had other things to consider. Her brother and his safety were first among them. Was her brother okay? Why hadn't he called recently to let her know how he was doing? If he had decided to end his hike and return home another way, he could have called. Letting Nathan into her thoughts about Blaine made her feel as if she was betraying her brother.

"Are you always this quiet when leading a hike?" Nathan asked.

"I'm looking for tracks to follow." She circled the scene, staying outside the crime tape wrapped around the surrounding trees and trying to determine which, if any, of the tracks belonged to the intruder.

If she could have looked at the ground before the FBI had arrived, it would have made her job that much easier.

Nathan walked alongside her, his long strides matching two of her own. "We saw the direction he ran. We could try to follow them, see if that narrows down the number of footprints."

"Let me see your shoes," she said. Nathan had given chase.

He held out his foot and she looked at its size and the footprints he had made behind hers. She found a long stick and carefully moved aside the leaves to see the mud and compressed leaves beneath. She stepped up her pace and followed Nathan's footprints. He hadn't been wearing hiking boots, and the flat presses into the mud were easier to follow and track than the dozens of hiking boot prints that the FBI had left in the area. One of the boot prints might belong to the Huntsman.

They lapsed into thoughtful silence as she tried to judge the direction, searching for trampled ground cover and broken branches. It was twenty feet away from the crime scene before she could see distinguishable prints.

They reached the spot where the Trail's Edge campground met the Appalachian Trail. The footprints intersected the main path and then stopped. Had the intruder turned onto the trail or continued into the backcountry? She guessed backcountry, but it was more of a sense than any facts guiding her. She made the decision to follow her instincts. "The white paint blazes mark the Appalachian Trail. We're going off the main trail. I don't recommend doing this unless you know this area well."

Nathan held up his hands. "Wouldn't dream of it without you."

Why did it send a thrill down her spine to think about Nathan staying with her, hiking together through the trail? Her entire life had been centered on nature. With Daniel, part of their connection had been the bond they'd shared with the outdoors. They'd liked to hike, fish, gather berries and shoot arrows at practice targets.

But that was where their chemistry had ended. Their escapades in the bedroom had been lacking. She'd known it but she couldn't determine how to bring it up to him. Whenever she'd made a suggestion, she'd ended up feeling like the clueless one. As Daniel was quick to point out, her other major relationship had been with a man who'd come out of the closet right before her senior prom. And since Daniel had no trouble finding other bedroom partners, she assumed the issue was her.

"You look like you bit into a sour berry. What's the matter?" Nathan asked.

Autumn wasn't aware he'd been watching her expression. "I was thinking about some things. Personal things."

"Tell me," he said.

As if it was easy to confide in someone she didn't know well. It was one of her lesser cherished traits. It took her a long time to trust someone and every time she was burned, she trusted a little less easily. Could she tell Nathan about Daniel and Ben? "I was thinking about Daniel and how much fun we had exploring the outdoors." That was easier to say without adding the part about their bedroom troubles.

"I'm sorry you lost your hiking buddy. With Blaine away, too, that has to be tough."

Tough and lonely.

He sounded sincere. Autumn wouldn't get emotional about it. Daniel had moved on and had moved on quickly. "Daniel and I weren't a good fit."

"Knowing that doesn't always make it easier," Nathan said. "I was married too young and I learned my lesson."

"What lesson was that?" she asked. Never to get married again?

"That relationships that are exciting are not always workable," Nathan said.

Exciting. It was a word she hadn't used before to describe a boyfriend. She wanted to change that. She wanted the opposite of realistic. She wanted fireworks. Could she have those with Nathan? He was closed off, but maybe that was okay. He wouldn't expect her to divulge her secrets to him and since he was around for only a short time, she could keep herself from getting emotionally involved. If the kiss they had shared was any indication, they had great chemistry.

Autumn concentrated on the path, the sights and smells. The path held an earthy scent, crisper when the leaves coated the ground. She couldn't remember the last time the trail was this unpopulated. Except for the killer. He was out here. "My brother and I grew up running up and down these trails. My dad had only one rule, and that was to be back to the cabin by dark." She pointed to some low-lying red berries. "Those are poisonous to eat. But those—" she pointed up the tree to small blue berries "—are not. Harder to get, but after Blaine and I learned to climb a tree, we were set."

"I'd have liked to see that," Nathan said.

She smiled at the memory of her and Blaine playing along the trail. "I ruined a lot of pants. My father had to learn to sew because new clothes were too expensive and the tailor charged too much for repairs."

"Sounds like your father was a good man."

Grief over her father hit her at strange times, and today, thinking about the late nights he would spend mending her pants, was one of those occasions. She blinked back the tears that burned behind her eyes and turned away, pretending to look around. "He was. He spoiled Blaine and me because he felt guilty about being a single parent." They hadn't had money, but they had long, wild summer days. It wasn't until Blaine got into trouble with a tough group in high school that their father implemented rules and jobs for them. It was his way of preventing Blaine from spending his time loitering in town and starting problems with the law.

"My father lived his dream, running the Trail's Edge and taking care of the trail." For the longest time, it had been her dream, too. But she hadn't expected to run the Trail's Edge alone. She had thought she, Blaine, her father and her uncle would do it together. But those idyllic days she remembered as a child were long gone. Life had taken away the people she loved, and without them, the Trail's Edge wasn't the same.

"And now you run this place," Nathan said.

It wasn't the business she had remembered. Without many guests recently, she missed those connections. She missed sharing her love of the outdoors with others and teaching kids to hike, fish and climb. "I have been running it for a few years, even when my dad was still around. When he got older, it was harder for him to do physical labor. His back hurt more and he got tired faster. At some point, he started taking naps in the afternoon."

That earned her a smile from Nathan. "My father used to fall asleep in front of the television. He said he was resting his eyes, but my mom and I knew better."

Fathers and their pride. Her father didn't like to appear weak or admit he was tired, especially in front of her and Blaine. For that reason, Autumn had always felt safe with her dad. She hadn't allowed ghost stories Blaine told her or tales of bear attacks and wolf maulings keep her awake at night. In her young mind, her father was invincible and he'd protect her from those things.

Was that why she loved having Nathan near? Because he brought with him the same sense of protection, that same quiet strength she had been missing since her dad died? "Sounds familiar," she said, not comfortable with how easily she was letting herself grow accustomed to having Nathan there and how easily she was opening up to him. He was around for only a few days.

She stopped and pointed to the rounded rock jutting from a copse of trees. "That's a landmark we'll use to know the path to return."

Autumn took a side trail that ran perpendicular to the main one. She hadn't cleared this path in some time and it was heavy with leaves and undergrowth. "Watch your step. Those leaves can hide slick mud and roots." If she didn't pick up the killer's trail, she'd trace back and look for prints along another route.

"Last thing I need is a muddy backside," Nathan said.

Autumn walked backward a few paces, looking again at the pants he was wearing. They were basic hiking apparel, probably from an outdoors store. They sat on the tilt of his hips and were fitted around the thighs without being tight. She hadn't known a man to look that good in hiking pants. "You'll be okay." She tore her eyes away from Nathan. "They're probably waterproof."

She focused on the trail, glad to have a place to put her attention other than Nathan. Keeping a steady pace, she scanned for signs of humans.

"Have you picked up the trail?" Nathan sounded winded and Autumn glanced over her shoulder to make sure he was keeping up. His cheeks were flushed and red, and he'd shed his jacket. Had she been moving fast?

"Not yet." She made a mental note to slow down. Her legs were accustomed to hiking long distances. Nathan's were not. "Do you need a break?" She handed him a bottle of water from her pack.

He took a drink. "No, I'm okay."

Autumn stopped and scanned the area, giving Nathan time to collect himself. Maybe male pride wouldn't allow him to admit he needed a break, but she could see it.

Birds moved from tree to tree, landing on branches and dropping leaves to the ground. Squirrels leaped across the forest floor, gathering the last of the nuts that remained. The wind whistled through the near-naked tree branches, brushing them together.

She scanned the ground and her eyes settled on

something unusual. Excitement rocketed through her. "The leaves are depressed there." Grooves the shape of a footprint lined the path.

Nathan moved closer to where she'd indicated. "Are you sure these aren't from an animal?"

Too large and shaped wrong to belong to an animal. "I'm sure. Those aren't hoofprints, paw prints or claw prints. Those are human."

"How many sets?" Nathan asked.

She circled the tracks to get a look at them from a different angle. "One person. Two if they were walking in each other's prints."

"Which way are they going?" His voice was a whisper, catching and holding on the air.

She studied them, but she couldn't conclusively decide. The prints were equally wide on each side, almost as if the person's foot was square. Who had square feet? Unless... "Both directions. To and from."

Had she found the intruder's path to and from the Trail's Edge? The same thought must have lit in their minds simultaneously.

Nathan reached to his side and unsnapped his gun's holster. "He could still be in the area."

She nodded once, her heart galloping. She didn't travel with her hunting rifle, but maybe this would have been a good time to start. They had a better chance against an attack when carrying protection.

Autumn looked around. Hiding in the forest was a simple matter. Was the Huntsman watching them? The hair stood up on the back of her neck. "He knows we're here."

Nathan pulled his gun. "How do you know? Do

you see something?" He circled slowly, looking around.

Instinct. "I sense it. We're being watched."

"Do you want to go back to your cabin?" Nathan asked. "I can return on my own."

Autumn shook her head. "You won't know how to track the path."

Nathan eyed her as if deciding. "Stay close to me. I'll keep you safe."

Autumn believed him. "The trail gets rougher ahead. It's hard to get past Rock Valley," Autumn said, thinking about the places where someone could set up shelter. Limitless possibilities, but some more practical than others.

"Rock Valley?"

She looked away from the footprints. "That's what Blaine and I call it. It's a pit about forty feet wide and twenty feet deep made of sharp rocks. You can climb inside, but it's not for the faint of heart."

Nathan shook his head. "We're going back."

Autumn narrowed her eyes. She wasn't ready to give up or turn back, not when she felt they'd found something important. This might be their only break. If the Huntsman knew they were out here, if he knew they were on his trail, he would relocate. Perhaps he would make a mistake defending his territory and come after them, giving Nathan a chance to apprehend him. "I'm your trail guide and I can help. These tracks are recent. We'll lose the scent if we don't follow them now. The more leaves that fall from the trees, the more they'll get covered." As if to make a point, more red leaves fluttered to the ground.

Nathan turned his attention to the path. She'd gotten her way if only due to his relentless need to find his sister's killer. "Why would he be that sloppy? We've found nothing at the other crime scenes. It could be a trap."

Autumn swallowed hard, a chilling sense of foreboding skittering across her skin. If they left now, the killer would be in the wind. She forced her mind to think of happy things, springtime on the trail, Thanksgiving dinner and decorated pine trees for Christmas. She wanted those things back in her life—warmth, safety and happiness—and with the killer loose, she couldn't have them. "A trap or no one else knows the area like I do. No one else had the right skills in the right place to track him."

The Huntsman wouldn't paralyze her with fear. The image of a scraggly mountain man with wild eyes flashed into her mind, and she stamped it out. The killer was one person. She and Nathan had each other.

Nathan cupped her chin in his hand, forcing her to look at him. "Stick to my hip. Do exactly as I tell you. If you see anything, if you find more evidence of a human nearby, alert me immediately. Got it?"

She nodded, her heart snapping up its pace. They'd been lucky to see the footprints, the slightest disturbance of the undergrowth. The brush and the leaves made it difficult to discern tracks in the woods. Where had the killer gone first—toward the Trail's Edge or away from it? Despite the quiver of fear shaking in her belly, she screwed her bravery up tight. Now wasn't the time for fear. She needed all the courage she could muster.

They were tracking a killer.

Chapter 4

It would be easy to become lost in the mountains. After a time, the trees began to look alike, the same evergreens, elms and oaks, their trunks identical, the stones and rocks dotting the way indecipherably different. The smell of pine and earth mixed with the cold air was numbing.

Autumn was at Nathan's right side, close enough he could watch her in his peripheral vision and scan the trail ahead of them. Not so close her scent would distract him or his eyes would fixate on her slim figure and he'd trip over his feet.

She abruptly drew to a stop, grabbing his shirt. She held her finger to her lips, indicating he shouldn't speak, and then pointed into the gorge ahead.

Her description of Rock Valley had been perfect. Gray and white stones covered the ground, some smoothed by the rain, others jutting raggedly from the dirt. On the far sides of the gorge, a full-grown bear and one smaller bear milled near the opening of a cave.

"Do you see a human presence?" Nathan whispered. After the few footprints had ended on the side of the trail, he hadn't seen other signs of the Huntsman.

She shook her head. "They're upset," she said, crouching down. "They're too restless this near hibernation."

Nathan watched them, fascinated. He'd never been this close to wildlife, at least wildlife not secured in cages. "I didn't realize bears were pack animals."

"They aren't. But they sometimes travel in groups. It's safer. We need to get away from here without disturbing them. Do not run. Do not turn your back on them." Her voice was calm, but her posture tense.

They stood slowly, backing away. When they were fifteen feet from the gorge, Autumn turned on a dime and froze. Her eyes went wide. A smaller black bear was meandering nearby, eating some berries off a low-hanging bush.

Nathan caught the sense of danger immediately and reached for his gun. They were between a bear cub and its mother. The bear cub wasn't as likely to attack, but the threat was imminent. The wind blew hard.

"Maybe she didn't see," he began, but the protective growl echoing from the valley answered his question. Mama bear had seen them or smelled their scent on the wind. He looked over his shoulder and saw the bear barreling toward them on all fours, zigzagging on the rocks, perhaps their only saving grace to buy them extra moments to flee.

Everything happened in an instant. He grabbed Autumn's forearm and they ran through the woods, knowing they couldn't outrun a bear, but hoping they could get out from between the mother bear and the cub and she'd decide they were no longer a threat and not worth giving chase.

"Shoot your gun into the air," Autumn said.

Nathan discharged his weapon into the trees, not stopping for an instant. He didn't need to aim. He needed noise to scare off the bear, possibly warn her of danger and make her reconsider pursuing them. They wove in and out of trees, branches thwacking into his arms and face. He did his best to keep Autumn behind him so the whip of the branches missed her.

Autumn stumbled and Nathan jerked her upright, preventing her from landing face-first in the dirt and hurting herself. He had to get her to safety. He had told her he would keep her safe.

They came to a stop behind a wide tree trunk. They were out of sight, but not likely out of mind.

He glanced around the trunk and, not seeing the bear, relief rolled through him. He gulped in the cold air. Autumn had kept a steady pace from the campground to Rock Valley and he'd been tired, but he had found the energy to run. An angry bear brought that kind of motivation.

He needed a place they could hide safely. "How far are we from the nearest shelter?"

Autumn pushed her hair behind her ears. "Miles."

"We could climb a tree and wait," he said. "Show me some of those climbing skills."

Autumn's breath came in gasps and she leaned forward, bracing her hands on her thighs. Her cheeks were red with cold and exertion. "Bears can climb, too. But faster and better. I think we were incredibly lucky. I don't think she followed us." She let out a noise of frustration. "I was so busy looking for human prints, I forgot to look for animal ones. I should have seen the signs before we were on top of them."

"Can you keep running?" he asked.

She took a drink from her water bottle and handed him another from her pack. He'd feel better if they could put more distance between themselves and the bear.

"I'm fine. We can't hike back in that direction. We need to circle around."

"Fine by me. No interest in returning to the bear's den," he said.

"We lost the tracks," Autumn said. She took out her compass and adjusted it. She looked at her watch and then to the sky. She pointed in a direction and started walking. "I didn't know black bears had made a home in Rock Valley. Maybe the tracks weren't from the Huntsman. They could have been from researchers or park rangers tracking the bears."

"Does that happen often?" Nathan asked.

Autumn shrugged. "Like I said, it's strange the bears wouldn't have been hibernating. It's cold enough they should be settling in for the winter. We can talk to Ben and the other park rangers and see if they have any bear population projects ongoing."

Autumn had a slight limp in her step.

She had tripped while they were running. He mentally berated himself for not checking if she was injured. "Are you okay?" he asked. He had some basic first-aid training and if she was hurt, he wanted to see what they could do now.

She bent to rub her knee. "I twisted my knee. I'm fine. I can walk it off."

He had a hunch it wasn't as minor as she made it sound, but he didn't push the issue. Not yet. "I'll carry the pack," he said.

She waved him off. "I'm fine. It's just a little sore. We should keep moving." She glanced behind her.

He looked over his shoulder, as well, half expecting to see a bear charging toward him. As they walked, he could see she was in pain, her eyes slightly narrowed, her lips pressed together to keep from grimacing. Twenty minutes later, she finally gave up and sat on a downed tree trunk, massaging her knee. "I need to rest for a minute. I have a general direction from the compass, but I don't know how far we are from the Trail's Edge or the trail itself."

Nathan stopped and squatted in front of her. They'd had an early start in the morning. They could find their way to the trail. As long as she could walk, they'd be fine. "Let me take a look at it."

It must have hurt terribly because she acquiesced. She rolled her pant leg up her shapely calf, past her knee. He rubbed his hands together to force out some of the cold and cradled her knee in his hand, gently turning her leg left to right. Her skin was warm and soft in his hand. Nothing was protruding, but he couldn't see the extent of the damage. It would probably bruise and make it difficult to walk. He needed to do something to make it easier for her. Seeing her in pain was difficult for him. It niggled at the protective part of his brain.

She slid her day pack off her shoulders and dug inside. She pulled out a long roll of cloth and held it up. "I'll wrap it to give it some support."

He took the roll from her hand, needing to feel useful. "Let me do it. It's easier from this angle," he said.

He held the bandage in his hand, started below the knee and wound the stretchy cloth up and around her leg several times, tightening the material around her knee to give support without cutting off the blood supply to her foot. "How's this? Too tight?"

"No, it's good," Autumn said, pointing and flexing her shoe, brushing his side with her foot.

Nathan ignored the warm shiver moving down his spine at the contact. When he ran out of cloth, he secured the edge and then pulled her pant leg over it.

"That should help," he said, setting her foot on the ground. He gave her his hand and helped her to her feet, another zap of heat striking him. He took the pack from her shoulders and stood on her right side, bending his elbow. "Use me as a crutch."

She bent and straightened her knees slightly, as if testing the injury. "I can't do that. We have a few miles to walk. I'll tear your arm from the socket."

He shot her a look that said *get real*. She was tall, but she was thin, and putting a little weight on him to take it off her knee would make the journey easier. "I'll hardly feel it, but if I have to carry you and our packs for miles, my bum knee will have problems."

Autumn looked at the sky. "Let's hope the weather holds. It will get more difficult if we have to hike in a snowstorm."

She took his hand, bracing her arm on his. Her hand was small, her fingertips cold. He closed his hand around hers, trying to warm it. She was relying on him, and though he was out of his element in the woods, he was acutely aware that taking care of her gave him a sense of rightness and completeness.

Thunder clapped in the sky. A storm was approaching. A light drizzle struck the trees. They had some shelter from the trees, but a small bit of water could soak them and cause hypothermia. Autumn withdrew two ponchos from her bag.

They could hunker down and wait for the storm to pass, but the poncho would help and home was the safest option.

As they walked, their pant legs and shoes grew muddy and wet. Nathan distracted her with tales of growing up, the pranks he and his friends had pulled, the trips they went on and the disasters they narrowly avoided. They'd never been chased by a bear, or gotten anywhere close to the den of a predator, at least that he knew of, but their antics had gotten them in more than a few scrapes.

He and Autumn found a white blaze painted on a tree two hours later. In a small celebration, they tore into granola bars she had packed, shoving the wrappers in their pockets. Autumn turned in a slow circle, looking at the treetops. "I've been this far before. We only need to go another twenty minutes, brisk pace."

He didn't point out he'd been setting a slower pace, not wanting to aggravate her knee injury. He could tell it was better with the makeshift brace, but the way she flinched every few steps told him she needed to get off it soon, maybe pack it with ice and keep it elevated.

"Is the trail always this deserted in the fall?" he asked.

"Because of the weather, it isn't prime hiking season. Between the Huntsman and the cold, I think people are finding other places to hike." Her tone twinged with sadness.

He patted the hand she'd looped through his elbow as they walked. "We'll get him and we'll put things back to normal."

Autumn glanced at him and then focused her attention on the trail ahead.

"What?" he asked, catching something in her eyes.

"I was just thinking that I'm not sure I want things back to normal. I want things to get better."

Autumn had begun letting him inside her private thoughts. He wanted to know more. He wanted to learn about her, what made her tick, what mattered to her. "What do you want to change?" he asked. Her life seemed to revolve around her business and the Appalachian Trail, and from what he could gather, she didn't leave the Trail's Edge unless she had no other options. Was she hoping to change that? Break out of her shell?

"I'd like to be able to talk to my brother," she said.

"We were close when we were younger, before my uncle died. But Blaine took his death hard and we drifted apart. He eventually shut everyone out. He didn't want to help run the Trail's Edge anymore."

A stab of disappointment pierced him. He'd wanted her to say she would make herself less isolated. He'd worry about her alone at her campground. Getting in touch with her brother was a start, though. "Maybe if you let him know how you feel, Blaine will come around."

Autumn shrugged. "I hope you're right. For Blaine's sake and for mine."

"Let's put some ice on your knee," Nathan said, helping Autumn up the stairs to her cabin.

Autumn unlocked the door and Thor greeted them, his tail wagging excitedly. Locking the door was a new habit she promised herself she'd commit to, and with her guard dog in place, she felt marginally safer.

"Have a seat. I'll get some ice," Nathan said.

Autumn grabbed her satellite phone and hobbled to the plush chair next to the couch, propping her foot on her ottoman and rolling up her wet pant leg. She unwound the bandage and rubbed at her knee. The injury couldn't have been too major or she couldn't have put weight on it. If it wasn't better by the end of the week, she'd make an appointment to have a doctor look at it. Her experience with twists and sprains was that given enough time and a little rest, they mended themselves.

Thor plopped beside her chair, his tail thumping against the wood floor rhythmically. She glanced over her shoulder at Nathan. He was breaking ice out of the tray she stored in the freezer and wrapping the cubes in a clean dish towel.

She faced the empty fireplace and closed her eyes, relaxing her muscles and letting the heat of the room seep into her bones. Nathan had been attentive and sweet, even though she had walked him into a dangerous situation. She'd forgotten basic rules for survival on the mountain. She knew better than to fixate on one thing and forget the world around her.

Her uncle had been an expert tracker and he had taught her tricks to finding signs of an animal—worn paths, paw prints and excrement. She was tempted to go out again, maybe in a few weeks when the bears were in hibernation, and practice her tracking skills. Though she hadn't been as expert as her uncle at tracking, so her skills had gotten rusty.

She sent a text message to Ben, asking about the bears in the area. He replied that he hadn't had requests from researchers to work in the area nor was he aware of unusual bear behavior. So much for that theory.

Nathan sat across from her. Her skin prickled in awareness. He was handsome, almost to the point that it hurt to look at him. She wasn't normally attracted to men who were polished and groomed, but on him, it worked. The mud on his pants and the dust on his face reminded her of a model in a fragrance ad, rugged yet refined.

She dreaded listening to her phone messages, likely more cancellations. Her reservations book was wide-open. If she didn't get some guests soon, she'd have to find another job to pay the mortgage. She shouldn't have remodeled the cabins all at once. She should have waited until they'd had the capital and taken each improvement slowly, over time. When business had been good, she'd calculated the investment would pay off in five years. At this rate, it was more like fifty.

She played the messages. The first two were silence followed by hang-ups and the third was Roger Ford, asking her or Nathan to call as soon as possible, an urgency underlining every word. She relayed the message to Nathan and handed him the phone.

Her heart thumped hard. If Ford was calling, it wasn't good news.

Her financial issues took a backseat to the problems with the Huntsman. When he was caught, she'd work to bring people back to the Trail's Edge.

Nathan made the call to Roger Ford while sitting on the couch. He listened for a few minutes, making sounds of acknowledgment. When he disconnected, his face was grim, his shoulders tight. "Ford wanted me to know they have a positive identification on the victim. It was a woman, early thirties, named Sandra Corvaldi. They are releasing her name to the media once the family has been notified."

Sandra Corvaldi? Autumn knew her, but not well. Should she tell Nathan that the Reeds had ties to her? She could trust Nathan, couldn't she? Once her name was released, Daniel would probably remind everyone that Blaine had been involved with Sandra. "Sandra dated Blaine in high school," Autumn said.

Autumn's stomach dropped. It wouldn't take long

for the FBI to connect her brother to Sandra. Once they did, it was another piece of evidence that pointed at Blaine.

Nathan plowed his fingers through his well-cut hair. "What was their relationship like?"

A fierce headache split through her mind. "What's any high school relationship like? Too much drama and lots of ups and downs."

It was how Sandra's friends and parents would remember the relationship, and they wouldn't be shy about sharing that information with the FBI.

"Did he tell you anything else?" Autumn said. Had a warrant been issued for Blaine's arrest?

"No. He shared the information because it was about to go live anyway. He wants to come back to the Trail's Edge to talk with you."

Autumn had to find something, anything to point away from Blaine before she spoke to Roger Ford. She wouldn't lie to him, but she couldn't throw more suspicion in Blaine's direction. "We'll go tonight to the coroner's office and talk to Natalie."

Nathan glanced at her knee. "You need to rest tonight. We can take a trip into town to see her tomorrow."

Autumn shook her head. "No. The medical examiner's office is closed Friday through Sunday. I don't want to wait."

"It's closed three days a week?"

Autumn shrugged. "It's a small town. Not much for them to do. At least, not much until now."

She thought again of Blaine. Why hadn't he called? It was impossible for her to guess where Blaine was on the trail. He could have taken a long detour or he could have kept a steady pace straight through.

"We'll find this guy. He'll make a mistake and we'll be ready for him when he does," Nathan said.

Autumn swung her legs to the side and stood, hobbling to the closet to get her knee brace.

"You could have asked me to get that."

Autumn sat and strapped the brace around her knee. "I'm used to doing things myself." She wouldn't rely on Nathan. He would leave and then she would be alone again. They were the cards she had been dealt and she wouldn't fixate on the situation too much. If she did, she would be lost. She couldn't walk away from the Trail's Edge. She was upside down on a mortgage and had few other marketable job skills. Where did that leave her?

"Hate asking for help?"

Autumn positioned the brace. "Not that I hate asking for it. Usually there isn't anyone around to ask. Thor's great, but he's not the best if I need something minus the slobber." A joke to make her loneliness sound less serious than it was.

"You don't get many visitors here? Besides the people who rent the cabins, that is?"

Autumn jerked her pants over the brace. It sounded pathetic, but no, she didn't have many friends who visited her and she hadn't dated anyone since Daniel. "I'm busy. I have a lot to do."

Nathan didn't say anything in response and his silence smacked of judgment.

Autumn pushed herself to her feet. "I know you're thinking I live like a hermit, but I don't. I'm social when I need to be. Just the other night, we went to dinner."

"I wasn't thinking you were a hermit. You didn't like being out. You couldn't wait to return to the Trail's Edge." Though the words were frank, they lacked any hostility or accusation.

What he'd said wasn't entirely true. At first, she had been hesitant to go, but once she'd been out with Nathan, she'd had a good time. She glared at him, trying to derail this conversation. She didn't want to discuss her social life. "I had fun."

"Glad to hear it. But you should practice not glaring at me. Our story about being involved goes right out the window if you're hostile to me in public."

"We're not in public now. And couples fight," she said. Why did he make her feel so defensive? She liked her life the way it was and nothing was wrong with keeping to herself.

"How do you want to play this out at the coroner's office?" Autumn asked. She had initially suggested Nathan flirt with Natalie, but now she was even less enthused by the idea. Natalie was sexy and feminine and could easily grab hold of Nathan's attention. As much as she tried to keep boundaries, Autumn liked Nathan's interest in her. She liked the sizzle and crackle of the chemistry between them.

Nathan rolled his shoulders. "We'll go in together. I can convince her to talk to us."

"Might not be that easy."

"I convinced you to help me. I convinced you to go out with me."

Nathan stepped closer to her. His eyes wandered

down her body, lingering a moment longer on her lips and her breasts. The suggestion was clear and it affected her the same as his hands and lips would have.

"You are a convincing man," she said.

She read the kiss in his eyes before he leaned forward to deliver it. When his lips touched hers, she melted against him, her hands going to his chest and her fingers fisting into the fabric beneath them. He had technique and heat, and the slow laziness of the kiss was thoroughly enjoyable.

He broke the kiss and she kept her eyes closed for a few extra beats, letting her lips tingle and her body ache for more.

With that, he left her hungering and scared of what that meant. Autumn's phone rang and she tore her eyes from Nathan and reached for the phone. "Hello, Trail's Edge."

"Autumn?" A voice from the past. She almost dared to hope the caller was not who she sounded like.

"Who is this?" Autumn asked, half hoping she had jumped to the wrong conclusion.

"It's your mother. I'm outside. Is it okay to come in?"

Her mother hadn't come to her father's funeral. She had called and left a message extending her sympathies. Before that, her mother had only bothered with a phone call a couple times a year to check in with her and Blaine. Anger surged inside Autumn. "What do you want?" Autumn heard the hostility in her voice. Her mother must have, too.

"I read in the news about the killing at the Trail's Edge. I'm here to see if you and Blaine are okay."

Did she care? Her mother hadn't been around for most of her life or for any of the important stuff. Why show up now and pretend to be concerned?

"Autumn?"

"I'm here," she said, still not making up her mind about how to handle her mother. Could it be a trick? Some mistake?

A knock on the door.

"Do you want me to answer it?" Nathan asked, touching the gun at his side almost as a reflex.

"I don't know," she said, still clutching the phone.

"Autumn? It's cold out here and I almost died driving up these slick paths in the rain. Can I come in?"

Nathan took the phone from Autumn. "Who is this?"

Protective and strong. Autumn could hear only what he was saying.

"I don't know if she wants to see you or not." Several beats. "That's something you should have thought of before showing up. Wait on the porch. I'll be out when she's made a decision."

Nathan disconnected the phone. "Autumn? Are you okay? I don't know what's going on with you and your mom, but if you want me to tell her to leave, I will. You don't have to see her if you don't want to."

Autumn's mouth was dry and her head felt foggy. Her mother. How often had she wanted to see her? How many nights had she prayed her mother would return to be part of her and Blaine's life? Those long-ago wishes had been fractured by time. "It's okay. She can come in." Autumn knew who her mother was. She was the person who'd given birth to her, but who hadn't thought it was important to stick around.

Nathan pulled open the door and Autumn's mother stepped through. Autumn took a deep breath, steeling herself against the battery of emotions. Her mother looked nothing like her. Even with a little rain on her shoulders from running from the car to the porch, she was glamorous and gorgeous, free-flowing hair and carefully applied dramatic makeup and form-fitting jacket and pants. She looked like the few pictures Autumn had of her, only older and happier.

Though she had every right to be angry, Autumn felt insecure and small. Her mother was happier because she wasn't part of Autumn's life. She had made a life somewhere else without her family. Old wounds ached.

"Autumn, you look beautiful," her mother said.

Autumn had trouble finding words. No one called Autumn beautiful, that is, except her father, who had seemed convinced his daughter was a ravishing beauty. "After all this time, you show up and comment on how I look?" All she could think were words of rage. No matter what her mother said, Autumn would take them as fighting words.

Her mother fiddled with the end of the glittery scarf she had wrapped around her neck. "I told you, I came to see how you and Blaine are doing."

Bitterness swamped her, poisoning every thought in her head. "You don't get to show up after a few sporadic phone calls and pretend you care. You didn't care when Dad died. You didn't care when Blaine and I cried every night for you. Why do you care now?"

Tears threatened, but Autumn refused to cry in front of her mother.

The woman lifted her chin and firmed her jaw. "I know I am not mother of the year. I know I don't get to be your mom. I have reasons why I did what I did."

Her mother didn't deserve an inch. "I don't want to hear them," Autumn said.

A lie. She wanted a reason from her mother's mouth as to why it was acceptable for her to walk out on them.

"Maybe one day you will feel differently and you'll listen to me. I've wanted to get in touch with you. I thought at first it was easier if I wasn't around and by the time I'd realized it was a mistake, I knew you and Blaine hated me."

Hate was a good word. A defensive word. "That sounds like an explanation."

"It's not the whole explanation. There are things you don't know. There are things that happened in the past that you need to understand."

"I don't need you to lecture me about what I do and don't need to understand," Autumn said.

"When I read about the murder, I had to come and see you. I took it as a sign."

Autumn snorted. Nathan was standing near her, watching but saying nothing. Though he was quiet, she felt his support. He wouldn't take sides against her or ask her to calm down. How she knew that, she couldn't say. She just did. "I don't believe in signs. I believe in people showing their true colors and holding themselves to those colors. I believe the best predictor of future behavior is past behavior. I believe once you have broken trust, it is fractured beyond all repair."

"I'm sorry to hear that," her mother said. A long, empty silence. "Is Blaine here?"

Autumn curbed the urge to swear. "He is not. He is hiking the trail."

"While the Huntsman is looking for more victims?" her mother asked.

"That was not his plan when he set out. I am aware of the danger. I've been trying to contact him. I am hoping that because he doesn't match the profile of the other victims, he's safe."

Her mother looked between Autumn and Nathan. She introduced herself as Blythe Ferguson, her maiden name, and Nathan gave his name, but not why he was with Autumn and not that he was an FBI agent.

Autumn didn't know where to take this conversation. "This is a bad time. Nathan and I have somewhere to be."

"Can we have breakfast tomorrow? Or lunch?" Blythe asked.

Autumn needed more time than that. "I'll let you know."

Her mother looked in her handbag and withdrew a card. "Call me. Please. We have much that we need to talk about."

Autumn threw the card on the counter. "I'll see if I have time."

Blythe nodded and swallowed hard. Though the initial charge of fury had passed, Autumn refused to feel bad about her rude behavior. Her mother had abandoned her and Blaine. Was Autumn wrong to be suspicious that her mother was at the Trail's Edge for a selfish purpose?

Nathan drove into town under the guise of needing camping supplies. After his and Autumn's night out, his appearance would draw attention. He guessed patrons of outdoors stores would be looped into what was happening at the Trail's Edge and on the Appalachian Trail. He was curious about Autumn and she seemed hesitant to tell him much about herself and the campground.

Along Main Street, a camping store called The Out House seemed like a good option. Nathan entered the store and strode to the checkout.

A woman was flipping through a magazine. She stood straighter and smiled when she saw Nathan. "What brings you in today?"

"I'm staying at the Trail's Edge. I need a few things to hike the trail."

The woman stared at him for a few seconds. "You're planning to hike the trail?"

"Yes."

"You've heard the news, right?" she asked.

"About the Trail's Edge?"

"About the Huntsman. And a body."

"I heard."

The woman circled the counter. "I would suggest hiking elsewhere. It's not safe."

"That's what Autumn Reed said, too."

"She would know. She never comes down from

the trail. I mean, maybe now and then for supplies, but otherwise, she's a hermit."

"Why do you think that?" he asked.

Though they were alone in the store, the woman—Linda her name tag said—leaned closer. "I think it's because her mother left her when she was a child. Blythe couldn't stand living there with her husband and his brother. Then after Autumn's father died, her brother left. She's basically alone in the world. Poor girl."

"She seems fine to me."

"That's the weird part. Everyone who stays there says the Reeds are so nice and accommodating. But to me, they are all crazy."

Autumn seemed levelheaded to him. What did this woman mean by crazy? "Because she lives alone?"

"In part. But she also used to date the sheriff and he says that she's broken. She doesn't connect with anyone. She lives alone and keeps everyone out."

Linda seemed to know a lot about Autumn. "Are you two friends?"

The woman waved her hand. "I was a year ahead of her in school. I just hear stuff, you know?"

He did. He knew that rumors could be soul-crushing and that Autumn was doing her best to hold it together. If half of what Linda was telling him was true, then he gave Autumn credit for maintaining her sanity. Everyone who loved her had left or passed away, leaving her to fend for herself with a killer stalking women on the trail.

Nathan pulled into the gravel parking lot of the medical examiner's office. He could practically hear

Autumn thinking about what had happened with her mother. She might open up and talk about it or she could seal off her feelings and shove them to the side.

Before they went into the ME's office, he and Autumn had to get on the same page and Autumn needed to relax. Under the circumstances, it was a tall order. He parked the truck and Autumn unlatched her seat belt. Before she pulled the door handle, Nathan touched her arm. "Wait a sec, Autumn. Are you okay? You haven't said much since your mother left."

Autumn looked away, but not fast enough for Nathan to miss the tears in her eyes. "Nothing has been okay about this. I'm not sure I've even processed her showing up."

He didn't know the details of her relationship with her mother, but he had gathered enough to understand it was bad. "She seems to care about you."

Autumn rolled her eyes. "I don't believe that. She left us. She's contacted us a few times over the years. That is not caring about someone."

"She seemed like she wanted to make amends. Not that she can easily, but she's trying."

"I can't think of any reason that would be good enough to excuse her," Autumn said.

"Not excuse, but she could give you closure," Nathan said.

Autumn sighed. "I thought you were on my side."

"I am on your side. I am on the side that means you get to stop hurting. I'm on the side where you get to feel better about something that happened years ago. I'm on the side that makes you happy. My sister and I had our share of problems. When she died, she had just gotten out of treatment for the third time for alcoholism. I wish I had been more patient with her. I wish I had told her more often that I loved her. Instead, I mostly think about the fights we had about her drinking."

Autumn touched the side of his face. The show of affection was enough to communicate her appreciation. "I'm sorry to hear that about your sister."

Nathan didn't like to dwell on it. But part of his guilt in looking for the Huntsman was to bring closure to that guilt and justice to his sister, who had suffered too much over the past ten years as she struggled with her addiction. "I'm telling you because I want you to think about how you would feel if your mother left and you didn't hear from her again."

"I will think about it. But I can't deal with my mom's drama now, too."

"Fair enough. But you know I will back you up. We're partners for the time being, and that means something to me."

Autumn nodded once swiftly. "I understand."

"Do you?" he asked. Had she ever had someone be a through-thick-and-thin partner? How could he show her how serious he was? She could count on him.

Nathan wrapped one hand around the back of her head and drew her closer. His mouth claimed hers, demanding she kiss him in return. Her jaw loosened, allowing his tongue to sweep inside her mouth. The taste of her exploded in his mind. Cinnamon and coffee. A small moan escaped from the back of her throat and Nathan fought the urge to deepen the kiss. Tilt back his seat. Pull her astride him.

His lips played with hers until she was sinking against him across the center console. He knew ten more seconds and his sense of decency would be gone. He drew away and took a deep breath.

"What was that for?" Autumn asked, sounding almost breathless.

Nathan had plenty of reasons, most centering on wanting her. Wanting to prove to her they had something real and strong. "Do I need a reason?"

"I'd like to know what brought this on," Autumn said.

Her trust issues were showing themselves plain. "You can count on me. That's all."

"For the time being, until another victim shows up down the trail," Autumn said.

He didn't have a response for that. He felt they were getting closer to finding the Huntsman, but if they missed their opportunity in Smithsburg, he wouldn't give up on finding his sister's killer. He couldn't. His family was counting on him.

He cupped her face and ran his thumb across her reddened lips. "We'll find him. We're closing in. Let's talk to Natalie and work our magic."

When Autumn strode to the door, Natalie perked up at her reception desk, setting down the pen she had been flicking against a stack of manila folders. She smiled at Autumn, but her eyes lit when she saw Nathan.

He had that effect on women, and it bothered Autumn more than a little. He wasn't hers. She had no claim on him. She wasn't sure any woman could make a claim to him. But knowing that Natalie, one of the biggest flirts in town, would be all over Nathan got under her skin.

Autumn introduced Natalie and Nathan.

Natalie stood and circled the desk. She extended her hand and clasped Nathan's in her French-tipped, manicured hands.

"What a pleasure to meet you. I can guess why you're here, and I have to tell you that I can't release any data about that poor woman, even if she was found at your place," Natalie said.

Nathan didn't appear the least bit fazed. "We know you have to protect the victim's privacy. Autumn was worried that Sandra suffered and I thought you could reassure her."

"How did you know the victim's name? That wasn't made public yet," Natalie said, regarding them warily.

"We're working the case and Roger Ford let us know they'd identified the victim." Nathan leaned on the desk, putting Natalie closer to him. Autumn almost slapped her when Natalie reached to her blouse and undid another button at the top.

"You're working the case with the FBI? You're an FBI agent?" Natalie asked.

Autumn rolled her eyes at her friend's blatant eye batting and starstruck expression. They lived in a small town and didn't have many federal agents around, but this was ridiculous.

"I'm a special agent with the FBI," Nathan said.

"Oh, well, let me see here. I don't know how to tell if she suffered…" Natalie said, returning to her chair and looking through the stacks of papers in front of her.

Nathan waited and when Natalie held up a paper, he smiled at her. Natalie almost melted on the desktop. "Do you think I could take a look at it? I can interpret the medical jargon."

Natalie waved the paper at him. "Sure, take it, take it."

"Thanks, Natalie. I owe you a drink," he said.

"Anytime," she said. "I'm free this weekend."

"I'm tied up with the case, but I'll let you know."

With a final exchange of pleasantries, Nathan strode out the door. Autumn followed after him.

"Do women always fall at your feet?" she asked.

"She didn't fall at my feet. She wanted to help," Nathan said.

"I'm surprised she just handed it over," Autumn said.

"People have a thing for titles. They're taught to listen to and obey authorities. This case has rattled the whole town. Everyone wants the killer caught and everyone wants to help catch him."

They climbed into their truck and Nathan started the engine. "Read the report. Out loud. Please."

Autumn did, disappointed Natalie had given them the two-page summary sheet. It was labeled sheets one and two of fifty. They were missing good information.

Once she started reading, she was grateful for having less to read. Sandra had been killed and then hung from a tree using vines as rope. The cause of death was the arrows in her chest. "Do you think she died quickly?" Autumn asked. The report did not mention it.

"Sounds like it," Nathan said.

It was hard to tell if he was saying it to make her feel better. Autumn wouldn't question it. She'd had enough trouble with what she'd seen when she found Sandra and didn't need to add terrible thoughts to it.

"What do you think?" Autumn asked, skimming the pages again. "If Sandra was already dead, why did he hang her in the tree? What purpose does it serve?"

Nathan turned off the main road and onto the path leading to the Trail's Edge. "The killer has a reason and we need to get in his head so we get a lead on finding him. He's in tune with his surroundings and he has some special relationship with the Appalachian Trail or nature, someone who has spent considerable time outdoors."

The killer didn't have the same respect she and her brother had been taught. Nature included humans. "What about the vines? Why the wrappings around the victim's body?"

"It's his signature. It has some significance to him." He sounded contemplative and she imagined him working over a number of theories in his mind.

The first flakes of a snowstorm traveled to the ground. A little snow could turn into a huge storm quickly. "First snow of the season."

After several moments, he replied, "Think it will last long?"

She looked at the sky, where the dark clouds were moving closer. "The storm could pass without leaving much snow or it could dump a foot of snow in a few hours." Autumn had seen both and preferred the former.

Twenty minutes later, Nathan parked in front of Autumn's cabin. Autumn opened the front door to the cabin and Thor bounded down the hallway and immediately went to his food bowl.

Nathan sat in the living room with the papers from Natalie. Autumn was putting Thor's food bag back into the pantry when Thor lifted his head and growled. A moment later, a knock sounded on the door. Autumn jumped.

"Are you expecting anyone?" Nathan asked, rising to his feet.

Autumn shook her head. Maybe her mother had returned to try again to talk to her.

"I'll get it." He strode to the door, gun in his hand.

Autumn's heartbeat quickened. The Huntsman wouldn't knock. His style was much stealthier. If it was one of the investigators, why wouldn't they call first?

She heard male voices and then the closing of the door. Nathan returned. "Hikers from the trail looking for a warm place to sleep before the weather hits."

It didn't sound right. Where had the hikers come from? With news of the Huntsman splashed on every news media outlet in the area for months, who ignored the warnings? The answer popped into her head—people like her brother who thought they were invincible. "Are you sure? I haven't had hikers from the trail in weeks." If Nathan's instincts said they were fine, Autumn would let them stay in one of her cabins. She wouldn't want her brother turned away from

shelter over someone's paranoia. Trail hospitality dic-
tated she welcome hikers in need.

Nathan shrugged. "They want to rent a cabin.
They're seventeen years old and have state IDs and
IDs from the local high school. It's your call if you
want to allow them to stay."

They needed a place and she had a dozen empty
cabins. Autumn hurried to the door to welcome her
first guests in weeks. She ignored the twinge in her
knee and made a note to put some ice on it later.

She led the hikers to one of the cabins she had
available and took pride in the way the teenagers
cheered inside the cabin, looking forward to the pros-
pect of a hot shower and warm beds. Even the most
rugged hikers could appreciate modern conveniences
when it was twenty degrees with the windchill. These
hikers were young and couldn't have had much experience on the trail.

Nathan stayed at her side, setting his hand on her
lower back, perhaps a subtle message to the young
men that they were a couple so they wouldn't think
to bother her. She ignored his hand as much as she
could and focused on settling her guests.

She reacted too easily to Nathan's touch. A quick
brush of his fingertips and her body urged her to lean
closer, to press against him and encourage his arms
to band around her and hold her. It wasn't like her
to lose her head this way or become internally giddy
over a man's casual touch.

She explained to the hikers how to use the fireplace and the heater and left them to wait out the
weather. The snow fell heavier through the trees, mat-

ting the ground and covering the brown beneath its icy coating. "Maybe I should get another couple of cabins ready so if we have more visitors, I won't have to run around in the dark." If hikers were on the trail nearby and the snow got too heavy, all except the most dedicated outdoors enthusiasts would need shelter.

"Sounds good. I'll give you a hand," Nathan said.

Autumn grabbed a few bags of supplies she liked to stock in the occupied cabins—packets of oatmeal, granola bars and cans of chili—and headed to cabin twelve. If no one else came that night, she'd retrieve the items in the morning. But if they did, they'd be grateful for the supplies and she'd be grateful to not have to haul them in the snow.

She unlocked the door to the cabin and reached inside, flipping on the light. The cabin was a chilly forty-five degrees, much warmer than outside but not warm enough to chase out the bitter cold that seemed to linger on her skin. There were footprints leading inside, muddy tracks, and irritation with Blaine for leaving a mess flashed through her, followed by the dawning of a terrifying realization.

Blaine hadn't been here in months and she'd cleaned and closed this cabin for the season a few weeks ago. Her bag dropped to the ground, the food spilling across the floor. "Someone was here. Is here." Fear and panic gripped at her throat and her legs tensed, anticipating the need to run.

"How do you know?" Nathan asked, pulling her out of the cabin and onto the porch and setting himself around her as if to barricade her from a threat.

"Muddy prints on the floor."

Nathan withdrew his gun. "Wait here."

Autumn peered around the corner, watching him. He stalked through the room, turning on lights, checking every possible hiding place. "It's empty. No one is here."

Autumn swallowed hard. "Sometimes hikers come off the trail and break in." The tremor in her voice shook her words. It wasn't the first time a visitor didn't pay and, in the spirit of the trail, she chalked it up to someone who was desperate and cold. But this felt different. An uneasy sensation rolled down her spine.

Her gaze returned to the muddy boot prints, dark mud and red…like blood. She clamped her hand over her mouth to muffle the scream that rose in her throat.

Nathan whirled to face her and followed her pointed finger to the floor. His gaze canvassed the room.

"He was here," she whispered. "The Huntsman."

"Could have been an injured hiker," Nathan said. "I'm calling Ford. He and the team need to see this."

Autumn wanted to look for herself. She wanted to see if the killer had used the bathroom. Slept on the bed. Lit a fire in the hearth. The violation of her privacy and her sense of security was complete. Her home wasn't safe. A Trail's Edge cabin had been used by a killer.

Chapter 5

The killer had been closer than he had known.

Had the killer taken shelter in the cabin after he'd killed Sandra Corvaldi on the trail? Was the substance on the ground wet mud or blood? If the blood was human, it might provide a lead, a possible DNA match if the killer was already in the system.

The FBI hadn't checked the cabins the night Autumn had found the body and Nathan cursed his oversight. He should have searched everywhere in the area.

Nathan called Ford and left him a message. He composed his next steps. He needed a cotton swab and a sterile bag to collect a sample. He'd send it to an independent lab and—

His thoughts cut off abruptly when his eyes fell on Autumn's face. She was deathly pale, and had her arms wrapped around her midsection as if trying to hold herself together. In two long strides he was next to her, gathering her in his arms and holding her against his body. He stroked her hair. "It's okay. You're safe."

She trembled in his arms and burrowed closer. "I don't feel safe. He was inside one of my cabins." The words came as a whisper. She'd been maintaining an amazing level of calm since finding the body and he hadn't stopped to consider how this would make her feel, how this could overwhelm her. Each incident weighed more and more on her until she would eventually break down. He'd seen it happen to every agent he'd ever worked with.

Nathan sat her on the couch. He started a fire and cranked the pellet stove, but she continued to shiver.

"I'll make you a cup of hot tea." He pulled the blanket off the back of the couch and wrapped it around her shoulders, tucking the ends underneath her thighs. Thor trotted over and lay across her feet.

In the kitchen, Nathan turned on the burner beneath a kettle of water and waited impatiently for it to whistle. While he watched the pot, his mind churned over the latest developments.

Keeping Autumn under watch and safe was a higher priority now. The killer hadn't been sloppy at any other scene and left evidence of his presence. If the boot prints in cabin twelve belonged to the Huntsman, they had been left deliberately. Just as with stringing the victim on her property for her to find, the killer wanted Autumn to know he was close.

But why? What connection did Autumn have to the killer?

Nathan felt like a traitor for thinking again of her brother. Though Autumn seemed convinced Blaine had nothing to do with the murders, the more they found, the more the evidence pointed to Blaine.

Nathan struggled to think of who else could be a suspect. Someone with a relationship to the Trail's Edge, perhaps someone Autumn knew through her work on the trail? A guest who had stayed at the campground?

Nathan's protective instinct flared. He wouldn't let the killer get close to her. Whatever games the Huntsman had planned to toy with her, Nathan owed it to Colleen to prevent the killer from taking another victim.

The kettle whistled and Nathan turned off the burner. The killer fixating on Autumn and the Trail's Edge was a dangerous matter. Nathan poured the hot water into a mug with a teabag he found in a box in the cabinet. Decaf. She didn't need anything else keeping her awake tonight.

The killer had been this close, left his mark and hadn't approached Autumn that she knew about. Had he talked to her in a seemingly innocent manner, perhaps even in a public place? Nathan had once worked a case where a serial killer had approached each of his victims in random ways, talked with them briefly and marked them for death.

Was the Huntsman waiting for a chance to get her alone? The thought strengthened Nathan's resolve tenfold. The Huntsman wouldn't have a chance to strike at her. Nathan would stay at her side around the clock until the Huntsman was in custody.

Her phone rang and Nathan grabbed it before it sounded a second time. Autumn was watching him with wide eyes filled with fear.

He answered the call and Roger Ford's voice came on the line. "I'm surprised you called."

Nathan wasn't playing power games with Ford. While he had no intention of backing away from the case, he wasn't planning to shut out Ford, either. They didn't see eye to eye on anything, but Nathan would still offer him professional respect and courtesy. "We've had a development in the case I thought you should know about."

Ford harrumphed as if he didn't believe Nathan's motives would be that honest. "We have problems here." Based on the background noises, he was in the middle of chaos. "One of the cars wrecked, blocking the road and we can't get up the terrain. It's a whiteout down here."

Nathan moved the kitchen curtain and peered outside. With the blockade of the treetops holding back some of the snow, he could make out the forest, but barely. "Everyone okay?"

"Minor injuries. Our truck skidded into a ditch. We'll be there as soon as we can. Maybe in two, three days. Try not to compromise the scene."

Frustration with the situation was evident in Ford's voice. Ford was trying to provoke him and Nathan ignored it. He had other concerns. Like being trapped on the mountain with Autumn and a few high schoolers for two days with no knowledge of where the killer was lurking.

A pregnant pause filled the line. "How desperate is the situation? Can you handle this or do you need me to snowshoe up there?" Ford asked.

Snowshoe up three miles of mountain? Ridiculous. That plan would lead to someone else being hurt. "I'll be fine. We have supplies." Nathan had his gun. It took only one bullet to stop a killer. "We've got three others up here. Walked off the trail looking for a place to stay."

An ambulance sounded in the background. "Give me their names and descriptions. We've had people stationed on the trail for days. I'll make sure they've been cleared and their story jibes," Ford said.

He didn't need to say he was also considering the boys could be the Huntsman. It was less common, but serial killings were sometimes committed by a group.

Nathan gave the basic description of the hikers, including the names they'd given Autumn to record to rent the cabin for the night. Static crackled in Nathan's ear. "Better make it quick. The phone connection is getting dicey."

"If you don't hear from me in the next hour, I will call Ms. Reed's sat phone from one of ours. I'll see what I can do about getting you support from the police or the park rangers to process the scene," Ford said.

"I'll wait to hear from you." Nathan disconnected the call. He sat next to Autumn by the fire. She watched him, her eyes filled with questions her mouth didn't seem able to form. "The FBI is having problems navigating the roads. They'll do their best to get here when the snow dies down. Ford is checking with the police and the park rangers to see if anyone else is available."

Autumn moved closer to him, laying her head against his shoulder. "If the FBI can't get here, it's no easier for anyone else."

The scent of her hair wafted to his nose and he fought the surge in his libido. Now wasn't the time to make a move on her or panic her with the worst-case scenario. He needed to keep her calm and thinking. "We'll see. It might be a day or two."

She sighed and rested her arm across her stomach. Comfort. She needed to be comforted. Nathan searched for words that would make her feel better. Coming up empty, he put his arm around her, securing her against him.

"At least this means I can put off seeing my mom for a couple of days," Autumn said.

"Do you want to call her to be sure she is okay?" Nathan asked.

Autumn closed her eyes. "I should at least call to see that she found a place to stay. Or maybe she changed her mind and went home. She's never had a problem leaving."

Autumn went to the kitchen and picked up the card her mother had left. Nathan listened to one side of a stilted conversation.

"I should have installed alarm systems on the cabins," she said, returning to the couch.

Nathan stroked her side, trying to infuse some relaxation into her tense body. "You couldn't have known you'd need it. And a cabin with an alarm system? May as well turn the place into a resort and be finished with the whole facade of an outdoor experience."

His teasing earned him a smile, the corners of her mouth lifting a few centimeters. "My dad said the same thing when I first told him about my plans to renovate. He couldn't understand why I'd want to tear up counters that were a splinter waiting to happen and install polished oak."

Nathan hadn't seen the before, but he knew the quality workmanship of the current renovation. "This is one of the nicest places I've stayed."

She lifted her head from his shoulder. "Really? Nicest places? Do you stay at a lot of places where a killer runs loose?"

Actually, yes. He worked in the violent crime division of the FBI, and many of his cases were related to serial killers. "I've worked in some difficult situations." He'd leave it at that. He wouldn't haunt her with some of the cases he'd handled. "I made you tea," he said, remembering the cup in the kitchen. He braced his arms on the couch to push himself to standing.

Autumn grabbed his shirt. "Don't go. Not yet. Can we sit here for a while longer?"

His heartbeat quickened. Settling back into the couch cushions, he let her nestle into the crook of his arm.

She inhaled and let out a heavy breath, tucking her knees to her chest. The crackle of the fire and

Thor's heavy breathing remained the only sounds in the room.

"What will we do about being trapped here?" Autumn asked.

He hadn't had time to formulate a plan. "Wait it out."

"What if the Huntsman's out there, watching and waiting? He might decide to come after us now when we can't get help."

Nathan was certain the killer wasn't far. But the Huntsman wasn't invincible and would need shelter from the snowstorm. "No one can survive in the elements without some protection. He'll be snowbound with the rest of us." With any luck, the killer was snowbound away from the Trail's Edge and would remain that way until Nathan could set a trap.

They sat on the couch, watching the fire. The warmth of the room and the slow letdown of adrenaline made Nathan's eyes heavy. He couldn't sleep now. Not until Autumn had fallen asleep and he'd secured the perimeter. It wouldn't be a bad idea to check on the high school boys in their cabin, either.

Autumn shifted beside him and he glanced down at her. Her eyes were closed, her breathing even. Standing carefully, he laid her on the couch, draping a blanket across her body.

Autumn's phone rang and he hurried to answer it, not wanting the noise to wake Autumn. Ford confirmed the hikers were enrolled at a nearby high school and they had spoken to an agent farther up the trail. The agent's notes indicated the young men believed they could take care of themselves on the trail and didn't see any reason to cancel their trip, which they had been planning since the previous spring before the killings had begun. They had no intention of wandering into the backcountry where other bodies had been found and they had planned to stick together. Since the Huntsman's victims had been females, they thought it bought them guaranteed protection.

They were young and foolish, a dangerous combination. Nathan used the internal phone system to call the other cabin and let the young men know there had been a break-in at one of the other cabins. He warned them to be cautious, stay in their cabin and not answer the door to strangers. They were to call him if they heard or saw anything strange. Hoping they heeded his advice, he hung up the phone and returned to the living room.

Autumn's eyes were open, but she hadn't moved from the spot where he had placed her on the couch.

"Why don't I take you to bed?" he asked, hearing the double entendre in his words, but refusing to let it elevate his lust. The investigator in him wanted to gauge her reaction, wanted to know how she would respond to his question. He'd been drawn to her from the beginning and that connection urged him to test the waters.

"Bed is good," she said, without giving away whether or not she'd thought of his question as anything more than an innocent query. She came to her feet and tossed the throw over the back of the couch.

Nathan walked her to her bed and peeled away the blankets. She looked at the bed and then to him, the sleep gone from her eyes. Her eyes flashed with fiery provocation and heat tore through him.

"Where will you sleep tonight?" Autumn asked, taking another step and closing the distance between them.

An invitation? Was he imagining the flash in her eyes? Did she want his honest answer? "Here. With you." A bold statement.

A long, heated moment passed between them. She looked from him to the bed, to the couch and back to him.

She grabbed his shirt and pulled him to her, fusing her mouth to his. She let her body fall against the mattress, taking him with her. Her ravenous kisses decimated every last shred of control and he let himself tumble with her, bracing himself on his arms over her, absorbing the impact.

His head warred with his body. Would he let this happen? He was on the edge of being mad with lust— his hands reaching greedily to stroke her side, over her hip, down her thigh.

He needed to focus on the Huntsman. Secure the perimeter. Check the other cabins for signs of the killer. Stay alert for changes.

He wasn't a possessive man, but something about Autumn, her gentle mannerisms, her confidence on the trail and the wildness of her spirit drew him irresistibly close to her, made him want to claim her and mark her as his. His time in the outdoors and nature had unleashed a primal and possessive element.

Outside her door lay a mess needing to be fixed, but the snow put it on ice. In his arms was a woman who wanted to make love. Her touch and her kisses made it plain, and hunger consumed him.

He tilted his hips against hers, drawing a moan from her lips. She held him close, their kisses taking on a mindless intensity. He reached his thumbs under the waistband of her pants and panties and slid them over her hips. She kicked them away and he stroked the curve of her hip, running his hand along the smooth skin of her thigh. Reaching behind her, he cupped her bottom and lifted, molding her body to his, pressing his arousal into her, and letting her feel his excitement.

Raw need thrummed in his veins. He couldn't get enough of her, every second that passed driving him harder, satisfying him but at the same time urging him to take more.

Her fingers forked into his hair, holding his mouth to her. He tasted her need, and his body was eager to sate her. His hand skated up her body and under her shirt and palmed her breast.

She let out a low moan and he squeezed gently, rubbing her peaked nipples between his fingers. Her legs went around his waist, hooking him to her, and she lifted her hips off the bed, grinding her body into his. He stripped off the rest of her clothes. Having her naked before him, bare, open, was unbelievably arousing. Lust enveloped his entire being.

Nathan lowered his mouth to her breasts, suckling and kissing until she was panting and tugging at his shirt, begging him to take it off. He shucked his pants and shirt and then covered her with his body. The heat of the skin-to-skin contact, her nipples pressed into his chest, her mouth devouring his, was almost more than he could bear. He thought he might finish on her thigh like a prepubescent boy and worked overtime to slow his intensifying excitement.

This was what got him into trouble with women. Lust ruled him and logic became worthless. He'd never felt quite this intensely about a woman, a woman who was complex and smart and beautiful in an easy, natural way.

They had all night, no rush. He reached for his pants and pulled out his wallet, withdrawing the foil packet and tearing it open. He covered himself and shifted his hips between hers. He wanted to make this good for her, make it last long enough to bring her pleasure.

Her voice broke through his mental coaching. "Nathan, please, hurry."

His control shattered. He reached between her thighs and found her ready. He gave up concentrating on moving slow and instead let his body free-fall into the rush of the moment. He guided himself into her, biting his lip to keep from pounding into her, giving her a moment to adjust. She shifted her hips left to right, taking him deeper, and arched her back. Her hands clamped down on his butt, holding him inside her, and she squeezed him tight, a smoldering look crossing her face. The heat simmering between them burst into an explosion as his body sank and held inside hers.

She moved her hands to his sides and he pulled away and slammed into her, the friction shockingly sensuous. He worked his hips, plunging into her with wild glides, losing himself in her, conscious thought slipping away until pleasure—hers and his—was his only goal. The sound of her moans urged him on, harder, faster, until she was crying out his name, her fingernails scoring his shoulders, and he felt the quiver of her body around his.

Only then did he let himself fall with her into ecstasy.

In Autumn's cabin, buried beneath a foot of snow, it felt as if they were the only people on the mountain. The hikers hadn't bothered them, likely holed up in their cabin.

The quiet of the forest amid the falling snow created a sense of peace and tranquility. Like animals tucked away for winter, he and Autumn stayed in her cabin, mostly in her bed, the heat roaring from the fireplace. His gun was always within arm's reach. The killer wouldn't catch him unaware, but as the hours ticked by, the stillness of the campground made him feel safer.

In two days, they got out of bed only a handful of times—food, shower, refueling the fire, basic necessities. Neither of them mentioned the case or any of the unsettling events that had occurred. It was an unspoken taboo subject. Discussing it would taint this time they had together. For the first time in his career, Nathan let himself become thoroughly derailed from an investigation. He reasoned protecting Autumn was most important now and she was safest in his arms.

Like all good things, it had to end, a point he was sure she understood, as well. When the snow melted and the roads became passable, he had to turn his attention to the case. He would continue to protect her, but he couldn't afford a distraction or the drama that relationships seemed to shower down on him.

Autumn shifted onto her back, her hair brushing his chest, her fingertips sweeping across his side. She'd showered a few hours ago and her hair smelled of pine, a scent he was fast associating with her. "What are you thinking about?" she asked.

His thoughts hadn't varied much over the past couple of days. "Just you."

She rolled over, pressing her breasts against his stomach. Her hair was wild around her head, her smile bright. She propped herself on her elbow. "Oh, come on, that was a line, right?"

He shook his head. Despite how enchanting he found her, she seemed to carry around threads of self-doubt about her femininity. Nathan would wager the ex-boyfriend had something to do with it, another strike against him. "Not a line." What else would he be thinking about? The snowfall had ground the case to a standstill.

She drummed her fingers against his bare flesh. "Then what were you thinking about me?"

He pretended to think hard, bringing his finger to his lips. "Just that I wasn't sure if I'd had you every way I could have you and wondered if I could talk you into another shower. With me." He waggled his brows at her.

She grinned up at him. "A shower, huh?"

He rubbed her arm. "Just you, me and the hot water."

She slapped him playfully on the chest, threw back the covers and sprang out of bed. "Race you."

She made it first to the shower and he rewarded her by making her the subject of his absolute concentration—her, her mouth, her hips, her legs, every inch of her skin was the object of his sheer adoration.

Autumn's skin was slick with sweat. The heat pouring from the fire, the pellet stove and Nathan's body had chased away the last of the cold that had set inside her.

Hadn't that been the point of the past two days? To forget about the Huntsman and the snowstorm and Blaine and Sandra and get lost in the moment. To see if she had it in her to be passionate and seductive. Nathan was leaving and therefore she risked almost nothing in sleeping with him. If the adventure had been a disaster, it wouldn't have mattered for more than a week. But it hadn't been a disaster. She had stoked passion in Nathan. He had responded to her touch. Sex had been good. Great. The best of her life.

Nearly two days of making love, eating in bed, building fires and cuddling ended in one sharp rap on the door.

Nathan unentwined himself from her, his posture abruptly changing. He didn't kiss her or sweep his lips across hers before he stood to answer the door. He didn't let his hand linger on her body as if contact was the only thing keeping him alive. It was a shift only she could have noticed after two days as his lover, two days of studying his body, watching his movements, his expressions. He was no longer Nathan Bradshaw, lover extraordinaire. He was Nathan Bradshaw, working a case to find his sister's killer.

She'd bet her role in Nathan's life had shifted, as well. Autumn wasn't his lover. Not now. Now she was back to being his partner in this investigation. A pang of sadness struck her chest, but she brushed it away. She'd known things would change when the snow melted, and she'd told herself she could handle it. More than that, a brief affair was all she'd wanted.

Nathan dressed quickly and she did the same, making the bed and trying to hide the evidence of how they'd spent the past two days. As a last-minute attempt to hide the evidence, she threw a pillow and blanket onto the couch.

She heard Ford's voice, and a chill of cold air blew into the room. The time she'd spent with Nathan was the longest she'd been cooped up inside since she'd had the flu as a teenager. Normally, she ached to be outside and exploring, loved opening the windows in the spring to let in fresh air and hiking the trail whenever possible. But being inside the cabin with Nathan, she hadn't felt trapped. He had made her feel free and uninhibited in a way she usually felt only on the trail.

"Autumn, Ford needs the keys to cabin twelve," Nathan said. For all the warmth in his voice, he could have been placing an order at a drive-through fast-food restaurant.

"Morning, Special Agent Ford," she said, tossing him a smile and hoping he didn't see through it.

"Terrible morning. The roads are practically impassable," Ford said.

Brushing aside Nathan's and Ford's brusque manner, Autumn scrambled to the kitchen, where she thought she'd left her key ring. She looked around for the keys, knowing Ford had to see the mugs and glasses everywhere, the mess they had let pile up in the kitchen because it hadn't been important to clean when they had each other. Autumn refused to focus on that. "Sorry to hear that. But you made it."

Autumn found the keys inside the kitchen drawer. She snagged them and handed them to Ford, hoping she gave away nothing of her hurt or confusion in her movements or in the way she looked at Nathan. He hadn't asked her to remain quiet about their love affair, but she knew he wouldn't want it brought to Special Agent Ford's attention. Or anyone else's, for that matter.

Keeping their love affair between them was fine with her. She wanted to hold that piece of her life close and private to her heart. She hadn't had time to process it. Putting a name on the emotion was difficult.

Was it love? No, not love. Love didn't grow that quickly. He had made her feel differently than any other man had, but now that it was over, would it make it that much harder to move on from the relationship?

"The hikers are staying in cabin seven," she said to Special Agent Ford. She didn't look at Nathan, afraid she would react and Ford would read something in her face. "I brought them food and the heat was working fine in their cabin. We've talked to them several times and they've been safe, just a little bored."

"I've spoken to their worried parents. I'll talk to

them and see if I can knock some sense into them and convince them to go home," Roger Ford said.

"I let them know to expect the authorities," Nathan said, his voice deep, hard. He grabbed his jacket, pulled it on and fled her cabin.

Autumn nearly flinched at his tone and his cold response. He was business as usual—no warmth, no emotion—while she was still reeling from the impact of their lovemaking.

Had it meant nothing to him? It hadn't dawned on her to ask if he cared for her. And now, the questions flooded into her mind, drowning out the rest of the world. She suddenly needed a sign that he cared.

She wasn't one of those women who fixated on a man after a couple of nights of passion. But now that she'd experienced the intensity of a night with Nathan, she didn't know how to walk away. And she hated that. She wanted to appear aloof and unaffected, as though the experience had been no more meaningful than doing her laundry. Or taking a shower.

The shower. She wouldn't think about taking a shower the same way again. Thinking of it brought the images of Nathan's hands on her breasts, on her hips, lifting her against the wall so he could slide inside her. She'd hooked her leg over his hip and he'd supported her weight on his hands while he'd moved, and the sensations pelted her as if she were still in that moment.

Nathan hadn't made any promises, but she was spiraling into her feelings, letting them consume her thoughts. She had other priorities. Blaine was missing. The Huntsman was looking for his next victim. That alone was terrifying. Adding the evidence that pointed to Blaine as a suspect, Autumn needed to work faster and find something to clear her brother's name.

After checking on the high school students in their cabin, Nathan waded through the snow, thigh high in places where the wind had blasted it into drifts. He checked each cabin, looking for signs that any of the others had been broken into.

The Huntsman's methods were becoming more ritualistic, more cruel. He was toying with Autumn and the authorities, leaving clues he was lurking and taunting them to find him. He didn't want to be caught, but it was his game to prove that he was smarter.

A gust of air tore through Nathan's jacket. Nathan had the oddest sensation of being watched. He turned slowly, scanning the area, peering through the trees. The wind had kicked up, sending flurries of snow from the treetops, limiting visibility. Combined with the sun reflecting off the white snow on the ground, it was nearly blinding. He shook off the sensation, refusing to allow the killer's head games to affect him.

Nathan pulled his sunglasses from his pocket and covered his eyes. With absolute certainty, he was sure the Huntsman was watching them, and taking great pleasure in staying one step ahead.

Nathan stopped at the steps of cabin twelve, waiting for Ford to look up from the notebook in which he was writing. "Something going on with you and Autumn?" he asked, stopping writing and looking at Nathan.

Talking about him and Autumn and how they had spent the past couple of days wasn't an option. His sex life was none of Roger Ford's business.

Would Autumn forget the whole incident had happened and move on? It was the best course of action, and though he considered it, it bothered him she might do the same. It had to be over, but he didn't want it to mean nothing. "Working the case together."

Ford sniffed. "Don't compromise the investigation."

"I'm not compromising anything. I've been investigating and tossing leads your way whenever I get them."

Ford narrowed his eyes. "Uncle Sam thanks you. But I've told you before. You're too close to this case. You're not thinking objectively."

Ford was right on that count, about him not thinking objectively. Nathan was a rational, logical man, but in this case, sleeping with Autumn had crossed a line. Protecting her had taken on new meaning.

"I'll find this guy," Nathan said, keeping his tone neutral, shoving thoughts of Autumn away.

Ford patted Nathan's shoulder. "I admire your persistence. To a point."

"Nothing's changed, Ford. I am not planning to back away from this. I will find this guy."

Ford shook his head as if Nathan was a lost cause.

Nathan returned to Autumn's cabin, knocking once before going inside. Autumn was curled in a chair with a book open in her lap. She wasn't reading it, just staring at the wall.

She looked over when he came into the room and

closed the book. "Did you find out anything from Ford?" Her eyes were wide, her lips slightly parted. His attention moved from her lips to her chest, rising and falling. The urge to gather her against him, maybe pull her onto his lap, was overwhelming.

He strode to the couch and sat across from her. He wouldn't bungle this by touching her or confusing her about their relationship. "Ford is still trying to keep us out."

Autumn inclined her head. "But we told him about the footprints. We've been looping him into what we've been learning. He has the mettle to shut you out?"

Though it irritated him, Nathan knew where Ford was coming from. Working for the FBI at Ford's level made it impossible to avoid politics. Missteps, even perceived missteps, would land Ford and his team in hot water. Giving away information to unauthorized civilians counted as a misstep. "He doesn't have a choice. The stakes are too high and getting higher every day."

Autumn sighed. "Then what's the plan?"

He didn't have one. He'd spent the past two days wrapped in her arms, not thinking much about the case. While he could have been building contingency plans and working to get a step ahead of the killer, he'd been taking a sexual vacation. "The Huntsman is close, watching and waiting. Possibly hiding out. Any ideas where he might take shelter?"

The color drained from her face. "Do you think he's hiding at one of the campgrounds along the trail? Or at the stops nearby?"

It was possible. "He's not done here." Nathan could feel it in his gut. One interrupted murder wasn't enough to sate him for long.

Autumn looked away and closed her eyes. She took several deep breaths and she turned her gaze to him, her chin tilted up, her shoulders pulled back. "The snow will limit where he could move and find shelter from the elements. Some mountain paths could be too difficult to navigate, even for an experienced climber. That narrows the list of possible locations."

"Can you point out the locations on the map?"

A long pause passed. "Some of these places are difficult to describe. The map isn't that detailed."

His mind jumped from the trail to the Trail's Edge campground and then to Autumn. She was comfortable out of doors, and she was skilled in traversing the mountains, but the Huntsman had proved he was stealthy, strong and quick. Autumn needed a place where she could be safe, and the campground was becoming one of the most unsafe places for her to be. "I think you should stay in town until we find him."

She narrowed her eyes at him. "What? I'm not leaving my home."

Angry Autumn was better than Dead Autumn. He stood by his suggestion. "It would be safer if you took a step back from this investigation."

She threw her hands in the air. "You just asked me to tell you about places where he could be hiding and now you want me to leave? I'm as safe as I was a week ago. Is your plan to go alone into the forest and look for a serial killer?"

She was wrong. Some things had changed. Autumn wasn't a stranger. She was someone he cared about a great deal more than he wanted to admit. The more connections she had to the case, the more letting her look for the Huntsman seemed too risky and unnecessary. Making love had shifted something irrevocably between them and had made her that much more precious to him. "I can do this alone."

She glowered at him. "Alone? You want to go alone? Not knowing the area and with only a map, you'll search for a serial killer?" She pushed herself to her feet. "You've made your point. I'll mark whatever you want on a map and you can stumble around until you find it. But I am not walking away from this case. My brother is out on the trail somewhere and he could need me. I know Ford considers Blaine a suspect. I won't let them pin this on my brother when I know he wasn't involved."

What did she want him to say? That he had come to care about her, and the idea of her involved in this case terrified him to a distracting point? That he wanted to put distance between her and the killer, regardless of how uncomfortable it made her? They hadn't addressed how their relationship had changed, and Nathan didn't think they needed to say more on the matter except that it had.

A knock sounded on the door, saving him from trying to guess the source of Autumn's irritation. Nathan stood, but Autumn held up her hand. "I'll answer it."

Nathan rubbed the back of his neck. A massive headache was forming at his temples.

He heard Ford's voice. "We've got another vic nearby. Off the Trail."

Blaine. Nathan surged to his feet and rushed to the door.

The room tilted and Autumn swayed on her feet. Another victim. "Is it Blaine?" Why else would Ford give her this information if he didn't believe it was Blaine? Until this point, he'd been closemouthed with them.

Nathan's arm went around her waist and she sagged against him.

Ford clasped his hands behind his back. "No identity yet. Been dead at least twenty-four hours, probably longer. The ME is having a hard time pinpointing a time of death with the weather and the condition of the body."

"What color hair?" Autumn asked, a tremble in her voice.

"We don't know," Ford said. "The body was burned like the others, but the snowstorm must have extinguished the flames." Ford looked away from her. "There's more left than usual. Part of the face remains."

Blood roared in her ears and her heart hammered so loudly she could barely hear Ford speaking, though his lips were moving. "Can you get a picture?"

"I'm going there now. The rangers have it locked down until I am on the scene. I can get a picture and bring it to you." To his credit, Ford sounded softer than usual, the hostility and brusqueness gone from his voice.

Autumn closed her eyes for a moment, absorbing the impact of the news. It could be Blaine who was dead on the trail. She needed to see for herself and she couldn't wait for Ford to return with a picture. "I'm coming with you."

Shoving away the horrific thoughts of Blaine as the Huntsman's latest victim, she grabbed her backpack and began throwing items into it. The essentials.

"Autumn," Nathan said gently.

She didn't answer him. He would try to talk her out of going or try to convince her it wasn't Blaine who was dead and alone on the trail in the cold.

Her mind fired denials at the idea of Blaine being a victim. It wasn't Blaine. Blaine had to be safe. He was the only family she had left.

"Autumn," Nathan tried again. "You don't know it's Blaine. It could be anyone. It probably isn't. Males aren't his targets."

Autumn whirled on Nathan, a jolt of outrage charging through her. She aimed a finger at him. "If it was your family, would you accept that and wait around for news? Or would you go and see for yourself?" She waited a beat. "Exactly," she said to his silence, and kept packing.

"Let me know when you're ready to go. I'll drive," Nathan said.

She paused for a minute and looked at him over her shoulder. "You're coming with me?"

"Yes."

Some of the tension unwound from her shoulders, and the hottest flames of fury quieted in her stomach. "Thank you, Nathan." At least she wouldn't have to do this alone.

* * *

Autumn watched the minutes tick by on the dashboard clock as Nathan drove the twenty minutes it took to reach the access point to the trail closest to where the victim had been found. The location was south of the Trail's Edge. Blaine liked hiking in Maryland. Could he have been in the area? If he had, why not stop by to see her? Or had he been planning to do just that before a killer stopped him?

Autumn had to believe that Blaine was still alive. Blaine was reckless, but was he wasn't stupid enough to go off trail into a killer's hunting ground. He had to have heard about the killer from other hikers and he would have taken the proper precautions.

Being familiar with the area, Blaine would have been cautious especially with the weather being volatile in the winter season. He would have seen the weather reports of snow, or at least seen the clouds, and stuck to the Trail. Blaine had a sixth sense about nature, knowing when it was most dangerous.

As much as she tried to convince herself that Blaine knew better, that someone as smart as him wouldn't tempt fate, a voice in her head taunted her.

Autumn squeezed her eyes shut, refusing to let tears spill down her cheeks. Keeping it together and staying strong would get her through this.

Nathan reached across to her and set his hand on her thigh. "It'll be okay. You can do this. I'll be right next to you."

She could scarcely draw a full breath, the emotions of the moment pressing on her chest. Anxiety. Fear.

The connection to Nathan her only savior, the only thing keeping her from breaking down.

Nathan turned into the parking lot and pulled into a parking space. The trailhead was locked down, allowing only the authorities entrance. The authorities and anyone who could ID the body. A cold shiver piped down her spine.

Was the Huntsman watching them, having a private laugh at their expense? While she and Nathan had been holed up in her cabin, the killer had been loose in the mountains, stealing another life. Though she couldn't have stopped him, guilt sliced through her.

Ford pulled into the parking spot next to theirs. He appeared concerned for her, borderline compassionate. It was an emotion she didn't associate with him, but she appreciated that he was allowing her to see the victim.

Nathan got out and popped the trunk to grab their gear. He pulled on gloves and a hat. "How long will it take to reach the scene?"

Ford touched the gun strapped to his side. "Thirty minutes, give or take. The ice and weather complicate matters."

Autumn tossed her pack onto her shoulders. The hiker couldn't be Blaine. She kept her tenuous grip on her sanity by repeating that to herself and relying on Nathan for strength.

"Autumn, can you do this?" Nathan asked, setting his hand on her upper arm, studying her face.

Her heart overreacted at the casual touch. "I can

do this. I'm fine. I need to see the body so I know it isn't Blaine."

Nathan didn't argue with her about the chances the killer's last victim was Blaine. It wasn't something she could allow to fully penetrate her mind. As when her mother had left them and Autumn had waited by the front window for her to return. As when her uncle had disappeared into the fringes of society and every holiday for years, Autumn had believed he would come home. As when her father had died, she thought there had been some mistake.

Her heart wasn't prepared to break again.

Forty minutes later, hot under her coat, her cheeks cold and numb, she waited with Nathan behind yellow tape surrounding the scene. The tape was wrapped around tree trunks, marking the area, and a small green tent was constructed around what Autumn knew was the victim. If the victim had been left in the manner Sandra had, at least the body had been taken from the tree.

Helicopters flew overhead, searching the area for the Huntsman, but he wouldn't be found. He was either long gone or blending into the terrain, undetectable from the air.

As she watched the agents process the scene, her muscles twitched. She was anxious to look at the victim, desperate to know if it was her brother. She shifted back and forth on her feet, trying to burn off the nervous energy that hummed in her blood.

"A couple more minutes," Nathan said, his voice low and soothing.

But her stomach was churning, her mouth dry and

the thumping in her head deafening. "Why are they making us wait?" An unneeded torture.

"They don't want us to compromise the scene. They have to make sure they've secured the evidence they need."

Autumn had half a mind to storm the scene. So what if she was arrested? She couldn't take this for much longer.

Finally, a man lifted the tape near where she was standing so she could duck under it. Her nerves tightened. "Please stay on the path, ma'am."

Autumn walked toward the green tent, aware of Nathan behind her. He was staying close, his hand on her shoulder, lending his support, his guidance. Having Nathan behind her took the edge off her terror.

As she got closer to the tent, she saw a black tarp covering a body, the tarp bulging—likely from the arrows that had speared the victim. No mistaking the form. She stopped abruptly and turned, shoving her face against Nathan's jacket. His arms went around her and he clasped her against him, his mouth close to her ear.

"You don't have to do this. You can wait until they move the body to the morgue or get pictures. This will be ugly," Nathan said.

She knew that. No way about it, this would be horrifying. Maybe the most horrifying thing she'd see in her life. She'd seen what the Huntsman did to his victims.

One thought shored up her strength and prevented her from having a complete breakdown. If it was Blaine, she didn't want him to be a nameless, faceless hiker on the trail. She wanted to take him home with her. She'd scatter his ashes along the trail so he would always be in the place he loved. The thought was so heartbreaking she thought she might collapse under the strain of it.

Deep breath in and out. She could do this for Blaine.

Autumn gripped the front of Nathan's jacket in her hands, needing the security of someone, of him. "I need to know now."

"Okay." His breath was hot against her ear, heavy with understanding. Had Nathan identified his sister's body? What had that been like for him?

She turned and his hands remained on her waist. He provided support, his strength the only thing keeping her standing.

Ten more steps.

She took each one with a growing sense of dread. Bile roiled in her stomach and a rush of fear tightened in her throat. Everyone on the scene had gone quiet and was watching her.

Then she was standing over the tarp, swallowing hard to keep from losing the contents of her stomach. How had her life shifted so dramatically in twelve hours? This morning, she had woken tucked against Nathan, the heat of his body warming her to her core. Now she was standing over the body of the Huntsman's latest victim, sick with dread it might be Blaine.

"You ready, ma'am?" the park ranger standing near the tarp asked.

She sent up a silent prayer for strength and leaned

against Nathan, needing to absorb support from him. She nodded numbly and the tarp was peeled back.

Burned tufts of hair remained. The scent was nauseating. Her muscles tightened. The victim's eyes were closed. Was it Blaine? High, strong cheekbones. The cheekbones were wrong. Not Blaine's nose. Not his mouth. Relief poured over her and she let her body collapse against Nathan, a prayer of thanksgiving running through her mind.

"Stop. Stop. It's not him." She couldn't look anymore, didn't want to see the injuries the Huntsman had inflicted. Relief mixed with guilt. Another person had been killed. Someone else's family member was dead. Someone else's daughter. Someone else's wife. They might not even know she was missing yet. They might be waiting at home for her to return. But the next time they saw her, it would be at the morgue.

The sadness was so pervasive, it cut her to the quick.

"It's not Blaine?" Nathan asked, taking her face in his gloved hands and forcing her to look at him.

She shook her head. "No. It's not him." A tear slipped from her eyes, an outpouring of the chaos of emotions churning inside her.

The relief on Nathan's face was plain and it caught her off guard. She'd expected the same stoicism he'd given her all morning. "Let's get you out of here."

He took her hand as they walked, him leading the way. Why had he allowed the intimacy of their clasped hands? Was he working on autopilot, dragging her as quickly as possible to the truck? She didn't want to linger at the scene, the entire situation eerie and unsettling.

"Was this what it was like for you?" Autumn asked.

She knew he'd caught her meaning immediately by the stiffening of his shoulders. "It was worse because it *was* her. She was alone in the backcountry. What was she doing there?"

He spoke the question as if to himself.

"That must have been terrible for you. I'm sorry," Autumn said.

"You don't have to be sorry. I want the Huntsman caught. I don't want anyone else to go through this. Everything he does is unnecessary. It's some sick ritual and he loves it and craves it," Nathan said, darkness entering his voice. "He won't stop until someone makes him."

They made it just outside the yellow tape.

"Nathan!"

Nathan drew to a stop and pivoted, releasing her hand, but staying close. "Special Agent Ford." His voice held the same coolness Ford's had.

A muscle in Ford's jaw jumped. "Could she ID the body? Look like anyone you know?"

Autumn shook her head. "It wasn't my brother. I didn't recognize the victim."

Ford swore under his breath. "Are you sure about that?"

She was sure. "I'm sorry. I'm grateful you let me come."

Ford rubbed a hand across his jawline. "We've got to find this guy before he strikes again. I have people posted everywhere along the trail. How is he getting by us?"

He didn't wait for a response, but walked in the opposite direction of where they were standing.

Nathan's arm went around her shoulders and steered her toward the trailhead. Sharp pleasure from being tucked against his body charged through her.

"What will you do?" Autumn asked, trying to ignore the pulse of heat where his arm lay across her shoulders.

"About what?"

"This case. The body."

"I'll put together what evidence and clues we can until I find this guy." Nathan kissed her temple. "I'll find him. If I have to chase him up and down the trail for the next decade, so be it. I will find him."

Chapter 6

Nathan took a step back from her and looked away. "There's a command center at the ranger station a short drive from here. I want to stop in and talk to the rangers who found the victim."

Nathan had kissed her temple, a casual gesture, but it had the same heavy impact on her. Did the kiss imply an intimacy? Was he attempting to recapture the closeness they had lost when the FBI had shown up that morning?

"Autumn?"

Oh, the command center. The rangers. She was familiar with the station, having worked a number of shifts when she had been a forest ranger a few years before. "Ford told us to back off. What makes you think the rangers will talk to us?"

Nathan smiled at her. "They might not talk to me,

but they might talk to their old buddy, former Park Ranger Reed."

How had he known she'd been a park ranger? She gave him points for doing his homework on her. "Which rangers found the body?" Autumn asked, thinking of Ben.

"I don't know yet," Nathan said.

Putting the rangers in a difficult position, a position where they had to choose between friendship and duty, didn't seem fair. It wasn't fair to her, either. "If they were told not to discuss the case, I can't ask them to disobey a direct order. They could lose their jobs."

Nathan stopped on the path and faced her, taking her hands in his. His dark eyes penetrated hers as if he could see straight to her soul, and his thumbs rubbed her palms in slow, soothing circles. "I wouldn't ask this of you, of them, if it wasn't a matter of life and death."

Autumn swallowed hard as the image of the Huntsman's latest victim sprang to mind. She saw the victim as she might have been in real life. With a family. Friends. A job. "What is it you need to know?" She pulled her hand away, confused by the message he was sending.

"I need information to catch the killer before he strikes again. I need the details of what they saw before they found the body. Was the area disturbed in some other way? Did they have a clue a body was waiting for them before the smoke started?"

"All right." Autumn tried to think about the trail in spring, the green and deep brown of the mountains, the heavy smell of earth, the freshness of blooming flowers—anything to blot out the image of the victim.

They walked the rest of the distance to the trail-head in silence and climbed into the truck. After throwing their packs in the backseat, she and Nathan fastened their safety belts and then Nathan pulled out of the spot.

The ranger station, a faded green trailer with wooden stairs leading inside, was a ten-minute drive away. A small crooked sign on the front of the building announced it was Ranger Station No. 403. Autumn knew the combination to the door, doubting it had changed in years. Nothing of value was inside. One unmarked car she recognized as Ben's and one ranger vehicle was parked on the stony lot that served as a parking area. They took the creaking wooden stairs to the door and Nathan pulled it open.

Ben and another ranger she knew less well, Mark, looked up from their desks and a modicum of relief washed over Autumn. They weren't sticklers for the rules and they were overall good guys.

They had been working hard, fatigue showing plainly on their faces. The ranger station was filled with more boxes and papers than normal.

"Hey, Mark. Hey, Ben," she said.

The men stood and Ben crossed the room to hug Autumn. His goatee tickled her cheek. "Long time since we've seen you here. Friendly visit or business?"

"Little of both."

Autumn introduced Nathan to Mark. "Nathan and I are working the Huntsman case."

Ben and Mark exchanged glances. Ben spoke first.

"We're not supposed to talk about the case without permission from the FBI agent-in-charge, Roger Ford."

Autumn wouldn't give up that easily. "How about we float a few theories and you can give us your impressions? We want this madman found. Anything you can tell us could be critical."

Ben shrugged and glanced at Mark. "I guess that would be okay."

Autumn hoped once they started talking, she and Nathan could derive the information they needed. "The killer has been striking along the Appalachian Trail."

Autumn stepped back, and let Nathan take the lead. "Initially, I ruled out territorial killer because the murders took place farther apart. But my working theory is that his territory is the entire Appalachian Trail." Nathan walked to the edge of a desk and propped his hip, looking relaxed and friendly. Autumn had no doubt it was intentional.

"The killer considers the trail to be his and he doesn't like anyone on it who doesn't follow his rules." Nathan rubbed his jaw. "Maybe his victims don't stay to the trail or maybe they disrupt the peace and quiet of his area. He feels as though he needs to rid the trail of people who break his rules."

Autumn's chest felt heavy. Nathan hadn't mentioned that theory to her before, nor could she imagine anyone thinking they owned the trail. The trail belonged to no one.

Nathan continued as the men listened, nodding their agreement. "He dominates the trail. If someone gets in his way, if they do anything to disturb what he considers his perfect paradise, he kills them."

"And hangs them so they can't touch the trail." The words popped from her mouth before she could censor them.

Nathan nodded. "I was thinking the same thing."

Ben shifted in his chair and looked at the ground. "I found that poor hiker." He rubbed his forehead, as if trying to summon the words, and closed his eyes for a brief moment.

Though their relationship had been underscored with awkwardness since Ben had come out to her in high school, Autumn didn't hold back. She slipped her arm around his shoulder and hugged him, wanting to give him support.

"I smelled burning in the morning. I was worried a hiker had gotten lost. I called Mark to tell him where I was going, gave him my GPS coordinates and started hiking.

"The body was swinging in the wind." Ben closed his eyes and a tear slipped down his cheek. "I didn't expect to find anyone the way I did. I hoped I wasn't too late, that maybe he or she was still alive." He shook his head in dismay. Park rangers didn't deal with murders often, and the brutality and senselessness of the Huntsman's murders were doubly difficult to understand. "No one has come around asking about a missing person." Ben's voice shook with emotion, and he seemed to push the words from his throat. "I should have stayed closer to the trail. The weather has been bad and I wasn't hiking in the storm. Maybe I should have."

"You couldn't put your life at risk. You had no way to know this would happen," Nathan said.

"You can't blame yourself for this," Autumn said, patting Ben's hand.

"We'll find her family," Nathan said. "Was there a car in any of the lots nearby?"

Ben shook his head. "Nothing."

"Any reason a hiker would go off the trail after the warnings posted everywhere?" Nathan asked. "Maybe a scientist doing research?"

Ben inclined his head. "We haven't had any local researchers call to let us know they were working in the area. Not since the killings started."

Nathan asked a few more questions, and when he seemed satisfied he'd gotten the information he'd wanted, the conversation turned to other, far less stressful topics. She didn't want to abuse their willingness to cooperate. After a casual exchange about their lives and families, she and Nathan said their goodbyes and left the trailer.

"What's the plan now?" Autumn asked, pulling her gloves on to her hands.

"I need to get inside the killer's mind."

She wanted to be as far from the killer as possible. "How do you plan to do that?"

"I want to walk where the victim walked. I want to walk in the killer's tracks. Can you help me do that?"

"If you think it will help," Autumn said, thinking again of the victim and of Blaine. She was at a loss for options, and if this was the best plan they had, she had no choice but to go along.

* * *

Autumn followed Nathan to the trailhead and then to the spot marked by a white paint blaze indicating a point along the Appalachian Trail. The trail was wet and slippery, the snow having melted in some places, making deep pockets on either side of the path where water collected and formed muddy pits. It was quiet as they began walking deeper into the forest's shelter. Even with the mostly bare trees, nature was an easy place to hide. Low-lying brush, rocks and fallen trees created an infinite number of concealed hiding spots.

"Impossible to find any footprints," Nathan said under his breath.

Autumn hadn't been looking for footprints. She'd been scanning for movement in the trees, expecting to see the Huntsman watching them, waiting to strike. She had hiked this area of the trail many times. It wasn't far from the Trail's Edge, maybe a few days at a quick clip. "The woman who keeps the hiker shelter near here also stashes a travel log for her visitors to write about their journeys. She's kept over ten years of journals. She types them up and posts them on a blog. It's good PR for the trail."

Nathan's eyes lit with interest. "Do you think our hiker left a message in her book?"

Autumn shrugged. "She—or he—might have if she passed that way. If she stopped to rest, she might have wanted to leave her mark on the trail and write a note that she'd been here. I doubt Hilde came out in the snow to collect the journal. Without people walking the trail as much this season, she wouldn't need to put out a new journal as often."

Nathan stepped up his pace.

The hut that Hilde Sinclair kept was a nicer one along the trail. She took pride in keeping it in good repair, not letting the roof leak or the shelter become overrun with rodents. It was hoisted on cinder blocks and three sides were made of sturdy oak. The front was exposed to the outside, oak covering about half of it. Hooks along the roof ridge allowed the opening to be closed off with a tarp to block the wind and rain.

The shelter was empty except for the bunk-style wooden platforms secured to the walls.

"She keeps the journal inside," Autumn said. She went up the stairs and scanned the little hut, half expecting the journal to be missing. But it was tucked inside the leather bag against the far wall, a few pens dangling from strings tied to it.

Autumn removed it with her gloved hand and brought it to Nathan. They set it on the floor of the shelter and opened it. She turned the pages carefully to about the middle of the book where the last words were written.

In tiny childlike printing, every letter lowercase, in dark print as though the letters had been traced repeatedly, it read, "This is a hallowed ground. Our timeless laws are to be revered and honored with endless duty. Be warned that you are to stay on the trail. The mother's secrets are not for all to know. They are mine to keep sacred."

The entry wasn't signed. It wasn't dated.

This wasn't a casual note left by a well-meaning hiker. No comments about the weather, interesting wildlife spotted in the area or good-luck wishes for other travels.

"He left this," Nathan said. He adjusted his gloves and turned the pages of the book. Scattered randomly through them was the same message repeated in the dark scrawl.

Nathan turned the book on its side and Autumn sucked in a breath. Maybe it was dirt. Maybe it was clay. But along the side of the closed pages was a red smear.

After so many months of eluding the police, the park rangers and the FBI, would the Huntsman leave DNA evidence behind? If it was blood, it could belong to any of hikers who had passed through and either read the book or left a message. The substance found at the Trail's Edge in cabin twelve could have been blood and if it was, could it be a match to the blood on the book? Autumn wished Nathan hadn't been shut out of the investigation so they'd know more.

"Has he ever done anything like this before?" Autumn asked. Leaving a message was risky. Handwriting analysis could provide clues or a fingerprint could give away his identity. How realistic was it to find a fingerprint on a page of a book that might have been touched by dozens of hikers?

Nathan lifted his eyes to meet hers. "He's never left anything behind to give us clues about his agenda."

"It could be a hoax," Autumn said, half wishing it was. A sick joke, some hiker leaving a message to frighten others.

"It's all we have to go on. Let's hope the last victim didn't come out to play a prank and get herself killed in the process."

Roger Ford was not pleased when he answered the phone. But Nathan couldn't have cared less what pleased Ford. From day one, he'd pegged Nathan as trouble because Nathan wasn't old-school and hard-nosed. Quickly marrying and then getting divorced from Ford's sister hadn't helped their relationship, but it was time to leave the past behind.

Calling Roger Ford in to help was necessary, and since Ford had allowed Autumn to come to the most recent crime scene, Nathan owed him. They had formed a reluctant working relationship. Nathan needed the crime lab to examine the book, and he wouldn't have access on his own to that type of evidence analysis.

The moment Ford arrived on the scene, as expected, he corralled Nathan and Autumn thirty feet from Hilde's shelter and told them to wait. Nathan had half a mind to leave—Ford couldn't require him to stay—but he wanted to know about that book.

"At least he didn't accuse us of committing the murders," Autumn muttered.

Nathan's gaze swerved from the crime scene—or what he could see of it—to Autumn. Every time he looked at her, he was taken aback at how beautiful she was. In the forest, with the backdrop of the trees, she was even more breathtaking. "It has to grate on his nerves that we've found more evidence than he has."

Autumn gave him a shaky smile. "We keep landing in the middle of the investigation."

"We're looking for evidence and hitting it lucky," Nathan said.

Autumn folded her arms over her chest. "How do you take the pressure? How can you do this, day after day?"

Nathan didn't always work active crime scenes. Much of his work was research, talking to people and reviewing evidence. "It's not always like this."

"This intense?"

Every case he worked was intense. From the time he began a case, he'd sink into it and absorb the pieces. "Most cases are intense. This one has a personal aspect to it."

Compassion was plain on her face. "Tell me about her. Tell me about Colleen."

It was still hard to talk about his sister. Nathan missed her so much. "Colleen was a good woman. But she had demons. Somehow, she couldn't shake them loose. Therapy and rehab and medications couldn't make her happy. She relied on alcohol too often. She had her life together when my niece and nephew were babies. When her husband left her and took the kids, she spun out of control. More recently, I thought she was getting better and maybe she'd get a fresh start. The Huntsman saw to it that it didn't happen." Talking about her sent an arrow of sharp grief to his core.

Nathan jammed his hands in his pockets to keep from reaching for her, from seeking out human contact as a salve on his hurt. Talking about this opened a fresh wound, left him feeling vulnerable and exposed in way he didn't care for. He could clam up, but he wanted Autumn to understand why it was so important that he find Colleen's murderer.

"What was she doing on the trail?" Autumn asked.

That part of the story was the dark aspect of their lives. He didn't talk about it much. "Colleen loved being outdoors. When Colleen and I were in middle school, our father walked out on us. Colleen had a lot of trouble with it." She'd run away several times, and while she always returned home safe, their mother was a wreck every time. After the first three times, when their mother called, the police stopped coming by or looking for her. "Colleen ran away from home and she caused a lot of problems with the family." It was Colleen's love of the outdoors that had saved her and cost her her life. "She needed that time. She said being outside was her therapy."

Nathan swallowed the thick emotion building in his throat. "She had arranged to go hiking with a friend, but at the last minute, the friend fell sick with the flu. Colleen decided to go anyway."

Autumn set her hand on his arm and squeezed. It was as if she'd flipped some switch in him, and the words and emotions he'd kept locked inside bubbled up in his chest. At Colleen's funeral, he'd remained stoic for his mother, former brother-in-law, niece and nephew. Nathan had been the person they'd leaned on, the calm and rational pillar of strength. He'd promised them he would find her killer. It wasn't a burden. He was honored to do this, to see that his family got resolution and peace.

Nathan didn't have the words. Instead, he settled

on a simple phrase, something to convey his gratitude to Autumn for helping him. She might not have
known how important this was to him, but she had
stuck by him and the case. That connection, that sense
that Autumn understood him, strengthened. "Thank
you."

Autumn wrapped her arms around him and hugged
him, letting her head rest on his shoulder. "For what?"

He dropped his cheek to rest on the top of her head.
He struggled to find the words, knowing they would
be awkward and weak. Before he'd settled on what
to say, Ford broke in.

"I need you to drive to the crime lab and get fingerprinted and swabbed for DNA."

Nathan's head snapped up and he took a small step
away from Autumn. Ford. The man had impeccable
timing. "We didn't touch the book without gloves."

Ford cracked his knuckles. "Don't care. Do it anyway."

The spell broken, Nathan sealed up the emotion
that pulsed from his chest. Ford might have the man-
ners of a mule, but he'd stopped Nathan from blub-
bering about Colleen and blurting out overemotional
mumbo jumbo that would only serve to complicate
matters in the future.

Another small opening in his defenses. Autumn
had felt the slightest shift in Nathan, from an investigator to the man he'd been in her bed. Almost as
abruptly, he'd closed himself off. His mixed signals
were sending her world topsy-turvy, and she worked
to steady her reaction. This situation was difficult for

him and his family, and she wasn't planning to complicate things with questions about them or about their future or about what being snowbound in her cabin had meant to him. Those things didn't rate. They were nonissues and she should stop thinking about them.

She and Nathan took the trip to the lab with the radio keeping them company. Swabbing for DNA and getting fingerprinted took less than twenty minutes and then they were back on the road, headed toward the Trail's Edge.

Autumn's thoughts wandered to the case, to the victim she'd found hung in the tree, to the blood in cabin twelve and to the victim she'd seen that morning. The journal didn't fit with the pattern Nathan had mentioned. The Huntsman didn't leave evidence behind. Like the boot prints in the cabin, was it deliberate? "Why do you think the killer left a message in the journal? He had to know someone would read it." If not other hikers, then Hilde, when she collected the journal.

"I've been thinking about that, too. He wanted his message found." Nathan drummed his fingers on the steering wheel. "Does the website where the messages are uploaded get a lot of traffic?"

"Maybe a few hundred, possibly a thousand people read it."

"He's working to put his message out."

Why? And what sense did the ranting make? If Hilde had found the writings first, she might not have put them on the blog. It wasn't Hilde's intention to scare hikers or drive them away from the trail. Autumn rubbed her forehead. "How did the killer know about the journal? Hilde doesn't leave signs on the trail."

"I'm sure he hasn't spent his entire adult life in the wilderness. At some point, he had or has access to a computer. He could have looked at hiking and trail sites for information about the Appalachian Trail and stumbled on Hilde's site."

Autumn laid her head against the window, exhaustion battering her, her eyes feeling gritty and heavy. The more she tried to sort the information and figure out the whys and hows of the case, the more confused she felt.

"You up for grabbing something to eat?" Nathan asked. "It might make you feel better."

"I feel fine." Her stomach growled and she pressed a hand over it. "Or maybe food sounds great." It would take the edge off her tiredness if she had some sugar in her blood.

Nathan pulled into a restaurant parking lot. It was one of the nicer establishments in town.

"I'm not dressed to eat here," Autumn said. Little black dresses and suits were appropriate for this place. She and Nathan were wearing tired, worn hiking clothes.

"I've wanted to eat here since I first drove by. We'll be fine."

Easy for Nathan to say. He blended in everywhere. People liked him and he always looked stylish.

When they arrived at the hostess station, the woman took one long look at Nathan and smiled brightly. "Come this way, sir."

He'd been right. No problems being seated. What

was it like to live life with a perpetual sense of confidence?

They were escorted to a window seat. Nathan pointed to a small alcove on the far side of the restaurant. "Any chance we could sit there?"

The woman smiled and escorted them to the private table Nathan had selected. When she left them alone, Nathan helped Autumn into her seat.

"How do you do that?" she asked.

"Do what?"

"You always get what you want," Autumn said.

"I ask for what I want. That helps."

Autumn sat and tried not to obsess about how she and Nathan had to look out of place. Her heart stopped and skipped a beat when Nathan sat across from her. He was a handsome man and when they were alone, she had time to look at him and drink in every ounce of his good looks.

"Are you doing okay? I've been worried about you," Nathan said.

"This hasn't been the best month of my life, but not the worst, either," Autumn said.

"I think Ford was hoping you'd recognize the body. He had to have a sense the body would be female."

"Maybe," Autumn said. She couldn't muster up anger even if Ford had been using her for a positive ID. If she had recognized the victim, the person's family could have been contacted that much faster. She wanted the same thing Nathan and Ford did: for the Huntsman to be found and stopped.

Her thoughts stuttered to a stop when Daniel and Francine entered the room. They were dressed for the restaurant, Francine in a knit dress that clung in the right places and Daniel in his crisp uniform.

Her heart lurched for an entirely different reason.

"Great," she muttered under her breath. After the day she'd had, her emotions had been jerked around enough that she didn't think she could handle any more problems. If she was lucky, Daniel would ignore her.

Nathan glanced at the door. "Is this going to make you uncomfortable? Because we can leave. We can eat anywhere you'd like."

She shouldn't care. She and Daniel were long over and now she had other things in her life to fill her time. "It's no big deal."

But the ache in her stomach indicated otherwise. It was the first time Autumn had seen Daniel and Francine together. She'd heard rumors about them being a couple. She'd seen each of them individually. Seeing them together struck a different chord. "I have to face them at some point." She felt less anger than she had expected, more the urge to flee. She was tired. She didn't want to deal with them.

"Ignore them. You're the most beautiful woman in this room and I want to look at you and talk about you."

Autumn cringed when Daniel strode in her direction. "He's coming this way."

He stopped in front of their table. "Hey, Autumn. What brings you out? I thought you only left the Trail's Edge once a year."

A common complaint he'd had about her desire to stay at the Trail's Edge.

How did he reduce her to tiny shreds? She wanted to appear confident and in control, as if her heartbreak was nothing and long over. It still stung to know he hadn't cared for her the way she'd cared for him. "We're having dinner. It's been a long day. Let's not do this here."

Daniel gave Nathan an appraising look. "Are you dating?" he asked.

Autumn wanted Daniel to know she had moved on from their relationship and was embroiled in a steamy affair with a hot FBI agent whom she had slept with multiple times in the past two days. It was shallow, but it would feel good for Daniel to know she could have something hot with a man. Since it was a man who looked like Nathan, double the bonus.

"You're interrupting our date, if that's what you mean," Nathan said. His hand moved across the table and covered hers. Along with the gesture, the searing look in his eyes nearly had her leaning away. Heat and desire smoldered in his expression.

Autumn's heart lifted. "Nathan's staying at the Trail's Edge."

"With you?" Daniel asked, straightening.

Before she could answer, Francine slipped her arms around Daniel in a proprietary gesture. "Daniel, let's go. I want to order. I'm hungry."

Daniel moved Francine's hands off him and held one of them in his. "Autumn is seeing someone new."

"I know. They came to the lounge the other night. People are still talking about them."

Autumn's ears burned. Gossip about her family was something she tried to avoid.

"You didn't tell me you saw them having dinner," Daniel said.

Francine rolled her eyes. "I don't give you a list of every person who comes into the lounge every day."

"We must have made an impression if people are still talking about it," Nathan said, perhaps picking up on Autumn's nervousness.

Francine waved her free hand dismissively. "New, sexy stranger, that's all."

Autumn relaxed. They were talking about Nathan, not her. She understood their interest. He was tall and darkly good-looking. "Yes, he is."

She smiled at Nathan and squeezed his hand, letting him know she appreciated him playing along in front of her ex.

"Come on, Francine, let's eat."

Francine waved over her shoulder as she and Daniel walked to their table.

"Thank you for that," Autumn said when they were out of earshot.

"For what?"

"For pretending like your interest is primarily me and not the case."

Nathan squeezed her hand. "I *am* interested in you. I've made that clear."

But they hadn't established what the turn in their relationship meant.

"Are you still in love with Daniel? I want to ask the blunt question because I've been in difficult relationships before where it gets messy because of a love triangle and unresolved problems."

In love with Daniel? Not even a little. "I am not

in love with Daniel." Autumn tried to explain more. "Daniel and I have a complicated history. He was Blaine's best friend and they had a falling out, and Daniel and I broke up because he cheated on me. It's a mess, really," Autumn said. "But that's what I've come to expect from my relationships. A mess."

"What makes you feel that way? Because of the way they end?"

Could Autumn tell him the most difficult part of her relationship history? While there wasn't one relationship that was bad, each had serious flaws. "My first boyfriend was a guy I dated for four years in high school. He told me the week before senior prom that he was gay." It had been devastating. Autumn had been planning a future with a man who didn't want to be with her, at least, not as a lover. She and Ben were on good terms now, but it had taken years to get over what had happened. She still carried around some of the insecurities that came with selecting and staying with a man who was so obviously not physically attracted to her.

"That must have been hard for you both," Nathan said.

It was. "We're on friendly terms now," Autumn said. "But I carried around a lot of baggage about it. It had nothing to do with me, but it made me feel…" Like less of a woman. Sexually clueless. Undesirable.

"Whatever it made you feel then, when I look at you, I want you to know I see a vibrant, sexy woman with so much to offer, so much caring and kindness."

Her cheeks heated with pleasure at the unexpected compliment. "That's how you make me feel." When they were together, boyfriends of the past were forgotten and her self-consciousness fled to the darkest corners of her mind. She was strong and capable and Nathan wanted her.

When he'd gotten cold and stoic that morning, Autumn hadn't known how to react. She thought maybe sex with her hadn't been as good for him as she'd believed. That maybe she'd misinterpreted his actions or was projecting her feelings onto him. "I'm glad to hear that."

Nathan was the first man who seemed to desire her as much as she desired him. He was the first man who made her feel good about herself in bed. He didn't have criticisms or complaints, at least none that he voiced.

Which amounted to fun in the short-term, but nothing in the future.

She had started the relationship believing she could maintain distance between them. He hadn't lied about his intentions or his priorities. But now she had to ask herself a difficult question, a question she might not like the answer to. How would she feel when Nathan left?

FBI agents were still milling around the Trail's Edge campground, taking pictures and searching cabin twelve for evidence. After overhearing that blood had been found in the cabin, Autumn kept busy with mundane chores, sweeping her floors, cleaning out her fireplace and taking the ashes outside, and feeding and playing with Thor. Nathan had returned to his cabin to review his case file. Alone, she had time to think.

Despite her body's exhaustion, her mind refused to settle. She ticked through the events —Nathan's uneven behavior, her fear for her brother's life, sadness at the loss of another hiker and terror upon finding the Huntsman's message. The wave of emotions was overwhelming, confusing and impossible to interpret and sort.

Nathan's actions were the hardest to understand. She hadn't expected him to be gooey and mushy while he was working, but he almost seemed like two different men: working Nathan and Nathan in bed.

For two days, he had been attentive and warm. When they'd woken up, he hadn't raced to get away from her. He had pulled her closer. Talking had been easy and natural. Only after Roger Ford showed up did Nathan behave distantly cool. Their relationship moved into flat-out uncomfortable. But then, at the restaurant, he had once again treated her like a girlfriend.

Confusion and exhaustion turned to anger, rage snapping in her blood. Why did Nathan think it was fine to turn on and off his emotions whenever he felt like it? She tried to put a lid on her anger, but it refused to simmer down. Thor was picking up on her mood, too, growling at the door and playing rough.

Too tired to fight it, she grabbed her keys and locked the door, storming across the grounds to Nathan's door. She pounded on it with her fist until he pulled it open.

He appeared surprised to see her. Surprised. Yeah,

well, she had things to say and he needed to listen. "Why are you pretending we didn't spend the night together?"

Nathan's face remained deceptively calm, relaying nothing, which infuriated her more. "I don't know what you mean."

He had to be kidding. "You were one way when we were together. Then as soon as people were around, you shut down and started pretending we're just colleagues working a case."

Nathan's eyes darkened for a moment, a muscle working in his jaw. As quickly as the expression passed over his face, it was gone. "It was a chaotic day. I'm doing my best to find my sister's killer and be a friend to you."

The coldness in his voice chilled her. She was intentionally provoking him, purposefully picking a fight, and he wasn't reacting.

She felt pressure building behind her eyes, and knowing she was overreacting, she blinked furiously to keep her tears from falling. She wouldn't give him the satisfaction of knowing he had affected her this deeply. Autumn didn't need to tell him that she wasn't a woman who slept around carelessly with men or that the night she had spent with him had meant something to her, even if it hadn't to him.

She suddenly wished she hadn't come to his cabin. What was she hoping he'd say? That he wanted her still? That he felt it, too, the electricity that never stopped flowing between them? Not likely. This would only end in more devastation—and embarrassment—for her. "Forget it."

It was a weak phrase, but right then, dismissing him was easier than dismissing her feelings.

She turned to go and he snagged her arm, stopping her from leaving. He spun her to face him, and in the next moment, his mouth was crushed to hers and he was kissing her, his lips soft and pliant. She struggled only an instant in anger and confusion, but he held her tight, his hand pressed to her lower back, coaxing, persuading. Then, she was giving herself over to the kiss and over to him. He pulled her into the cabin. She was distantly aware of the door closing behind them and then of his bed at the back of her knees.

His teeth skimmed along her neck, nibbling, tasting. "How can you expect me to forget anything when it comes to you?"

She lowered herself onto the bed and slid back, bracing her arms behind her. He ran his hands down her legs, stopping at her feet and pulling off her shoes, letting them clunk to the floor.

He was hovering over her, his body straddling hers, his mouth dipping down at uneven intervals to kiss her, taste her, as his hands slipped along her body, sending her sensitive skin blazing.

"Tell me if you want to stop," he whispered.

She paused and he stilled. Did she want this? She'd come looking for answers and now all she felt was… what? Lust? Wanting? In the space of a minute, he had diffused her anger and her frustration, and she was fixated on one thing—him. How it would feel to have him in her arms, moving over her and sliding inside her. She felt powerless to resist.

She skimmed her hand over the hard lines and

planes of his body and he closed his eyes when her fingers made contact.

"Is that a no?" he asked.

"It's a please-don't-stop," she said.

He groaned and reached for the hem of his shirt, peeling it over his head and tossing it to the floor. Her shirt came next, then her pants. He took every scrap of clothing away until they were pressed together, his skin hot against hers.

She was unable to do anything except feel. His hands skated over her body, just shy of rough. His lips moved along the column of her neck. He asked her a question so explicit, she could respond with only a nod and the release of a quavering breath.

He reached into his wallet and pulled out a condom, sheathing himself quickly. Nudging her knees apart with his, he positioned himself over her and drove inside her in one long glide.

She nearly vaulted off the bed as he filled her. She followed his rhythm, making amazing, slow love to him. He hadn't said anything to assuage her fears, but what he was doing made her feel incredibly, unspeakably precious.

He rocked against her, working his hips into her, and they crashed together in a flurry of heat and excitement. He thrust gently as her climax eased and then they lay together, intertwined and lost in their thoughts until sleep claimed them.

Autumn awoke in Nathan's arms and looked at the red numbers on the alarm clock. It was nearly 9:00 p.m. They hadn't resolved anything, and the familiar sensation of self-consciousness shimmered across her chest.

How would Nathan behave now? Would his attitude toward her be as dismissive as it had been earlier that day once they were no longer alone?

She moved to get out of bed, sliding his arms from around her and holding the blanket close to the bed to preserve the heat.

"Hey, where you going?" His sleepy masculine voice carried straight to her heart.

He'd noticed she'd left his bed. That was something. "I need to go back to my cabin. Thor needs to be let out."

"Give me a sec. I'll come with you."

Her heart soared and she stifled the smile that sprang to her lips. She was letting her heart run away with her, and it wouldn't happen again. She wouldn't make the same mistake twice. Losing her heart to Nathan wasn't an option. She didn't know what they had, but she knew it wasn't a future.

Chapter 7

The sound of scratching at the front door and the jiggling of the front door handle woke Autumn. Thor growled from the foot of her bed and Nathan bolted upright beside her. Autumn looked at the clock. 3:00 a.m. Nathan was tugging on his pants, gun in hand, when the front door opened.

"Don't move," Nathan growled, stalking toward their intruder.

The intruder's hands went up. "If you hurt my sister, you son of a—"

"Nathan, stop. Don't shoot," she said. The intruder was Blaine. Hearing her brother's voice, relief and joy fogged her brain. Autumn raced to him. "Blaine?" She threw herself against him. He was home. He was safe. He smelled awful and his clothes were grimy, but she didn't care. He was alive. Thor bounded over, shoving his nose in between them, barking and trying to get attention.

Autumn released Blaine and fumbled for the light in the kitchen. Blaine closed the door behind him.

He and Nathan sized each other up, long and hard. Thor paced the kitchen before settling near his food bowl.

"Who's he?" Blaine asked, shrugging off his backpack and letting it slam to the floor. He stood with his feet spread apart, his arms crossed over his chest and his bright blue eyes narrowed. He was in need of a shave and haircut, his brown hair long and curling around his ears and his beard scruffy.

Autumn scrambled for a believable answer. Blaine wouldn't buy that Nathan was a federal agent watching out for her. First, his jeans were unbuttoned, hanging low on his hips, making it obvious he was naked beneath them. She was wearing Nathan's T-shirt and her pajama pants, the only articles of clothing she had been able to find in the dark.

How could she describe Nathan?

Friend. A nice neutral word. "This is my friend Nathan. He's been staying with me."

Blaine's gaze sharpened on her. "You just broke up with Daniel. What do you mean by 'staying with you'? For how long has this been going on? Is this a rebound?"

She dreaded answering his questions. She and Nathan hadn't known each other long enough to garner her brother's approval for what they were doing, and despite her age and the fact that neither of them were virgins, Blaine's acceptance was important to her. She couldn't tell him the truth, which was that she knew Nathan was leaving and she was along for the ride until that happened. She changed the subject. "Sit down. We need to talk. I've been trying to get ahold of you for weeks."

Blaine took the chair closest to the door, looking between Nathan and Autumn. Mercifully, he didn't press her for an answer about their relationship. Yet. "Satellite phone broke and I fiddled with it, but I couldn't get it working."

Next time, she would insist he check in with her every few days. Borrow a phone. Go into town and pay for one. Whatever it took. "What about the Huntsman? Have you heard about the problems on the trail?"

Blaine scratched the back of his neck. "Sure I did, but I assumed it was a rumor. Wasn't until the last few weeks I started to believe it. Found a couple of newspaper clippings on it posted in one of the trail shelters."

Though he was safe and in front of her, she couldn't ignore the stab of fear that Blaine had been alone. "Are you hungry? Do you want something to drink?"

They fell into a familiar pattern. She started heating water for tea and preparing food for an early-morning breakfast and Blaine told her about his trip. Nathan watched this exchange from his position leaning against the counter. He'd found another shirt and had buttoned his pants, but his presence was no less distracting.

"Do you want me to sort your pack?" Autumn

asked. Besides his needing a shower, Blaine's pack was likely filled with muddy, damp clothes and his equipment would require a thorough cleaning.

"Nah, I'll take care of it at my cabin."

Autumn refilled Blaine's cup with hot water, leaving his tea bag floating. "You'll want to shower here. I turned down the water heater at your place to save a few dollars."

Blaine let out a sharp bark of laughter. "I must smell like I've rolled in trash. You should have said something. After two days on the trail, the smell stops bothering me. I forget civilized people aren't used to it."

Nathan moved to take a seat at the opposite end of the table from Blaine. His posture was relaxed, nonthreatening, but Autumn saw the telltale glint in his eyes. He'd given her and Blaine time to talk, and now he'd want to know about the trail. "What are hikers on the trail saying about the murders?"

Blaine's fork paused midway to his mouth. He set the fork against the plate. "Not too many hikers are on the trail, but the ones I spoke with are saying to be careful and stay close to the main path. And sleep with one eye open."

"Have you spoken to any federal agents along the trail?" Nathan asked, leaning forward in interest.

Blaine normally provided one-word answers when it came to strangers. That his answers were a couple of sentences was remarkable. Whatever technique Nathan was using to disarm Blaine, it was working. Autumn didn't like the idea of Nathan working her brother, but she wanted the Huntsman caught and

Blaine could have good information. Hiking alone, he wouldn't have the distraction of other people to absorb his attention. He'd have walked the trail, his thoughts and observations keeping him company. He might have noticed something that could help them.

Blaine shook his head. "Haven't seen any federal agents."

A sudden coldness hit her core. Agents were posted along the trail for miles. How had Blaine missed them? Was he hiking the backcountry, staying off the main trail? The backcountry was the Huntsman's primary hunting ground.

Nathan raised his eyebrow. "The FBI has people stationed in the area."

Blaine returned to his food, lowering his eyes to his plate and offering no response.

"You should be careful. We have reason to believe the killer is in this area now," Nathan said.

Blaine took another bite of his eggs and shrugged. "I'll be fine. I know what I'm doing."

How could he know that? Maybe Blaine thought he'd been on his own long enough that he didn't need anyone to look out for him. Maybe he felt safe at the Trail's Edge or on the Appalachian Trail, where his skills and wits would keep him alive.

"Blaine, I'm not trying to scare you, but you need to be careful. I found a body on the Trail's Edge grounds. The FBI's lead investigator has been looking for you and asking me about you. Daniel told them about you, and whatever he told them has the FBI very interested in your whereabouts."

Blaine looked between Autumn and Nathan. He

let go a curse. "Daniel's a lying snake. He has it out for me. Forget him and his lies. Tell me more about what you found."

Autumn told Blaine what she and Thor had discovered at the Trail's Edge. "What's worse is that the victim is someone you know."

Blaine's eyes grew wide. "Who? Tell me."

"Sandra Corvaldi," Autumn said.

Blaine closed his eyes and inhaled deeply. "Not Sandra. Her poor family. She didn't deserve to die that way. No one deserves to die that way."

"It's awful. Absolutely terrible," Autumn said. From Blaine's reaction, it was difficult for her to imagine he was lying or that he had known about Sandra.

"I'm sorry I wasn't here when you needed me," Blaine said. "Are you doing okay?"

Autumn continued to see the image of Sandra hanging from the tree. An image that terrible didn't go away completely. "I'm handling it. It helps to have Nathan close. Being alone up here can be difficult. There's more you've missed," Autumn said. "Mom showed up."

"Mom? Here? Why?" Blaine asked with equal parts anger and confusion.

His emotions echoed her own. "I didn't talk to her long. She wanted to speak to me and have lunch, but I put her off."

"I think we made it known we don't want her around. Whenever she calls, we're clear about that. What does she want? Another chance with us?" Blaine asked.

"She said she wanted to explain," Autumn said.

"Forget it. I don't want to hear anything from her," Blaine said.

Autumn's initial reaction had been similar. After having a few days to cool off and after talking it over with Nathan, Autumn was beginning to think her mother's arrival presented an opportunity to get answers to long-held questions. "I might talk to her again."

Blaine inclined his head. "You know what Dad and Uncle Ryan said about her. She's a liar and a manipulator. She'll hurt you all over again."

"I'm not a child, Blaine. I am not planning to accept everything she says as fact. I am capable of making my own decisions about whether what she tells me rings true," Autumn said.

"Don't meet with her. You're making a mistake," Blaine said. "You let people do this to you. Tell you their sob story and you believe them when they're obviously lying."

"Obviously?" Autumn asked. Was he talking about Ben and Daniel here, as well? Blaine knew her dating history.

"Come on, Autumn. Do you think a woman who walked out on her children is someone you want in your life?" Blaine asked.

"I didn't say I wanted her in my life. I said I wanted to hear what she had to say. It's my mistake to make," Autumn said. "I would like if you came to listen, too, but I understand if you don't want to."

"I don't want to," Blaine said.

Autumn didn't want to fight with her brother. He

had been gone for so long and her gratitude at having him safe was still fresh. "Why don't you stay with us here?" Autumn asked. She wanted to keep Blaine close.

Blaine blinked at her several times. "I'll pass. I'll be fine."

Autumn sighed in frustration. "You need to take this seriously. The Huntsman is in this area. We've also had a break-in at one of the cabins."

Blaine shrugged. "We've had break-ins before."

Autumn tamped down her frustration and tried again to convince him of the danger. Was he in denial? "Not a break-in by someone who left blood in the entryway."

Blaine was quiet.

Autumn added the last critical piece of information, hoping it would sway Blaine. "The Huntsman killed another victim less than two miles from here."

Blaine swallowed his food. "I know."

She darted a look at Nathan. Lines had formed around Nathan's eyes. "How do you know?" she asked.

They'd found the body only the day before, and public information hadn't been released yet about the killing or about the victim.

Blaine set down his fork and pushed away from the table. "You hear things on the trail. I want to get to my cabin, take a shower and hit the hay. I stopped by to tell you I was home."

"Are you planning to stay for a while?" Autumn asked.

"No," Blaine said.

Her heart fell. Her brother's wanderlust was in full control and Blaine was running away from his problems. "The FBI wants to talk to you. You should at least stay around and meet with them. You can give them your alibi and clear the air," Autumn said. Maybe they could convince Blaine that being on the trail was dangerous.

"I'll see," Blaine said, not looking at her. What was he not saying? His tone had changed when she'd mentioned the most recent victim.

Roger Ford wanted Autumn to alert him when she'd heard from Blaine. Could she talk Blaine into meeting with Ford? Her other options were to withhold the information from the FBI or rat out her brother. Where did Nathan stand on the matter? Would he call Ford to inform him that Blaine had shown up at the Trail's Edge?

"Offer for the shower stands," Autumn said.

"By the time I clean my gear, the water will be hot. Night, Autumn. Night, Nathan."

As abruptly as he'd arrived, Blaine left, closing the door behind him.

Nathan hadn't moved from his chair. He ran his hand along his jaw. "That's strange."

People had been saying that about Blaine's behavior all his life. "He's not normally so cranky or standoffish. He's probably tired."

"Not that. He was vague about how he knew about the latest vic."

He'd picked up on Blaine's change in tone and behavior, as well. Autumn felt torn between Nathan and Blaine. While she didn't believe her brother was involved, she didn't want to raise doubts in anyone's mind. To this point, Nathan had been firmly on her side and in the Blaine-is-not-guilty party.

Something in Nathan's tone sent a torpedo of worry to Autumn's gut. The urge to defend her brother rose in her chest. "He needs sleep. We'll talk to him tomorrow. He's not much of a talker anyway. My dad and uncle used to joke that Blaine spoke a hundred words a day. We probably got as much as we did from him because he's been alone for months and has barely spoken a word to anyone. He had those hundreds saved up."

Her attempt at humor didn't lift the corners of Nathan's mouth or scrub the look of concentration from his face. "He knows something about the victim he's not telling us."

Autumn didn't care for the implication Nathan was making. Blaine was not involved with the Huntsman or the murders. She ruffled Nathan's hair. "Don't get FBI on him. He's just quirky."

Nathan smoothed his hair. "You mentioned that Blaine was a loner and had some trouble in high school."

Was Nathan profiling her brother? Building a psychological sketch to use against him?

The adrenaline rush from her brother's visit had subsided, and in combination with the interrupted sleep and the early-morning hour, irritation rose in her veins. "I didn't say he was a loner. I said he was hiking the trail alone. And most people have some problem or another in high school."

Nathan stood. "I'll talk to him alone tomorrow."

Autumn stared at Nathan, shocked she had fallen into this emotional pit again. Nathan, the man who had made love to her hours ago and held her tenderly, was gone. Blaine's presence had brought back Nathan, Special Agent. The distance widened between them and a chill speared through her.

She turned away, unable to look at him. She might shatter if his eyes were cold and expressionless.

"Ready for bed?" he asked.

She was angry at his accusations and frustrated by his attitude, but she didn't tell him to go to his cabin. She was physically exhausted, emotionally wrung, and being alone wasn't high on her priority list, especially with a killer lurking in the area.

She crawled into bed and shut off the light at her bedside. Nathan climbed in beside her, but he didn't reach for her. Closing her eyes, she tried to fall asleep, willing her restless mind to quiet.

An hour later, still wide awake, she rolled over and found Nathan was also awake, staring at the ceiling. She set her hand over his chest. "What's the matter?" she asked. Was he thinking of the same things she was? Or was he thinking about her? Wondering how she felt?

"The case," he said.

A bruise to the heart, but not a break. When did a man ever admit to his feelings? "What about it?"

"Trying to put the pieces together."

She'd thought up until now they'd done a good job working as a team. "Anything in particular you want to share?"

"Nothing yet. Get some sleep. The sun's almost up."

Dismissed. He had shut down emotionally and he had shut her out of his thoughts, out of the case.

She rolled away, tucking herself under the blankets, and squeezed her eyes shut, promising herself it was the last time that she'd let Nathan Bradshaw bruise her heart.

Blaine might know something about the murders. His evasive answers replayed in Autumn's mind. At 6:00 a.m., Autumn showered and dressed and took care of a few chores. Unable to think of anything except the Huntsman, she knocked on her brother's door until he answered it.

Despite the late hour when he had arrived the night before, Blaine was awake and coffee was in the pot on the kitchen counter.

"Let me pour you some coffee. You seem wound up," Blaine said. He poured her a cup and handed it to her, then walked out onto the porch.

Autumn followed. "Blaine, if you know something about the Huntsman you have to tell Nathan."

Blaine sat on the wooden chair facing the Trail's Edge entrance. "I don't have to do anything."

Autumn dragged a seat in front of Blaine and sat, forcing him to look at her. "This is important, Blaine. This isn't high school pranks or practical jokes. People are getting hurt."

"What makes you think I know anything?" Blaine avoided making eye contact and took a sip of his coffee.

"Cut the bull, Blaine."

Blaine narrowed his eyes and a long pause passed.

"I don't know anything for sure, Autumn. I just have theories. The killings. Something about the killings is strangely familiar." His voice took on a haunted tone.

An uneasy feeling skittered down her spine. "Familiar? What do you mean? We've never had murders along the trail, at least, not like this."

Blaine rubbed his bearded jawline. "What about the locations of the murders?"

"You mean the one between here and the trail?"

Blaine shook his head. "I can't figure that one out. Think about the other ones."

"Backcountry. Less accessible to most hikers," Autumn said, trying to guess where Blaine was headed with this line of thinking.

"Not just that. What about the hanging from a tree? It's almost ritualistic."

Nathan had used similar terms in describing the Huntsman's killings. "No doubt, it's creepy. Nathan thinks it has something to do with keeping the trail clean."

Blaine stood. "Do you have Dad and Uncle Ryan's nature books?"

Autumn came to her feet. "I have a few. Why do you want them?"

"Get them. Please. Don't tell your boyfriend I want them."

Autumn didn't bother correcting him about Nathan. It didn't matter what Blaine thought and she didn't waste time explaining. Autumn jogged to her cabin and went inside, trying to think what she could tell Nathan. Turned out, she didn't need to tell him anything. Nathan was gone. A note on the counter had his cell number and a message. "At my cabin—work."

At least with him gone, she wouldn't need to lie about what she was doing. She retrieved the box of books she had crammed under her bed. After removing her books, layered on the top, she reached the ones that had belonged to her father and her uncle. They were among the few items she had kept to remember them. The books had belonged to her grandfather and he had passed them to his sons. Lifting the box with the remaining books, she carried it to Blaine's. She dropped the box at his feet. "I haven't read these in years."

Blaine picked up the first book and turned it over in his hand. "I saw the last victim. It was a woman. Expensive equipment. Her boots weren't even broken in. She had no business being on the trail and I told her so. She had a fancy camera and said something about working on a thesis project."

Autumn froze and her eyes snapped to Blaine's face. What was Blaine saying? "Why didn't you say something to Nathan when he asked what you knew about the victim?" The FBI could still be looking for her identity. Blaine could have helped them.

"She was burned almost beyond recognition. At first, they didn't know if she was male or female," Autumn said.

"It's always females," Blaine said, a heavy edge on his voice.

Autumn watched her brother, growing afraid to ask more questions while feeling compelled to know more. "Blaine, what are you saying?"

Blaine ran an agitated hand through his hair. "I don't want to get involved in this. I can't get involved in this."

"We're already involved. We're part of the trail. We can't turn our backs and pretend otherwise." If he knew something, he had to tell the authorities. The FBI had dozens of agents on the case. If they found anything that implicated Blaine, they'd be thrilled to have a suspect in custody.

Blaine set his jaw. "Things haven't been right since Dad died."

Following the jump in conversation, Autumn knelt at his side. "I know what you mean, I feel—"

Blaine cut her off by slicing his hand through the air. "You've kept going, Autumn. You're running this place and you're living your life. But I can't shake it. It catches me off guard, and I can't handle it. I'm angry. I'm angry at Dad for dying and angry at the world that doesn't care. We've lost everyone except each other." Blaine looked at the floor as if embarrassed by his emotional outburst.

Autumn hadn't realized her brother had been having this much difficulty dealing with his grief. Losing their father had been hard on them, and Blaine hadn't spoken much about it since the funeral. She'd assumed he'd coped as she had, with time alone, reading and thinking. She couldn't give a precise explanation for how she'd managed, but somehow she had. Her grief wasn't nearly as raw as it had been in the months following her father's death. Day by day, it had gotten easier for her. Had Blaine not felt any healing change?

Autumn set her hand on his arm. Blaine didn't pull away, so she wrapped her arms around him, hugging him, wishing she could take some of the grief from him, if only for a little while. "I'm sorry, Blaine. I didn't know you were having such a rough time. You can talk to me about it, if it helps. I'm there, too. I know it hurts and it sucks and it's a total awful time."

Blaine let her hug him for a few moments, then shoved her away abruptly, squaring his shoulders and lifting his chin. His eyes were damp but his cheeks dry. "Why did you keep these?"

She'd kept the books for their sentimental value. They had been a part of her childhood, her father teaching her and Blaine lessons from them, basic first aid, essential information for living in the forest. Now it was quicker and easier for her to look up information on the internet.

"I wasn't ready to throw them away. They were Dad's and Uncle Ryan's and they loved them. But I don't know what this has to do with the murders."

Blaine squatted next to the books and pulled each out, setting them on the floor in a stack. Near the bottom was a maroon-colored leather-bound book with the gold-embossed title on the front, *Nature's Secrets*.

It had been a favorite of their grandfather's and their uncle Ryan's, listing plants and their healing properties, how to create headache medicine from boiled leaves and soap from mashed roots. He held up the book, shaking it in his hand. "Do you know what this book says about purifying the land?"

Autumn shook her head, uneasy about where this conversation was headed. Blaine had seen the victim and he'd lied to Nathan about it and now he was obsessed with these books. "Blaine, tell me what's going on. You're freaking me out."

"It talks about removing litter from the land," Blaine said, opening the book and holding it in his palms. He started flipping through the pages.

Autumn shivered. "I don't understand what that has to do with the murders." She didn't want to make a connection between the murderer and her brother. Blaine was all the family she had left. He wouldn't hurt another hiker. It wasn't in his nature. But his behavior was bizarre, and her stomach knotted with worry.

Blaine's gaze shot up. "The vines around the bodies. Didn't you think that was weird?"

When Autumn had told Blaine about the body she'd found, he had been so blasé about it. Now, the intense look on his face caused her to lean away. "I guess so. I didn't know why someone would do that."

"The hiker on the trail, the last victim, was moving quick, too quick to have any idea what she was doing. She would have exhausted herself in hours. When I saw her veer off the trail, I followed her, wanting to warn her."

Autumn wished he would stop. She didn't want to hear this. But the words caught in her throat.

"Because of the weather, I lost her. I set up camp for the night and the next day, I found her. She was swinging from the tree. She had an arrow through her chest and the vines wrapped around her. The way the body was burned, I knew she was dead."

Autumn's stomach twisted in a mixture of horror and fear. Blaine had been in the vicinity, in the backcountry where another killing had taken place. Why had he been spared? Blaine was quick and quiet in the woods. Had the killer not seen him? Was one victim enough? She grabbed Blaine's forearm. "You have to tell Nathan what you saw."

Blaine shook his head adamantly and pushed his unruly dark hair away from his face. "I can't. Come on, Autumn. I'm telling you because it's been eating me, but if I tell him, he'll haul me in for questioning. He might even think I'm involved."

"If you tell the truth, you have nothing to worry about," Autumn said, in that moment putting more trust in Nathan than she had in any other man, outside her father. Nathan would treat Blaine fairly, hear him out and give him the benefit of the doubt. He wouldn't snap to judgment or twist the facts against Blaine.

Blaine closed the book and threw up his hands. "Get a clue, Autumn. This is real life. The police and the FBI want a suspect. They want someone on the hook for these murders. Look how ready Daniel was to point his finger at me."

"You can trust Nathan to do the right thing."

The look on Blaine's face told her he didn't see things the same way. "Don't be naive. He might be your boyfriend, but he has no reason to help me. You do not have good taste in the men you choose to date."

"That's not true," Autumn said, knowing it was.

Blaine looked at her sideways. "Come on, Autumn. Ben? Daniel? Now this guy? Are you even sure he's not using you to get to me? Or using you to work an angle? He could do this with women at every location."

Autumn shook her head. Nathan wasn't using her. "Nathan and I are a team."

Blaine sighed. "I hope for your sake you are right about this. I know how this looks for me. With my record, how long I've been on the trail, my history with Sandra and now a victim I spoke with dead, no one will believe me." His voice had taken on a panicked hitch.

"I believe you. Whatever you tell me, I'll believe it." She knew Blaine wouldn't intentionally hurt someone. "I don't understand what that book has to do with the vines." She couldn't remember anything in the pages about the topic.

Blaine blew out his breath in a huff. "The original pantheistic settlers in this area had beliefs that stemmed from a love of nature and a reverence for its power. They believed they could bind evil using vines. They'd wrap vines around criminals to prevent them from hurting someone else as part of a cleansing ritual."

Autumn recalled something in the book about ceremonies and beliefs along the trail. She'd thought it was folklore, an exaggeration of a story to scare people into respecting the land.

"Are you saying the Huntsman is a descendant of the original settlers? Someone who still practices pantheism?"

"It's a working theory," Blaine said.

Autumn didn't know anyone who openly prescribed to pantheistic beliefs, but plenty of nature lovers put the land first and believed in the earth and nature as their higher power. "Let's take a few deep breaths and calm down."

She didn't suggest talking to Nathan again, but maybe once they discussed this a little more, Blaine would agree to tell Nathan his theory.

Blaine took her arm. "I am calm, Autumn. I won't tell anyone about this. I have no proof it means anything about the Huntsman or the murders." His eyes bored into her and she shrugged Blaine's hand away. She needed to convince Blaine that he should come clean about what he knew.

The sounds of cars approaching had Autumn turning toward the entrance of the Trail's Edge. Police cars and the FBI. What had happened now?

As the cars approached, Autumn saw Nathan exit his cabin, striding toward Blaine's dwelling. Had they found another victim? Or caught the killer?

Special Agent Ford approached at the same time Nathan did, holding up his hand to Nathan. "Stay out of this, Bradshaw."

Nathan didn't budge. Four police officers got out of their cars.

"Blaine Reed?" Ford asked.

Fear skittered across her spine. Autumn stepped in front of Blaine. "He just arrived home a little while ago. What's going on?"

Ford didn't look as if he believed her. "Our video surveillance confirms he arrived sometime early this morning. Were you planning to let me know?"

Autumn didn't answer. They'd had her under surveillance? Had that been the sensation she'd felt of being watched?

Ford continued. "Step away from Blaine. Mr. Reed, don't make this harder than it needs to be. We have questions for you."

Blaine looked between her and Special Agent Ford. "I've done nothing wrong."

Special Agent Ford looked amused. "Really? That's mighty interesting. DNA tells us otherwise."

DNA? What DNA? "Someone needs to tell me what's going on," Autumn said, refusing to step away from her brother. She glanced at Nathan for an explanation, but he seemed as confused as she was.

"Your DNA is a close match to the DNA we found on that book from Hilde's rest spot and at the Trail's Edge in cabin twelve," Ford said to Autumn.

It couldn't be. Blaine had not done this. Confusion swamped her. Before she could form a coherent question, Special Agent Ford continued. "Blaine, we have questions," Ford said. "Step away from your brother, Ms. Reed."

Horror washed over her. They couldn't take Blaine. The DNA test had to be wrong, a mistake of epic proportions. She'd wanted Blaine to tell Nathan what he knew about the killer and the latest victim, but if Blaine broke during questioning and told Ford what he had witnessed, he'd destroy his defense. "You can't take my brother. There's some other explanation."

Ford reached into his back pocket and withdrew an envelope. "This warrant says we can search the premises and we can arrest Blaine Reed." Search the premises? Would they see the books and question them?

Blaine stepped around her. He patted her shoulders lightly. "It's okay, Autumn. I'll be fine."

She heard something in his voice, an ominous threat. He wasn't planning to tell them anything, but he didn't want to upset her. "Blaine, don't say anything without a lawyer. Nothing."

Blaine walked to the police car and smiled over his shoulder at Autumn as if they shared some secret. Which they did. But it left her feeling cold and terrified.

Nathan was at her side a moment later. "He'll be okay."

She turned to Nathan, clutching at his shirt. "Blaine didn't kill anyone. He's innocent. There's been some mistake, an error at the lab." She needed someone to believe her. For someone to be on her and Blaine's side.

"You need to hire a lawyer for your brother."

Her mouth fell open. Didn't he believe her? Blaine was innocent. Was Nathan taking Ford's side against her and Blaine? "You think Blaine is guilty?"

Nathan took a step away and rubbed the back of his neck. "It doesn't matter what I believe. What matters is taking care of Blaine. Ford is out for blood. He wants to lock Blaine away. You need to protect him."

One of the police officers was handcuffing Blaine. The officer put him into the back of the police cruiser.

As they drove away, Autumn tried to hold herself together, tried to think logically without allowing emotion to fuel every thought. She wrapped her arms around herself. What could she do? Following them to the police precinct seemed pointless. She needed to find Blaine help. Which lawyer? She racked her brain trying to think of someone she knew who practiced law. Not environmental or family law, but criminal law.

She needed someone to direct her. She hadn't been in a situation like this before. "What should I do now?"

"I'll follow them to the station and see if I can do anything. You need to call a lawyer. Henry Summers. He'll help you."

A name of a lawyer. That helped. "Can you call in some favors? Pull some strings? Blaine will be miserable in jail. He needs to be outside in the fresh air."

Nathan appeared apologetic. "I can't pull strings on this. I'm not on the case and if they have DNA evidence, that's not good for Blaine."

Terrifying for Blaine. What had Blaine gotten mixed up in and how would she get him out of it?

Autumn wrapped her hands around the mug of hot tea, but nothing warmed her. She'd gotten in touch with the lawyer Nathan had suggested, and Henry Summers had agreed to represent her brother. To secure his services, she'd given him every cent she had remaining in her savings account, a mere pittance of his normal fees. Since she'd been referred by Nathan Bradshaw, Henry had said they'd work out the rest of his fee later. While that had a fateful sound, Autumn wouldn't worry about it now. To protect Blaine, she'd sell everything she had, even the Trail's Edge.

Henry hadn't been able to convince the judge to release Blaine on bail or to persuade any of the court officers to allow her to visit with her brother. However, by some act of extreme good fortune, the FBI had decided to hold Blaine overnight in the local jail, as opposed to transporting him the nearest maximum-security prison.

Being in jail wouldn't be easy for Blaine, a man who needed the outdoors as much as he needed oxygen, but a maximum-security prison would be worse. How long could he stand being locked in a jail cell?

She looked at the list of tasks she had composed. She needed to talk to the bank about getting another mortgage on the Trail's Edge. She had to find another job, something that would pay Blaine's legal bills. She needed to support Blaine, to provide whatever Henry required to prove Blaine was innocent.

She nearly laughed aloud at the last note. As if finding evidence was that easy. She and Nathan had been looking for days to find something, anything to lead them to the Huntsman. Every bit of evidence had pointed to Blaine as the guilty party.

A knock on the door sounded and Autumn almost decided she was too tired to answer it. But if it was a hiker looking for shelter, she couldn't afford the loss of income. Not now when Blaine needed her. Thor lifted his head, but didn't follow her to the door. He was as exhausted as she was.

She looked through the peephole and sighed. Her mother. This was not a visit she wanted to have now.

Autumn opened the door. "You picked a bad time." Although she couldn't see any better times on the horizon.

"What were those police cars doing? What happened? I was worried about you," Blythe said.

Autumn considered blowing her off, but it would be faster to tell her the truth. "Blaine came home last night and the police arrested him. They think he's the Huntsman."

Her mother gasped. "It's not possible."

How would she know? Blythe didn't know her or Blaine.

"How can I help?" her mother asked.

"Do you have fifty thousand dollars to spare to pay for Blaine's defense?" Autumn asked drily.

"I don't," her mother said and chewed her lip. She shoved her way into the cabin. "Autumn, I need to talk to you."

"Again, this is not a good time. I have things I need to do." She didn't need more drama. Nathan's words ran in her head and she thought about what had happened to Nathan's sister. She was open to the possibility of making amends with her mother. Healing the old wounds between her and her mother would take time and energy she didn't have at the moment.

"This will only take a minute," her mother said.

Autumn was about to firmly, rudely, whatever it took, kick her mother out, but gathered what remained of her patience and energy. Could her mother know something about the pantheistic beliefs along the trail? Could her mother know more about who might be part of a group with those beliefs? Her parents had lived at the Trail's Edge for years before Autumn and Blaine had been born. "Can you tell me anything about pantheism?"

Her mother scrunched her nose. "Is that what you call worshipping Greek gods?"

It had been worth a shot. "Nothing to do with Greek gods. It was a theory Blaine had about the Huntsman."

"Autumn, I want to help you. I want to help Blaine. I think I have some things to tell you that might shed some light on the past."

Autumn waited for her mother to continue. She hadn't visited them in years. Did Autumn really need to talk about the past now?

"It's no secret that your father and I had a difficult marriage. The problem was that it wasn't just the two of us in that relationship. There was a third person."

"If you are about to tell me that Dad cheated on you or you cheated on Dad, that'll only make me feel worse about everything," Autumn said.

"Not cheating. Just an interloper. Your uncle. He drove me away. He never liked me and he made it impossible to have a normal marriage to your father."

Autumn lifted a brow. "From how Uncle Ryan spoke of you, he wasn't a fan."

Her mother stiffened. "I'm sure he wasn't. After I left, it was the fuel his fire needed to cast me as the devil."

Her uncle had never used those words, but he hadn't said anything good about their mother, either.

"Then tell me what he did that drove you away. Tell me what he did that made it possible for you to leave me and Blaine."

Her words found their mark and her mother flinched. "I know you think I'm a bad person for what I did. But I felt like I had no choice. Nothing I did was good enough for your uncle, and he spread his venom to your father. I didn't know much about hiking. I didn't like hunting or fishing. I didn't cook. I didn't sew. I didn't do any of the things your uncle thought I should in order to be a good wife to your father."

Her mother's eyes welled with tears. She swiped at them, smearing mascara across her temples. "Your uncle criticized everything I did. Your dad defended me, but as the years wore on, he decided ignoring it was better. Then he started to believe it. I couldn't take it anymore. I thought if I left, you all would miss me so much, you'd beg me to come back."

Autumn and her brother had begged every night in their prayers for their mother to return. "Blaine and I missed you terribly."

"When I called, your father said you were fine."

"And you believed that?" Autumn asked, now angry with both her parents.

"I thought I was wrong for you and wrong for Blaine and you'd be better off without me."

Autumn stared at her mother. "That is ridiculous. You might not have been a chef or a very good maid or outdoorswoman, but you were our mother and we loved you."

"I made a tremendous mistake," her mother said and began to cry softly. "Not a day has passed that I haven't thought of you and Blaine. When I've called, you and Blaine were so distant. I thought about coming to your father's wake, but I knew I wouldn't be welcomed and I didn't want to put you through more of an ordeal."

"So you waited until now, when things are bad, to show up?"

"I thought I could help," her mother said.

How? What could her mother contribute? "I don't think you can help," Autumn said. "But I appreciate your honesty." It wasn't forgiveness she was offering, but it was the best she could give at the time. "I have a lot to do. We'll talk later."

"We will?" her mother asked.

"Yes," Autumn said, not comfortable with the idea, but knowing a "no" wasn't a response she was ready to commit to either.

Her mother left and it took Autumn an hour walking the trail with Thor to calm down enough to center herself. When she returned, Nathan was sitting on her porch, looking through a file folder.

Emotionally wrung, she didn't know if she should pretend she hadn't seen him and return to the trail. Whenever they were together, her emotions became a loopy mess.

He stood. He'd seen her. It was too late to run. "I've been worried about you."

She took the stairs to the porch and her heart had the same reaction it always did when he was close; it skipped to a faster beat as she drank in the sight and the smell of him. "How's Blaine? Do you know anything more?"

Nathan studied her face for a moment. "That's why I'm here."

His tone was serious and sullen. Her stomach and heart twisted. "Tell me what happened."

Nathan took a deep breath. "He won't provide a DNA sample."

Autumn took a moment to process what he'd said. Was Nathan here to plead for the prosecutor? "He's taking the advice of his lawyer. The lawyer you recommended."

"It makes him look guilty. They already have your DNA. They know that he left blood on the journal."

Autumn felt her anger simmering. She didn't care what Roger Ford said. It wasn't Blaine's blood on the book or in cabin twelve. "What do you want me to do, Special Agent Bradshaw? Help nail my brother for a crime he didn't commit?"

She spat his title and name at him, furious that he wasn't on her and Blaine's side. This was when she needed his loyalty the most.

"Autumn, don't do that. I'm here to help you." He reached to cup her chin and she whipped her head away, taking a step back from him. Thor growled in his throat.

"I'm not the enemy."

She took another step back. "You work for the enemy. With the enemy."

He advanced a step. "I don't work for anyone. I'm trying to position myself to best help your brother. They will get a warrant for his DNA. It looks better for him to be helpful."

Autumn retreated and felt the wood railing at her back. "If the FBI and the police were doing their jobs, they would have followed the correct evidence and they would have found the real killer and not wasted my and my brother's time. The killer is still out there." If she was the only person who would believe in Blaine's innocence, then fine. She would not waver.

"If he is innocent, then giving us a DNA sample wouldn't matter," Nathan said.

"Blaine admitted he was on the trail. That doesn't mean he killed anyone, but his DNA could be on Hilde's book."

Nathan set his hands on either side of her against the railing, his legs braced apart so they were almost nose to nose. She turned her head to the side and crossed her arms. She could have shoved him away or lifted her knee and done some serious damage. But her heart wouldn't let her. Her emotions reveled in his smell, the scent of him that clung to her sheets and in her clothes long after he left. Too easily, she remembered their nights together, the endless passion, the explosive chemistry that set him at odds with the man he could be at times—cold, distant, focused on the case.

"Let me help you and Blaine," he said.

Autumn looked at him, and their eyes met and held in an electrically charged moment. "Are you trying to help Blaine and me? Or are you here for the FBI, to make progress in the case?"

"I'm here to help you."

Nathan wanted his sister's killer found to bring closure to him and his family. "What do you want me to do?"

"Tell Blaine to get the DNA test."

That did it. Forget love. Forget lust. Nothing came between family. She shoved him away with all her might and Nathan fell back a step. She would have had some satisfaction if he had pretended to stumble. "I won't talk my brother into anything except following the advice of his lawyer."

"Henry is good."

She didn't reply to that or thank him for the referral. She was too angry to give him any ground. "If that's all you need to say, please leave. I'm tired."

Nathan stared at her for a heated moment. "That's not all, Autumn, and you know it."

Every muscle in her body flexed in awareness. The look in his eye. The intensity on his face. She affected him, and that knowledge sent a surge of power through her. But having him wrap his arms around her and comfort her was a temporary fix. She wouldn't toss her heart to him for the night, knowing come the morning, she'd be emotionally devastated all over again. The situation with Blaine was using every inch of her emotional capacity. "Please leave." The words stuttered from her lips. She wished she could have spoken them with more conviction.

"Let me stay with you. I'll sleep on the floor."

Autumn couldn't give in knowing even now he was breaking down her defenses. The close quarters of her cabin would melt away her resistance, and by morning she'd be in his arms.

She needed something to throw at him, something to get off the defensive and protect herself. The rejection she'd felt when he'd been cold as ice was a near and painful memory.

"Why? What do you want, Nathan? To sleep with me? Is it still a challenge for you? Isn't it old hat now? You won! You got me. We had sex. Mystery is over, Great Detective." The words hurt to say, and she realized she half believed them, half believed he'd had an agenda and had used her to achieve it. She changed the subject, the knife twisting in her heart too painful. Why wasn't it easier to write him off? "Or is it Blaine you need to figure out now? Ask me questions to dig into his past so you can tell the jury what a mixed-up little boy he was? You know my mother left and my father's dead. Why don't you twist those things into a noose and hang us both? You want closure for your sister, but you won't find it by investigating the wrong person."

Nathan seemed momentarily taken aback by her words and for the first time since she'd met him, he looked unsure of what to say. "Is that how you feel, Autumn? That I'm using you to get at your brother?"

No. She tilted her chin, hoping he didn't see through her false confidence. "Yes." At the same moment she spoke the word, she wished she hadn't.

Nathan winced, an injured shadow passing over his face. "Don't do this. Don't shut me out like you have every other person in your life. Don't put me in the same box with that other loser you dated."

Autumn felt the knife hit to the heart and struggled to recover. "I don't shut anyone out." She'd give him that Daniel was a loser.

"You live in this secluded area, you hate going into town, you've constructed so many walls around yourself, it's a wonder you can see anyone else. And now you're worried about Blaine, so your instinct is to reinforce those walls and shove me out. Maybe if you weren't so worried about getting hurt, you'd let someone who cares for you help you. You can't even talk to your mother when she is standing in front of you, asking for forgiveness."

He had no right to judge her for that. She had been through a lot in her life. Her family had left her. Her fiancé had betrayed her. Her business was failing. Wallowing a little was allowed. "I'll have you know that I did speak to my mother. But you have no idea how much history is there. You're one to talk about shutting people out. When other people are around, you pretend as if we have no relationship."

"I don't pretend we don't have a relationship. I put some distance between you and how I feel about you and this case. I don't want to think about the Huntsman getting close to you or hurting you," Nathan said.

She didn't know what to say to that. They stared at each other for several long moments.

Nathan backed away from her. "I have no right to tell you how to live your life. I've said too much. I'll go."

As he walked away, she knew everything he'd said was the truth, and it burned her to the core.

Chapter 8

"Hey, Mom," Nathan said when his mother answered the phone. She sounded tired. Had she been sleeping? Worrying? This was a call he had been dreading since Blaine had been arrested.

"Nathan, we've been following the news. Do you have anything to share?" his mother asked.

The news that the FBI had a suspect in custody under suspicion of being the Huntsman was a national headline. Blaine's identity hadn't been disclosed, but Nathan knew it was only a matter of time. Local gossip was already buzzing about Blaine Reed.

If only Nathan believed Blaine was guilty, he would enjoy sharing what he knew with his family. But Nathan believed the Huntsman was at large. "Still investigating, but we're getting close."

"The FBI made an arrest."

"Yes, they did."

"Why aren't you elated? This is what you've been working for," his mother said.

Her voice had taken on a color of hope and Nathan hated to white it out. But he wouldn't lie to his mother. "I am not sure they have the right person."

His mother sighed. "I knew something was off when I saw the news and you hadn't called."

"I'm sorry, I wish I had better news," Nathan said.

"I know you're doing everything you can," his mother said.

His best hadn't been enough. Not enough to shield the Reed family and not enough to find Colleen's killer and stop him. He would take more lives. At least at that point, the FBI would have to admit they had the wrong man in custody.

"I miss your sister every day," his mother said.

"I know you do, Mom. I do, too."

"I think it's my fault."

He and his mother harbored guilt that they had a role in Colleen's death. If they had been able to quiet her demons, she wouldn't have needed time away so desperately that she'd been willing to ignore conventional wisdom and hike alone.

"It's no one's fault but her killer's."

Her mother's breath hitched on a sob. Nathan wished he was with her. He heard his niece and nephew running and playing in the background and his heart ached. They'd lost their mother. They were confused and grieving and because of how up and down their relationship with their mother had been, they hadn't fully grasped what had happened to her.

Nathan's mother had stepped up to help his former brother-in-law with the children and making the adjustment, but they deserved better. They deserved their mom in their life.

"Tell me how you are, Nathan," his mother said.

Should he tell his mother about Autumn? "I met someone." Someone who was important enough to mention to his family.

A pregnant pause. "Who is she?" his mother asked.

"She found one of the victims of the Huntsman," Nathan said.

"Nathan, you know how bad it is when you get involved in drama," his mother said.

He did know. He was aware of his dating pathology and the mistakes he repeated in relationships. His first marriage had been fireworks and excitement and had imploded because it was too much too fast. "It's not like that," Nathan said, but he could point to many times over the past several days when his and Autumn's relationship had been intense and over-the-top with problems and excitement. "I like her. I like her a lot."

"If you like her, then you know I will, too. Just be careful. I don't want you to be hurt again," his mother said.

Nathan talked to his mom for a few more minutes, said hello to his niece and nephew, and then disconnected the call. Letting his family down hadn't been an option, and now he had someone else important he couldn't disappoint. Autumn needed him to find the Huntsman and prove Blaine wasn't the killer.

* * *

Nathan shifted in his sleeping bag, turning his back to the wind. Autumn's porch provided some shelter, but sleeping outside alone wasn't his idea of a good night. Returning to sleep in the cabin he'd rented was tempting, but he wasn't leaving Autumn alone and unguarded.

The FBI was thrilled to have a man in custody under suspicion of being the Huntsman. Blaine fit the profile and the timeline, and DNA at the scene pointed to the Reed family, but his gut told him Blaine wasn't guilty. Nathan had no proof Blaine was innocent of the crimes he was accused of, but with even a 1 percent chance that the Huntsman was at large, Nathan had to keep Autumn safe—and that meant staying close to her.

Nathan had called Henry, an old pal of his, after Blaine's interview with Roger Ford. While his friend wouldn't betray attorney-client privilege, Henry indicated Blaine had a good defense.

Nathan hoped so—the evidence stacked against him was strong and incriminating. What did Henry think he had? Pinning most of the evidence collected on circumstance?

Nathan closed his eyes, but couldn't sleep. The case he could shut out and he could ignore the cold, but he couldn't forget the look on Autumn's face that night. He'd hurt her, and that didn't sit well with him. She'd been upset about her brother, and he shouldn't have pushed her. She'd needed him to be a friend and he'd been an investigator.

Perhaps just shy of regret, she was confused about

their relationship and scrambling for more stable ground. He'd known Autumn was a closed book and he'd tried to stay away from her. Tried to construct some boundaries and keep them from being crossed. But he couldn't.

Even tonight, with the anger spewing from her lips, he'd wanted to take her in his arms and convince her everything would be fine. He wanted to run a trail of kisses down her neck, flick his tongue over the soft skin of her collarbone, and lower to her breasts, suck her nipples in his mouth... He groaned and rubbed his hands together, trying to generate some warmth inside his sleeping bag. Thoughts like that would get him nowhere, and he had a long, cold night ahead of him.

He tried to block thoughts of her, but they filled his head. He was awake when she turned off the light in her kitchen, and he imagined her changing into her soft pajamas and slipping between her sheets. Sheets he wanted to be on with her.

Closing his eyes, he let thoughts of her drift him to a dreamless sleep.

He jolted awake when her screen door hit him in the cheek. He rolled to the side so Autumn could step onto the porch.

"What are you doing?" she asked, more surprise in her voice than anger.

He peeled his sleeping bag away, hating the frigid cold that seeped into his bones. "I slept out here. I didn't want to leave you alone."

She angled her head, her eyes narrowed. "You've been on my porch all night?"

"Yes." And it had been brutally cold. Next time he was in town, he was buying some breakable heat packs to stuff in his sleeping bag.

"Alone?"

He looked around and lifted a brow. "Yup. Just me and the bears."

She folded her arms over her chest. "Why didn't you sleep in your cabin?"

"Because I can't hear or see you from my cabin."

This morning she was the image of warmth. She wore a scarf around her neck, a plush coat around her body and thick pants on her legs, and he'd bet beneath it all, she was fresh from a hot shower.

"Why do you think you need to hear or see me?" she asked, inclining her head, her ponytail dropping to the side.

He rubbed his hands together, trying to get the blood flowing in his arms. "The Huntsman is still out here. I don't think you're safe."

Something flared in her eyes. "You think Blaine is innocent."

He didn't like the word *innocent*. Everyone was guilty of something. "I don't think he killed those people. I don't think Blaine is the Huntsman."

Autumn's shoulders relaxed a fraction of an inch. "I have some errands to run." When she spoke, her words were soft.

Didn't she realize he was on her side? Though he had asked her to help him, now that the situation was reversed, he wouldn't walk away. "I'm coming with you." He came to his feet. He needed coffee, food and a hot shower. But it could wait. Autumn shouldn't be moving around town without protection.

"I'm fine on my own."

He shook the cold from his limbs. "I'm coming." His instincts told him not to leave her alone. The media would soon figure out that Blaine was in custody, whether from rumors or someone spotting him at the jail. When they did, they would descend on Autumn and the Trail's Edge. They would invade Autumn's privacy, and given how much she liked the quiet of her cabin, it would be hard for her.

Autumn sighed and glanced at her watch. "Come inside. I have a few minutes. You can get a shower and I'll make you breakfast."

Had he convinced her that he wasn't working against her and her brother? "You don't have to do that. I'm fine."

"You slept on my porch in the freezing cold. I owe you a hot shower and some warm food."

When she turned and went inside, he didn't argue. He just followed after her.

"I'd like to go into the bank alone," Autumn said, gathering her folder of paperwork from the backseat of the car. She had the loan documents from the remodeling of the Trail's Edge tucked inside. If she could get another loan or extend the one she'd taken, she'd have cash on hand to pay Blaine's legal fees. She wouldn't take another loan unless it was an emergency, and Blaine needing legal aid more than qualified. Increasing her mortgage payment made her feel sick, but somehow, she'd fight through this.

"I'll come with you and keep my distance," Nathan said from the passenger seat.

She hadn't been wild about him coming on her errands, but she had agreed because he'd shown such dogged persistence. He had slept on her porch the night before when he could have been warm and comfortable in his cabin. It had given her a secret thrill that he cared enough to stay when her words should have sent him packing. He'd believed Blaine was innocent. He and her mother might be the only people who did. Nathan was methodically breaking down her defenses and the reasons to keep him away.

She needed more people on her side, especially now, when she felt so alone. If only her father were here or even her uncle. Anyone who knew Blaine would know he was innocent and help her do what was needed to defend him. She thought again of her mother, but what could she say to her? How could she tell her mother what she needed?

"Have you considered how the town will react to Blaine being arrested?" Nathan asked.

She hadn't, but at that moment, the memories of the vicious rumors that had spread through town about her mother and her uncle hit her with force. They had hurt. As a child and then as a teenager, she had turned away and tried to hide. She was stronger now than she had been and if she had to listen to someone accuse Blaine, she wasn't sure she would stand and listen quietly. But starting a fight that might bring Daniel to the scene would be worse. He would take the side against her. He would like to have her and Blaine locked in jail. "I'll be careful. I can do this."

He relented, nodding his agreement that she would go into the bank alone.

Autumn left him in the car, glancing over her shoulder once, expecting him to follow her. He didn't. Her tension dropped a few notches. It was embarrassing to be in this financial situation. She had nothing except the Trail's Edge and the loans that went along with it. Blaine's lawyer hadn't cashed the check she'd given him, but unless she wanted to bounce a check for Blaine's defense, she couldn't spend any more money. She went inside the bank, its tinted windows and deep brown bricks preventing Nathan from watching her when she was inside.

She needed privacy to deal with this matter. It wouldn't be pretty.

After waiting for twenty minutes, she was led to the desk of a loan officer. Autumn pleaded her case and showed sales records and explained her slumping income by pointing out the problems with the Huntsman, letting the loan officer know she wholeheartedly believed that when the killer was caught, occupancy would increase.

"My understanding is that the FBI has arrested your brother in connection with the murders," the loan officer said.

Small-town gossip infuriated her. Autumn worked to stay calm. She wouldn't let facts fluster her. "Our lawyer is working to have him released. My brother is innocent."

"But that situation is pending a trial," the loan officer said.

Autumn checked her patience. "The case won't go to trial. There is no concrete evidence against my brother."

The loan officer seemed skeptical. She glanced at the paperwork Autumn had brought. She gathered it into a pile and handed it back to Autumn. "I know this must be hard for you, given your family's history, but we can't entangle ourselves in a criminal case."

"I am not asking the bank to be involved in any criminal case."

"Your business is floundering. You have no income from the campground. We can't extend you any further money."

Autumn had known this was a possibility, but she had hoped that something would go her way. "The Trail's Edge has been in operation for fifty years. It's a sustainable business."

The loan officer shook her head. "I'm sorry, Ms. Reed. We cannot help you."

Autumn took her papers and fled the bank, catching her reflection in the glass door. A face filled with disappointment. Tears threatened to spill down her cheeks, and her throat was tight. Given her nearly nil income over the past few weeks, the bank wouldn't help her. She had no one to turn to and nowhere else to go. She climbed into the truck and closed the door harder than she intended.

Nathan didn't speak, but offered her a nod of understanding. Her face made it plain it hadn't gone well.

She wouldn't make this his problem and she certainly couldn't look at him. She'd burst into tears, confide in him and share the burden. But this was her baggage to carry.

Autumn was tired, she was frustrated and she felt cornered. She hadn't had much sleep the night before since she'd been up late organizing her financials. Her thoughts were hazy. How could she fix this?

She hit the steering wheel with the palm of her hand, trying to force out some of her aggravation.

"Tell me what's going on so I can help."

A command, not a question. "Help? How will you help?"

Nathan rubbed his stubbly jaw. She'd offered him a fresh razor that morning, but he'd declined. The effect of a day's worth of growth on his face made him more handsome, more rugged and devastatingly masculine. She tried to steel herself against her feelings for him, but one look and she melted.

"I assume this errand has something to do with Blaine. I'll talk to Henry and see if he'll take the case pro bono."

Her internet research on Henry Summers the night before had revealed he was no small-time lawyer. He was a founding partner of his impressively sized law firm and had a nearly impeccable record of successes. "Why would he do that? He doesn't know Blaine or me. I don't even know if he believes Blaine is innocent."

"I didn't think you would accept his help if you knew it was a favor to me, but this is beyond pride. You need my help and I want to help you. Henry and

I go back to college. He has a philanthropic streak in him and besides that, we trade favors often enough."

A mental image of Blaine in a jail cell crushed her pride into silence. "Thank you. That would be very kind."

"It's no problem."

She took a deep breath, pulled out of the parking spot and navigated to the trailhead near where they'd found the journal. She parked in the sun, hoping its rays would keep the vehicle warm.

"Am I allowed to ask what we're doing here?" Nathan asked.

In troubled times, she could rely only on family. It wasn't just her future at stake. It was Blaine's, too. But Nathan had been strong and true. She'd be cautious in what she'd share with him. Now that Blaine had a lawyer, she should consult him on everything to be sure Blaine was protected. If she got Blaine into more trouble, she would feel terrible. "We found a small piece of evidence when we found that book at Hilde's. There might be more out here. Something to prove Blaine is innocent."

What else could be waiting on the trail that would free her brother?

"The crime scene investigators have gone over the scene," Nathan said.

"They don't have as much experience as I do in the wilderness," Autumn said. Her eyes were more attuned to nature and looking for footprints and other signs that humans had been present.

Autumn climbed out of the car, her boots crunching against the gravel of the lot. After popping the trunk, she circled the truck to lift it. She grabbed her pack and threw it over her shoulders. Though the sky was clear, the smell of snow was heavy in the air, the crispness biting at her nose.

"Good thing I brought my pack," Nathan said and grabbed it from the trunk.

She tugged a pair of ear warmers over her head and ignored him. She wanted to find the location where Blaine had slept when the last victim was killed. Knowing Blaine, he would have built a fire, meaning the remnants might still be there. Maybe there would be a second fire—anything to corroborate Blaine's story that there had been three of them—the victim, Blaine and the Huntsman—that night in the backcountry.

Nathan caught her elbow. "I'm here. I want you to remember that. I'm here for you."

Autumn started to turn away, but Nathan pressed a kiss to her lips that melted her from the inside. She leaned into it, sinking into soft, slow kisses. Nathan groaned and Autumn broke the kiss. Her relationship with Nathan had swung again from bitter cold to far too hot.

"We should focus," Autumn said.

"I've been telling myself that since the day I met you."

"What's your secret?" Autumn said.

"Fake it, mostly," he said. "But I'm here to support whatever you need. I want the Huntsman caught, too. If that means hands to myself, then okay."

Autumn and Nathan set out on the trail, clomping over snow, careful of the places where ice had formed in small puddles. A few hundred feet away stood the hut where they'd found the journal.

Not surprisingly, the perimeter was marked with yellow crime-scene tape and a police officer was standing nearby, looking bored. Keeping her head down and staying off the main trail, Autumn circled around it. To his credit and her surprise, Nathan said nothing, followed close and didn't make a sound. He didn't question her dodging the police officer, nor the exact reasons for this trip.

When she was out of sight of the officer standing near the hut, she returned to the trail. She looked around, searching for any hint of where Blaine might have gone. In their youth, Blaine would take off when he found something he thought was worthy of inspection—following a stream to the source, examining a peculiarly shaped rock or hearing the sound of a bird or animal he wanted to investigate. He'd said he'd followed the hiker. Where had they peeled off?

She walked slowly, looking for boot prints, but it was impossible to distinguish one print from another, and with the snow leaving its heavy imprint on the land, most trail markings were smeared together. This path had been well traveled, likely by law enforcement on their way to the hut. She wouldn't think about the possibility the snow had covered Blaine's camp or had blotted out evidence to support Blaine's story.

She'd find something. She had to help her brother. He was counting on her.

She pressed on, her feet slipping several times on the ice. She managed to keep her balance and avoid falling and caking herself with mud. It was too cold to be wet and she didn't have time to stop and make a fire to dry herself. She reached subconsciously for the striker and flint around her neck, her companion on the trail, especially when she ventured into unfamiliar territory.

Though she didn't relish it, she could survive in the wilderness for a number of days as long as she could make fire and find clean water. Her father had taught her and Blaine how to survive.

One of his first lessons was to stay calm no matter how difficult the situation became, and that lesson was helping her now. She was keeping it together for Blaine. She couldn't help him if she was dissolving into tears every few minutes, giving in to the heavy ache of anxiety and fear that weighed on her.

She trudged on, barely hearing Nathan behind her. Several times, she pretended to check her compass to be sure he was following. She didn't want him hurt or lost, and while he could protect her from a killer, she could protect him in the wild.

She hadn't been paying as much attention as she should have to the location of the latest victim. She'd been worried about Blaine and distracted about the possibility of finding him dead. She hadn't taken detailed notes of her surroundings. Asking Nathan would tip him off. Though she could confide in him, telling him her plan put him in a difficult place. He was her friend and her lover, for now, but he was also an FBI agent and the brother of one of the Huntsman's victims.

She remained quiet and looked for anything familiar.

Autumn continued along the trail and stopped when she heard the distinct sound of rushing water. With the snowstorm, smaller steams may have frozen over, but the sun and the press of a fresh water supply up the mountain would break them open. A stream. Blaine or the hiker might have decided to follow a stream to keep from getting lost.

Reaching into her backpack, she withdrew her camera and took a picture of the area. Scanning close to the ground and not seeing a footpath, she made her own.

"I didn't sleep with you because it was a challenge."

Autumn whirled and nearly stumbled over an exposed tree root. They were the first words he'd spoken to her since leaving the truck. Why was he bringing that up? Any other time, he'd acted as though nothing had happened between them and he was fine with it. Now, when she was on a mission, he wanted to talk about their relationship. It hurt to talk about, hurt to acknowledge this thing between them that had started out with promise and was now confusing and sure to end in heartache. "Then why did you?"

Why did she ask questions to spur the conversation forward? She didn't want to talk about this now. She had to concentrate on helping Blaine.

"It felt right."

She scrutinized those three words. *It. Felt. Right.* And now? Did it feel wrong? She couldn't bring herself to ask. She could live with him getting lost in the moment and sleeping with her, couldn't she? She was a big girl. Her heart had taken worse beatings, and this one stung only because it was fresh.

She lifted her chin. "Glad to hear it."

"I know you're guarded. I've known from the first moment I saw you."

"Then why bother getting involved with me? Or was that what you wanted? Something superficial and uncomplicated? You wanted someone closed off so you didn't have to get involved." As she spoke the words, she was aware they were her thoughts, as well. At least at first, she had wanted a torrid and sexy affair. Something to stroke her ego, and having a man like Nathan in her bed did just that. But then it had morphed into something else, and she was unprepared to cope with that.

Nathan didn't answer immediately. He seemed to draw the words from somewhere in his soul. "I saw beyond those defenses to the bright, vibrant woman you are. Maybe I could see so easily because I have some of those same barriers. I am involved with you. What do you call what I'm doing right now?"

His admissions surprised her. "You can turn your emotions off like a switch." She couldn't do the same with hers. Letting Nathan past her defenses, going into town with him, taking him to her bed and spending time with him amounted to one clear, heavy conclusion. She was in love with him and she had no idea what to do about it.

He shook his head. "I can turn off displaying them. I've had relationship drama in the past and I want to avoid that. The more I'm attracted to a woman, the more drama seems to start. I've been attracted to you, almost impossibly so, from the first moment I met you. I didn't want what we had to turn into fighting and tragedy."

"From the moment you met me?"

Nathan threw up his hands. "Of course. I don't know what happened to you to make you so reluctant to believe it, but know this. I am attracted to you. More than I've ever been attracted to another woman in my life. You are beautiful and smart, and being with you is an adventure. I'm sorry if I've hurt you."

An emotional admission and an apology? It was a lot for her to process. "Don't be sorry." Why was it hard for her to accept that she and Nathan had the right chemistry? "Come on. We've got miles to go."

Spinning on her heels, she proceeded along the path, trying to put herself in Blaine's frame of mind. The stream. He would follow the stream. The snow wasn't as heavy in this area, the trees holding a good portion of it in their branches.

"Will you please stop storming off every time I speak to you?" Nathan asked behind her.

She quickened her steps. Their conversation was taking a turn she wasn't capable of handling. A few words couldn't erase years of self-conscious thinking. If they kept speaking, she would confess she loved him, and then it would be so much worse. He wouldn't say the words in return. She would have pulled the pin on a grenade and tossed it at him. "I am not storming off. I am trying to help my brother. If you'd rather not be here, then wait in the car."

When he didn't respond and it grew quiet, she felt a flare of panic he might have listened to her and given up. She looked over her shoulder to see him following, but at a farther distance.

A smug smile traced over his face. "You don't want me to leave."

Her cheeks heated. "I was making sure you were okay."

"Sure." He caught up to her and took her elbow. A course of sensual lightning ripped through her.

She faced him, holding the straps of her backpack to keep her hands from reaching for him. She might not be able to calm her heart's excited reaction to him, but she could control her body. They weren't animals.

"I know you're scared your brother is in jail. I know that you think you don't have anyone to lean on. But you can lean on me. You can count on me to be there for you through this. You want me to stop shutting you out. You have to do the same."

Old insecurities flared. She didn't want to misunderstand him and take a fool's chance with her heart. "What part of this are you referring to? The investigation? The trial? What if my brother is wrongly convicted and goes to jail? He didn't kill those people. He didn't kill anyone." Now that he'd started her on this topic, she couldn't let go. If he wanted to know what she was thinking, if he wanted her to let him inside her most private thoughts, she would let him have it. "When we were children, Blaine could hardly stand to see an animal wounded much less another human. My dad and I were certified in first aid, but not Blaine. The sight of blood and injuries makes him sick. He didn't kill those people, and while the FBI is wasting their time building a case against Blaine, the real killer is planning his next move."

"If the Huntsman strikes while Blaine is in police custody, that will look good for his defense," Nathan said.

"If I'm lucky, I can find proof to free Blaine and find the killer before he kills again."

"A tall order, but I'm with you. What proof do you think we'll find? What do you think you'll find that hasn't been brought into evidence by the rangers and the FBI?"

Could she risk telling him? Could she trust him? She chose her words carefully, hoping if this went wrong that Blaine wouldn't blame her. "Blaine sometimes takes side trips off the trail."

"You think he came out here." He paused. "If you prove he was out here, you're building a case for the prosecution."

She gave him a cutting glower. "He wasn't out here alone. The victim, the killer and Blaine were out here. Three of them."

Nathan adjusted his pack. "How will you prove that?"

She hadn't worked through those details. Her search was an act of faith mixed with a little desperation. "If I find more than one camp, if I can prove in the same time frame that the killer, Blaine and the victim were out here, that constitutes reasonable doubt." Didn't it?

Nathan continued up the mountain. "It's a long stretch. You'd have to prove the other campsites were from the same time period."

Determining when a fire was built, especially after a snowstorm, was close to impossible. But what about Blaine's thoughts about the vines? Should she tell Nathan that Blaine had a theory about the Huntsman and his methods? "I can't sit around and wait for Blaine to go to jail." Doing something was better than nothing.

"You realize that anything I see I have to report as evidence."

She huffed indignantly. "Oh, I realize it. What you don't realize is my brother is innocent and anything we find will only help his defense." She hoped. To date, the evidence she and Nathan had found had made it worse for Blaine.

Nathan grinned at her. "That's the other thing I knew about you from the start. You're loyal to a fault."

"Blaine is family. Nothing is more important than family," Autumn said.

"I feel the same about my sister," Nathan said.

Sometimes she momentarily forgot she and Nathan were working this case for the people they loved. "When this is over, we'll get what we want. You'll find Colleen's killer and Blaine will be free."

"What if that's not everything I want?" Nathan said. He looked her over from head to toe.

Autumn shivered. The implication that he wanted her was flattering, but impractical. They weren't a couple that made sense. They didn't have a future. "I belong at the Trail's Edge. It's my home. It always has been. You belong to the FBI."

She didn't need to state the obvious. Their worlds had collided for this investigation, but otherwise, they were too different to work together.

* * *

The hike to the top of the stream took most of the afternoon. The ground was uneven and the brush thick and gnarled. Ground cover clung to the soil partially hidden by snow, making natural trip wires Nathan caught in the tips of his boots several times. When they reached the place where a larger river fed the stream they'd been following, Autumn shrugged off her pack and sat on the ground.

Nathan did the same, sitting across from her, forcing her to look at him. "Do you need water?"

She shook her head and patted her pack. "I have some."

Autumn's belief her brother was innocent was unwavering and she seemed convinced she would find something to prove it. He didn't think an old campsite proved anything. He didn't voice those opinions. She was edgy enough.

He should have expected her reaction—the anger, the irritation and even the flashes of warmth, yet he was unprepared for his reaction to her. He'd sworn that any future offer of protection or rescue was in the vein of his job as her partner in finding Colleen's killer. But being alone with Autumn tore the best of intentions to shreds. He couldn't stop thinking about the leanness in her legs and the firmness of her butt as she walked ahead of him. The brown fabric of her pants highlighted her natural slenderness. Autumn looked graceful as she hiked.

She pushed his buttons and she didn't seem to realize she was doing it.

That her brother was a suspect didn't dampen his

lust for her. That he was dedicated and focused on the case, to finding Colleen's killer, didn't squelch the need to take Autumn in his arms and taste her, touch her and hold her. Even her anger, which thinly masked the fear she was carrying, didn't turn off his raging libido. Instead, it made him think of having fast, heated sex with her, followed by slow, passionate making up.

Autumn came to her feet and brushed off her backside. "He'd probably make his camp beneath a tree. He wouldn't chance looking for a cave that might already have animals in it. Blaine is terrified of bats and of being cornered by an animal."

Nathan rolled to his feet and took a step closer to her. Even with a half day's grime on her, she smelled delicious and looked even better. A few strands of hair had worked themselves loose from her ponytail and she had a brush of dirt near her temple, likely where she had tucked her hair away from her face.

She glanced toward the sky, shielding her eyes with her hand. She pointed to a location about fifty feet away and three hundred feet up. "I want to see this area from the top of that peak."

The stone ledge jutted from the ground, the river intersecting it, an odd structure in an otherwise fluid incline.

He lifted a brow. "How do you plan to get up there?"

"Climb." She said it matter-of-factly, as if it wasn't dangerous and risky. He wasn't a skilled climber and wouldn't be able to keep up with her.

"Is it safe?"

She shrugged. "Maybe."

He didn't like the sound of *maybe*, not when they were talking about her life. "Why don't we scout the area first and save the climbing as a last resort?"

"We're losing daylight. Once I find Blaine's site, I need to track it to the location of the victim and look for evidence someone else was here."

Something wasn't adding up and his instincts prickled. It was as if she had a plan more detailed than looking for campsites. Stomping around in the forest looking for evidence that could be anywhere was ludicrous. She wasn't an illogical woman. She knew something more. "Tell me what's going on."

A trace of mistrust lit in her eyes and it wounded him more than he cared to admit. She didn't trust him. After all they had been through, her walls were still in place.

"Don't get in my way, Nathan."

With that, she marched in the direction of the peak, along the river.

He could physically stop her, possibly carry her down the trail kicking and screaming, but she would return the moment she could, her anger for him multiplying. He followed, unsure how to talk her out of this. The river was wide near the base of the rock structure, narrowing as it moved jaggedly down the mountain.

"Can we walk around and move up the peak where it's less steep?" he asked. Another path had to lead to the peak.

She threw back her shoulders. "It will take too long."

Nathan gritted his teeth. The more he tried to convince her not to do this, the more she would insist she follow through.

She pointed a few yards down. "I can chimney climb up that way."

A chimney climb involved her bracing her weight on her legs on opposite sides of the opening and maneuvering between the large rocks. She wouldn't have a safety harness, and from her vantage point, she couldn't see clear to the top of the peak.

His gaze swung from the top ledge to the ground. "With the river beneath you?"

"Water is better than rocks beneath me."

Comforting. "You don't know how stable the ledge is."

"It's rock. I'll be careful."

She riffled in her backpack for a rope, looping it around her arm. "I might be able to repel down once I get to the top."

Though he wasn't a particularly religious man, he sent up a prayer she could make it to the top without breaking her back.

"Can you give me a boost?" she asked, after she had adjusted her equipment, leaving her backpack on the ground.

To climb onto the peak, she would have to either stand in the water, soaking her clothes, or have help. He wanted to refuse, demand she tell him what she was thinking and then talk her out of this crazy scheme. But he'd seen her determination, and she'd risk the water and hypothermia to scale to the top of it if it meant it would help Blaine.

Nathan laced his fingers together and gave her a boost. Her foot landed on a thin ledge and she wobbled.

He reached to steady her, setting his hand on her thigh. "Be careful, Autumn."

"Always am."

He watched her scale the peak, moving slowly, checking each foothold with a stomp before setting her weight on it. She was halfway up when he heard the breaking of rock above him.

Autumn hadn't stumbled, but she was looking around in confusion, pressing her body against one side of the structure, her arms stretched to the other wall. Fear pelted him. He shouldn't have let her climb the peak. He should have insisted they come with a team of professionals. Something, anything to keep her out of harm's way.

Another splintering of rock and Autumn began moving away from the peak. She looked over her shoulder and shouted at him. Nathan couldn't hear her over the rush of the river's water.

Rocks were breaking above her. She hadn't stumbled. Someone was shooting at her!

Another blast and Autumn fell from the peak, disappearing into the water below. Adrenaline shot hard in his veins and he raced for the water, his rescue instincts springing to life.

Autumn was in the water. Had she been hit by a bullet? Was the river washing her downstream? He had to reach her, even if it meant putting himself in the crosshairs of a killer's arrow.

Chapter 9

Nathan pulled off his boots, threw his gun to the ground and shrugged off his pack, scanning the waterline for any sign of Autumn. She had minutes before hypothermia set in. Nathan dived into the water. It was shockingly cold and he struggled not to gasp in the icy liquid. He had to remain calm and find Autumn. He'd always been a strong swimmer, but the water pressed against him, the cold numbing his arms and legs, making him feel powerless against the force of the river.

Nathan searched for her, his arm striking something sharp. A jagged rock? Or had something struck him? A bullet from above? Fearing someone was shooting into the water, he looked more frantically for Autumn. The bottom of the river was lined with pointed rocks. If she had hit her head, she could be unconscious, breathing in water. He blotted out that thought. He had to think positively.

His lungs screaming, he peered through the murky water. A flash of green fabric caught his eye, and he reached to latch on to it. Autumn? His fingers skimmed her arm but not enough to grasp her. He needed oxygen, but he was afraid of surfacing for air and being unable to find her again. He tried again, this time making contact with her pants, slipping his fingers through her belt loops and dragging her against him. He fought the strength of the river, grateful they weren't in white-water rapids, and hauled her to the surface. He gasped in air, pulled her head out of the water and labored to shore. He shoved her onto land and then dragged himself out after her.

She was icy cold. She had been in the water less than thirty seconds, but the blue around her lips told him hypothermia would set in soon. He pressed on her chest, once, twice, and she coughed. He sat her up and water poured from her mouth. She gasped and sputtered.

His muscles trembled with cold and exhaustion. He had to get her warm and dry. Whoever had been shooting had stopped. A warning? Or was her attacker circling around for a better shot? In this position, they had no protection and nowhere to hide.

Nathan snatched up their packs, knowing seconds were precious but whatever supplies were inside might save their lives. He lifted Autumn, cradling her against him, realizing his body heat wouldn't keep her warm, but it was something.

She blinked, breathing hard. Her eyes opened. "I can walk. Put me down. Please."

Nathan set her on her feet. They had to make tracks. They ran in the opposite direction of the peak, away from the river, skidding and sliding down the hill. They needed shelter and they needed warmth. They wouldn't make it to the main trail in this condition.

Autumn slammed to a stop against a tree trunk and tugged him to the left. He didn't question her. They darted across the steep incline, the numbness in his arms and legs making him feel as if he wasn't the person in his body. A small cave came into view.

"I don't think it's inhabited," Autumn said.

After a run of bad luck, they were due for a stroke of good fortune. They approached cautiously and, finding no evidence of animals inside, they ducked inside the opening. Without the wind blowing through them, Nathan felt warmer. Autumn snatched her pack from him, spilling the contents on the ground. She seized a small wad of sticks and pulled a striker and flint from around her neck.

"We have to warm up and dry or we'll die. Find wood," she commanded. She continued to strike the flint, her skin deathly white and her fingers shaking. Sparks flew, but the wood didn't catch.

As she worked to light the tinder, he searched for dry wood, a nearly impossible task with the recent snow.

He managed to find a few pieces in the immediate area that weren't soaked through. They would have to do. Autumn had gotten a small fire started and was blowing on it, building its strength with twigs and brush and leaves.

Nathan positioned the sticks over the small fire, leaving air for the flames to breathe.

"Take your clothes off," she said and removed her shoes and her pants, then her T-shirt. He scanned her for injuries and she froze, her wet shirt still on her arms.

"Are you hurt anywhere?" he asked. He handed her his dry jacket and she pulled the rest of her shirt off and wrapped the coat around her shoulders.

She shook her head and squatted on the ground, reaching into her pack and removing a folded blanket. "I'm fine. Here," she said, handing him the cloth.

He unfolded it and wrapped it around him. It wasn't as thick as he'd have liked, but it was something. He opened it to her. "Come here. We'll share the heat."

She hesitated only a moment and then opened the jacket to him. They readjusted the few dry clothes they had, his jacket warming their upper bodies, the blanket wrapped around their legs, putting them in an intimate position, chest to chest, thigh to thigh.

Autumn shifted, her soft skin brushing against him. "I was afraid he would hit me and I dropped from the peak into the water."

Were he not half-numb from the icy water and the frigid air, he would have gotten embarrassingly excited. They'd been shot at and nearly frozen to death. The last thing on his mind should be how good she felt pressed against him.

"Did you see who it was?" he asked.

"No. But he was shooting arrows at me. I saw one where it bounced off the rock and tumbled into the water."

Arrows, as he'd feared. The Huntsman's weapon of choice.

They huddled near the fire, teeth chattering. Naked in thirty-degree weather wasn't good, but wet and naked was a far more dangerous option.

"Whoever was chasing us will see the smoke," he said.

She rubbed her hands together. "It's daylight. We might get lucky. It's this, or die. Do you think he followed us?"

Nathan scanned the area but didn't see any movement through the trees. "I don't know." The shooter could be stalking them through the woods, closing in on them.

"He stopped shooting. Maybe he ran away. Did you take a shot at him?" Autumn asked.

Nathan rubbed his thighs, trying to scrub some heat into them. "Couldn't get a clean shot. I didn't see anyone. I heard rocks breaking and then saw you fall into the water."

The feeling returned to his arms. They lay in the cave, the fire growing steadily warmer and their body temperature returning to normal. She shifted, sending sparks shooting to his groin. He groaned slightly.

"I need to check the clothes. They might be dry enough to put on." Her voice was muffled against his chest.

Did she know what she was doing to him? The impact she had? Lust wound tight inside his chest.

She rolled away, depriving him of her warmth, of her body. She patted the clothes. "They're wet."

"It's cold. They'll take a long time to air-dry."

She spread them out in the sun near the fire they'd built. She scampered back and snuggled in next to him. "You are so warm," she said.

He grunted, trying to keep his cold hands and feet away from her. Her hot body wiggled against his. It took everything he had not to grasp her waist and hold her close.

He still wanted her. For all his promises to himself to behave like a professional and focus on this case and finding his sister's killer, this situation was undoing every last thread of his control.

"Why did you jump in the water?" she asked, tucking her head beneath his chin.

The answer was obvious, wasn't it? "You went in and you didn't come up."

It might have been his imagination, but her heartbeat kicked up a notch.

Autumn moved her arms, bringing them closer, resting her hands on his chest. "I thought some rock was crumbling above me and by the time I realized someone was shooting arrows at me, I was just trying to get to the ground."

"Did you tell anyone you were coming out here?"

"I didn't even tell Blaine. No one knew my plan," she said.

Nathan shifted, flexing his feet to get the blood flowing into them. "Someone is trying to warn us off this case."

The fire was to a full roar now, and inside the

cave, despite the cold rock pressed to his back with only a blanket and jacket between it and him, he was warming up.

"Truth time. Tell me the rest of the reason you came out here," Nathan said.

Autumn shifted, pushing her elbow into his rib cage. "I can't betray Blaine."

She'd said her brother didn't know she'd come out here. "You can tell me," Nathan said.

"I hoped I would find vines or arrows or a stockpile that the Huntsman used in his killings," Autumn said. "He moves along the trail, but he has a ritual that requires supplies. Does he carry everything with him? He may not, not while he's actively hunting."

"Interesting theory," Nathan said, wondering if she had caught a thread he and the FBI hadn't considered. The FBI knew the arrow shafts were hand carved, but the points were from an outdoors company, available at hundreds of hunting stores, including The Out House in town.

"Our pants should be dry. Shirts will be damp, but we should be able to hike to the car."

"I might not have found exactly what I set out to find, but I found what I was looking for. I have proof a killer is out here. Blaine is in custody and the Huntsman shot at us."

Proving it to a jury was another challenge. "We'll need those arrows. Forensics might be able to tie them to the arrows at the other scenes."

Autumn rolled off him and threw his jacket over his body. He sat up and watched her tugging on her clothes. "We need to circle back and collect them."

"Autumn, no. It's too dangerous. He's watching. He's looking for us. We'll need to come out with a team when it's safer."

The acquiescence in her eyes told him she knew he was right. "Clothes are dry enough. Let's hurry. The faster a team gets out here, the less likely the evidence will be washed away."

A strange tension built between them as Nathan and Autumn drove toward the campground. Maybe it was the cold or the danger, but they were on edge. Her name was like a litany in his brain. Arousal consumed him and he waited for her to make a move. Afraid to cross a line with her, he bided his time.

She had asked him to drive her truck and she was in the passenger seat, her feet on the dashboard. The sun was angled in through the window, casting a warm glow across her face. Every time he glanced at her, she stole his breath.

"Are you okay?" she asked.

"Fine, why?"

"You keep looking at me."

"You're something to look at," he said.

She jammed her fingers into her damp hair. "I'll bet."

Other women might need hair dryers and makeup to look amazing, but Autumn had a natural quality he found tremendously appealing. "You look great."

She slipped her hand across the console and over to his thigh. She gave him a light squeeze. Before she moved her hand away, he covered it with his and slid it higher to where his erection strained against his pants. "Do you want to start this now?"

Another light squeeze and he had his answer.

He pressed harder on the gas, pushing the vehicle as fast as the winding and narrow roads leading toward the Trail's Edge allowed.

He stopped the truck in front of her cabin and they raced up the porch to the front door. She scrabbled with her keys and he grabbed her and turned her, pressing her up against the door with his body. He kissed her and her mouth opened beneath his. The heat of her lips burned him.

He pushed her hands above her head and took the keys from her. Without breaking the kiss, he opened the door. They fumbled inside and he kicked the door closed. He spun her so her back was against the door. He needed her now.

Pulling her shirt over her head, he made quick work of undressing her. He peppered a trail of kisses down her neck, across her collarbone and down between her breasts. All his life, he'd been waiting to find someone like Autumn.

She inhaled sharply when he rubbed his hand lightly between her legs. "Nathan, please hurry." She pushed his hair away from his face, and the pleading in her eyes nearly undid him.

After removing one shoe, he stripped off his shirt and unzipped his pants. He was frantic to be inside her. Seeing her in danger had triggered something even more possessive and protective, and the safest place for her to be was in his arms.

He lifted her, holding her bottom in his hands, and

she wrapped her arms around his neck and her legs around his waist. He surged inside her, and her tightness and heat consumed him. He moved slowly for a few thrusts, and finding her wet with need, he went faster, setting into a relentless rhythm.

She wiggled her hips against him, taking him deep, making him crazy. She was right there with him. Her breaths were coming in shallow pants, and he felt his body getting tighter when rioting spasms brought him over the edge with her. His muscles felt weak, but he kissed her before releasing her. They slid to the floor and he gathered her in his lap.

"How about a shower?" she asked, her eyes closed.

He rose to his feet, still holding her in his arms, and carried her to the bathroom. He had thrown caution to the wind, and as much as he had wanted to remain focused on the case, he had lost his heart to Autumn.

Autumn waited in the interview room of the police precinct. Henry had finally arranged a meeting for Blaine and Autumn to talk.

The small windowless room was like something out of a television crime drama—scarred metal table, four mismatched folding chairs and cinder-block walls that had probably been eggshell white when painted, but that were now dull gray. The scent of sweat and cigarette smoke clung to the air.

The entire room felt cramped. Was Blaine being kept in a room like this? Or someplace worse? For someone who loved the openness of the outdoors and craved the freshness of clean air, he had to be suffocating. Autumn's stomach knotted and her heart sank. Thinking of her brother locked in a small space was difficult.

The door opened with a creak and Blaine entered, escorted by a uniformed police officer. Blaine's wrists were cuffed and he wore a bright blue jumpsuit. He looked at the floor and took a seat in one of the chairs.

Henry Summers entered a moment later, setting his leather briefcase on the table. His suit was immaculately pressed and tailored, his hair trim and neat, his face clean shaven. "Are the cuffs necessary?" he asked the officer who'd brought Blaine into the room.

The police officer nodded. "We're taking every precaution."

Autumn opened her mouth to protest, to defend her brother. He wasn't a monster and he hadn't committed those murders. Henry must have sensed she would speak and shot her a silencing look. She clamped her mouth shut. She needed to trust him. He was a good and capable lawyer.

"I feel perfectly safe with my client and his sister. Please remove the cuffs."

His voice left little room for argument, and Autumn cheered him silently.

The police officer shrugged. "Your funeral." He removed the cuffs and with a look of disgust at Blaine before fleeing the room and bolting the door behind him.

Only then did Blaine look at her.

His eyes were red rimmed, his face drawn. He looked broken, as though the fight had been driven from his soul. "Hey, Autumn."

Autumn struggled to control her emotions, feeling her chin tremble and her knees weaken. She sat, no longer caring how dirty the table and chair were. "How're you holding up?"

"Too much time to think. Can't sleep. Every time I close my eyes, I hear them describing the crimes. Crimes they say I committed."

"I know you didn't hurt anyone on the trail." Autumn reached across the table and covered her brother's hands with hers. His hands were cold and shaking. Her brother was slender, but his hands felt feeble.

Henry opened his briefcase and pulled out a thick stack of paperwork. "Your sister has some information that might help your case."

Autumn nodded and cleared her throat. "I went out to the spot near where the journal was found looking for your camp."

Blaine's eyes widened. "Did you find anything?"

"Nothing good, but while I was looking, someone shot at me. With arrows."

Henry removed a copy of the pictures the FBI had taken of the arrows found in the area from his briefcase. They had recovered a few and had sent them to the lab for testing.

Blaine lurched to his feet. "Autumn, don't go out there again." He ran a hand through his hair. "I told you it wasn't safe. Go somewhere else until the police catch this guy. Get out of town. He's dangerous. Look at what he did to those women. You look like those women. The next victim could be you."

Autumn stood. She wouldn't let anyone make her

run from her home. "I'm staying until you're found innocent. I'm not leaving."

"Did you read about the vines, like I told you?"

Autumn nodded. She'd read the chapter from *Nature's Secrets* on binding. She had it memorized. "I read it and I told Henry about it."

"Did you mention it to Nathan?" Blaine asked.

Autumn shook her head. "Not yet, but it might be a good idea. He's on our side."

Blaine groaned in frustration. "Autumn, you have to be careful. You have a track record of picking crappy men. Men who lie to you and keep secrets from you."

It was Autumn's turn to feel defensive. "If you mean what happened with Daniel, that's in the past."

Blaine punched the table. "I do mean what happened with Daniel. And what happened with Ben."

"I've learned my lesson since then. I know to be more careful."

"Do you know why I left the Trail's Edge? Do you know what happened with Daniel?" Blaine asked.

"I know you two had a fight," Autumn said.

Blaine threw up his hands. "The entire town knew Daniel was cheating on you. He was making a fool of you. While you wore that cheap ring he gave you, he was flaunting his affair," Blaine said. "I told him to stop embarrassing himself and you. He told me that he was only engaged to you because he felt sorry for you. Because of what happened with Mom, Uncle Ryan and Dad. He feels bad that we're alone."

The hurt knocked the wind from her. Daniel cheating on her wasn't new information, but the reminders of the people they had lost stung.

"I can take care of myself, Blaine. I know Daniel was wrong for me. I wasn't in that relationship for the right reasons, either. I was lonely."

"I can't trust myself, Autumn. I'm too angry about what happened with Mom, with Dad and with Daniel. I need distance and space to think."

Henry interrupted. "I don't mean to cut in, but we're on borrowed time. Can you tell me more about the vines?" Henry turned to a page in his folder.

Blaine sat down. He rubbed his temples. "Lore says that binding a person with vines prevents his or her evil nature from spreading and poisoning the trail."

Henry tapped his pen against the pad. "How do you know this?"

Blaine rolled his shoulder. "I've read everything I could about the Appalachian Trail from the time I was a child. The vines were documented in a book my father had."

"But how can we prove it wasn't Blaine using the vines?" Autumn asked. "If we present the vines as a symbol of a ritual, the judge and jury will want to know how we came to that theory. It doesn't prove Blaine's innocence." It was another piece of evidence that made Blaine appear guilty.

"I'm hopeful the crime lab will make a connection between the arrows at the scenes and the killer," Henry said. "But we need more. I need to build a solid case that the prosecutor can't twist into a conspiracy, like say, accusing your sister and Nathan of leaving those arrows to help your case."

"We didn't!" Autumn said. "Nathan would never."

Henry held up his hand in a calming gesture. "I know. But the FBI and the police need to pin these murders on someone. It helps careers and the public's sense of safety to have a suspect. I have to anticipate they'll challenge the evidence I bring."

They looked to Blaine. He sat with his elbows on the table, his head in his hands. "When I was young, Uncle Ryan took me hunting. After every kill he left a vine at the scene."

Autumn and Henry seemed to come to the same conclusion at once. Henry spoke first.

"Where is your uncle now?"

Autumn's heart fell heavily to her shoes. "We haven't seen our uncle in years. He's dropped off the map and we've presumed dead."

Creases formed around Blaine's eyes. "Autumn, I was trying to tell you before I was arrested. The vines at the scene made me think of Uncle Ryan. That book was one of his favorites. I remember him talking about it, describing nature and living harmoniously with the land."

Autumn's head throbbed. She didn't want to believe what Blaine was suggesting. The DNA test. The blood on the book didn't point to Blaine. Blaine thought it pointed to their uncle. "Are you telling me you think Uncle Ryan did this?" They hadn't seen the man in years. If he was hiking the Appalachian Trail, wouldn't he have stopped at the Trail's Edge? Wondered where their father was?

Blaine leaned back in his chair. "I don't know what to think. Dad said after Desert Storm, he wasn't right. Something happened to him overseas."

Panic made her dizzy and sick. Suddenly, the room felt too small and Autumn had trouble drawing enough oxygen into her lungs.

"A DNA test will conclusively prove I'm not the one," Blaine said.

It would also prove the DNA belonged to their uncle. "But then what? They'll start a manhunt for Uncle Ryan."

Blaine shrugged and Autumn swallowed the bile that rose in her throat.

"Why don't you get something to drink?" Henry suggested. "Take a break and let Blaine and me discuss this new information."

Autumn stood shakily and went to the door. She knocked twice and instead of the police officer opening it, Nathan did.

"You okay?" he asked.

She wasn't okay and didn't bother lying about it. "You were waiting for me?"

He nodded. "I wanted to make sure you were all right."

She drew in a trembling breath. She wasn't ready to cope with the idea that the Huntsman was her uncle any more than she was willing to accept it was Blaine. "I'll manage." She should be rejoicing that Blaine would take the DNA test, it wouldn't match and the FBI wouldn't have evidence to hold him. But thinking of her uncle made her stomach turn. "Blaine agreed to take the DNA test."

"That's good," Nathan said. He brushed a stray

lock of hair away from her face. "But the DNA found at the scene points to a relative."

Autumn jolted at his words. "I shouldn't talk to you about the case." Why was she feeling defensive about her uncle? She wanted the Huntsman stopped and he was the only other suspect. If he was the Huntsman, he'd tried to kill her.

She could have sworn she heard a growl low in his throat. "Don't shut me out. I want to help you."

"I don't need help." Didn't want help. Didn't want to admit she was in over her head.

"You look like you do." Nathan took her arm and led her farther from the interview room, away from the hustle and bustle of the precinct. Hardly anyone was paying attention to them, but Nathan didn't stop walking until they were alone, standing next to a nearly empty vending machine.

He lifted her chin, forcing her to look at him. "I know it wasn't Blaine. I know it was your uncle. I figured it out last night after we talked with Henry."

Her heart picked up its tempo. "Why are they still holding Blaine?"

"Until the DA has proof otherwise, they're keeping someone on the chopping block. It's politics. But Henry is a good lawyer. He won't let Blaine be a patsy. With the right evidence, he'll help Blaine."

Autumn wrapped her arms around her midsection, trying to hold herself together. Blaine was trapped like a caged animal and her uncle was being hunted. Had her uncle known who she was when he shot at her? She hadn't felt so alone in her life. She closed her eyes and wished she had her father to lean on. Someone to lean on whom she could trust. Then it dawned on her. She had Nathan. He wasn't the most open man, but he had been solid. If she wasn't already in love with him, she would have fallen right there with that realization.

Mustering her strength, she opened her eyes. "What can I do?"

Nathan searched her face, appearing concerned. "Can you think of any way to find your uncle? A place he used to go, an old hangout? Friends he might have been in contact with?"

She shook her head. "As a last-ditch effort, I tried to find him after my father died so he would know what had happened. I wanted him to be able to say goodbye and to come to the funeral. I asked everyone I could think of if they knew where he was. I called a few of his old war buddies. I came up empty-handed." His years of silence, and coming up empty had led her to believe he was dead.

"Then we'll have to draw him out."

Autumn rubbed her forehead where a massive headache pounded. "How? I don't have any way to lure him. He must not care about Blaine if he let Blaine get arrested as the Huntsman. He killed someone near the Trail's Edge and left boot prints in one of my cabins. He shot at me. I don't see him caring enough to seek me out to talk."

Nathan rubbed her arms. "Why do you think he went after those hikers to begin with?"

Autumn shivered and rubbed at the goose bumps that sprang up on her arms. She didn't understand how her uncle could be a serial killer. He'd been different after the war, but she remembered him as he was before his military experience took its toll on his mind—a kind, gentle man who took her and Blaine hiking. He'd told them legends of the Appalachian Trail, taught her to fish, and had treated her and Blaine as if they were his.

Her father hadn't allowed her and Blaine to be alone with their uncle when he'd returned home. Her uncle had become a different man. The urge to explain kicked up in her gut. "He's a sick man. He went to therapy after the war, but nothing helped. He became obsessed with living off the land and taking care of Mother Nature. The hikers must have done something he didn't like and he associates them with an evil he needs to contain." As bizarre as it sounded, it was her best guess.

Nathan studied her face, as if he'd find answers hidden in her eyes. "Then you think he's still on the trail."

Would he have a reason to leave? "He could be anywhere. But if I had to guess, he's still on the trail."

"He might not know about Blaine being arrested."

"Or he might not care."

Nathan inclined his head. "There has to be something important to him we can use to find him."

Autumn shook her head and tried to bring some order to her thoughts. "To be honest, Nathan, I don't know what to believe. If he's the Huntsman, he's a sick man and I don't know if he can think clearly enough to care about anyone."

Henry joined them in the hallway and Blaine was led away in cuffs. "What's the plan, Nathan?"

Nathan looked between Autumn and Henry. "We'll have to hunt for a killer."

Chapter 10

"Hi," Autumn said. She hadn't wanted to call her mother, but she wanted to tell her that Blaine was okay and would be doing better soon. Twenty seconds and then she could go back to ignoring Blythe.

"Hi, Autumn. I'm so glad you called."

Her mother sounded surprised and Autumn was almost as astonished she'd decided to call her. "Blaine was released today. You can't let anyone know. They're trying to keep it out of the media."

Her mother huffed. "They had no trouble allowing it into the media that they'd arrested a suspect. And have you heard the rumors around here? Everyone knows Blaine is the suspect."

"The FBI has another person in mind."

"Who?" her mother asked.

"Uncle Ryan."

"I see." Her mother didn't sound upset or surprised.

"You don't sound like that's shocking to you."

"It's not. I tried to talk with you about this before. Your uncle had some problems even before I left. I heard from your father a few times after he returned from Desert Storm."

"You heard from Dad?" Autumn asked. She hadn't realized her parents had been in contact after her mother had left.

"Now and then, a couple of times after your uncle disappeared."

Her mother had been a topic she and her father had never discussed. "Do you want to come by the camp today?"

"I'd love to."

Autumn's nerves tightened. Should she not have invited Blythe? She and Blaine had been carrying a grudge for a long time, but Nathan's words about his sister echoed through her thoughts. Life was short. She would probably regret not talking to her mother more than she'd regret seeing her.

"Mind if I join you?" Roger Ford asked Nathan, Autumn, Blythe and Blaine. Blaine had been released two days ago and this meal at the diner was to celebrate his freedom.

The Reed family was willfully ignoring the pointing and staring from other patrons. Nathan was proud of Autumn. She and her family had been through too much to let gossip bother her. They had chosen a quiet table near the back of the diner. It wasn't as crowded as the Wild Berry had been the time Nathan had been there. Despite whispers, the Reed family seemed in high spirits.

Nathan looked up from his hamburger. "Please, sit down."

Nathan couldn't put his finger on the precise moment it had happened, but he and Ford had formed a shaky trust. They were sharing information, and though that was hard for an inflexible agent like Ford, he'd bent his rules to include Nathan. They would never be friends, but a working professional relationship was best for both of them.

Ford sat next to Blythe. "We've been doing research on Ryan Reed."

Blythe stopped eating and turned to face Ford. Genuine fear shone in her eyes. She waited for Ford to continue.

"We've pulled his service records. We've spoken to psychologists who counseled him after he returned to the United States. The diagnosis is severe post-traumatic stress disorder."

Nathan knew people who had behaved out of character when they were suffering from PTSD. Why was Ford sharing this with them? Though he might have been doing so in the spirit of cooperation, Nathan guessed there was more to it. What did Ford want from the Reed family?

Ford ordered a cup of coffee from the waitress who came to their table and waited for her to leave before continuing. "We believe he is still in the area, likely keeping an eye on the case. He has a fascination with his crimes and he wants his message delivered to as many people as possible."

It fit the profile Nathan had sketched of Ryan Reed. Together with the words Ryan had scrawled in the journal, they were developing a clearer picture of the man's psyche, enough to understand what made him tick.

"We're looking for a way to draw him out. He's too smart to fall for an obvious trap. We need something to dangle out to him that he can't resist," Ford said.

"The newspaper didn't work? No sign of him?" Autumn asked.

The FBI had left a phony newspaper in the shelter closest to the Trail's Edge with an article inside about Blaine's arrest, stating he had been released on bail, and including a quote from Autumn indicating she planned to sell the Trail's Edge to pay for her brother's legal fees.

From what Autumn had said, that wasn't far from the truth.

The FBI had been staking their bets that if Ryan Reed believed the land that had once belonged to his father and then to his brother was being sold to the highest bidder, he would confront Autumn.

Agitating him was a calculated risk. Sending him over the edge and out to hunt for more victims wasn't their intent. Until Ryan Reed was in custody, Nathan wasn't letting Autumn out of his sight.

Autumn's mother touched Ford's sleeve. "Special Agent Ford, you could use me."

Ford stared at Blythe a few beats before speaking.

"Use you to do what?" he asked, his voice sounding gruff.

"Ryan Reed hates me. He holds me responsible for the trouble we've had at the Trail's Edge and for getting between him and my ex-husband. If I'm around, perhaps he won't be able to resist the urge to try to kill me."

"Mom, you can't put yourself in the line of danger. You need to stay somewhere else until he is caught," Autumn said.

"If he sees you, he could fly into a rage," Blaine said. "You know Dad and Uncle Ryan had short tempers."

"If he flies into a rage, he's more likely to make a mistake, like stepping out of the shadows into the sun, into a place where the FBI can catch him," Blythe said. Blythe's flair for the dramatic had grown on Nathan, and he believed Autumn was enjoying being with her mother, too.

"We're not sure what triggers him to kill," Ford said. "We have female agents in the backcountry trying to entice him. So far, he's not shown his face. Maybe we have to raise the stakes, make the trap impossible to resist."

"No," Autumn said. "You are not using our mother."

"I agree," Blaine said. "Too dangerous and he's too unpredictable."

"We'll be there. We'll be around and close in before he gets near Blythe," Ford said.

Autumn appeared uneasy and Nathan seconded her feelings. Ryan Reed was a trained military man and he was capable and savvy in the wilderness. They were working from a position of weakness. If anything happened to Autumn or her mother, Nathan wouldn't forgive himself. "We can have an agent stand in as Blythe."

"No time to find someone who looks enough like her. He could be watching and know what to expect. He could move on to the next location or the next victim. I want to keep him rooted here," Ford said.

"I can do this," Blythe said, flattening her hands against the tabletop.

"I think you are underestimating how dangerous Ryan Reed is," Nathan said.

"He's sick," Blaine said.

"Which makes him unstable," Autumn said. She turned to her mother. "You don't have to do this. You don't have to prove anything or try to make amends to Blaine and me for the past by putting your life at risk."

"The faster we move forward, the faster we'll get a killer off the trail," Ford said.

Pressure was getting the better of Ford. The FBI didn't use civilians except in extreme cases. A dangerous killer might be considered extreme, but adding to the body count in a rush to find him wasn't a reasonable risk.

"It's not for anyone else to decide," Blythe said. "I will do this. I can do this." She tipped her chin proudly. If she had looked at the faces of her children, likely the very people she was trying to impress, she wouldn't have been so sure. Blaine appeared sickened and Autumn seemed afraid.

Ford stood from the table. "I'll meet with my team to discuss the details and I'll be in touch soon."

* * *

Autumn was waiting for an arrow to slice through the air and directly into her mother's chest. Every snapping of a stick or crunch of leaves and she jumped.

Nathan set his hand on her lower back. He was adding to her nervous energy. He was sticking close to her. If her uncle had been watching them since Nathan had been staying with her, his presence now was less suspicious than that of the other agents who were positioned around the campground.

"What if something happened to him? What if he's already dead?" Autumn asked.

"I don't think he's dead," Nathan said. "We'll take each day one at a time, and we'll stop him before he hurts himself or anyone else."

"You're the first person who's mentioned not hurting him," Autumn said. "Ford and the FBI don't seem to care if Uncle Ryan dies."

Nathan's eyes were soft as he regarded her. "I care, Autumn. I know he means something to you."

"He killed your sister." They were hard words to speak. Her uncle had killed someone whom Nathan loved. Could he ever forget that? Would some part of him always harbor resentment for her? "I'm sorry," she said, knowing the words didn't make things right, but feeling that they needed to be spoken. Her uncle may not be capable of apologizing or seeing what he did as wrong.

Nathan took a deep breath. "I don't blame you for the mistakes your uncle has made." He gathered her against him. "I know you think we're on opposing sides, but I need you to know that we're on the same team."

Autumn looked up. "I feel like it's been a long time since someone has been on my side. Really on my side. Through everything and unconditionally." Blaine disappeared when life got rough, her mother had walked away and Daniel had cheated on her. Nathan was proving to be different, unwavering. He'd been constant and steady. Her love for him surged and she wondered if he could read it on her face. She wanted to hide it. After all, once her uncle was caught, Nathan would leave. Their relationship would be over.

She had long known it was the case, but standing at the end of something that mattered to her, it was hard for her to let the relationship go.

Nathan kissed the top of her head. "I'm on your side and I'll prove it to you. I will be here for you through all this. I won't walk away and I won't let you down. I promise."

Instead of immediately dismissing the promise as a well-intentioned lie, Autumn chose to believe him.

Autumn heard her mother shout. She and Nathan spun and raced in the direction of the cabin where Blythe was staying. Nathan had his gun drawn. Autumn's heart raced. Had the FBI captured her uncle?

"Stay away!" Blythe said from the porch of cabin nine. She was kicking her legs as she was dragged out of her cabin by a man. Her uncle? It was hard to see.

Though she couldn't see them, Autumn knew FBI agents were close.

Autumn ran toward her mother. Her uncle was

pressing a gun to her mother's head and holding her in front of him as he pulled her away.

He looked different from what she'd remembered. Years older, years that had not been kind to him. Scraggly hair and long beard, dirty, worn, mismatched clothes and boots that looked black with grime.

"Back away. Do not come close to me or I will kill her. This is her fault!" Ryan Reed said.

Blaine stood on the porch of his cabin, appearing shocked. This was what they had been waiting for, but it somehow seemed to be going wrong. Why hadn't the agents swooped in to save her mother?

"If anyone follows me, I will kill her," Uncle Ryan said.

"Uncle Ryan! Stop! Don't do this!" Autumn shouted.

He paused for a moment, scrutinizing her. Autumn felt as if he was peering through her. Did he realize who she was?

"She did this! She is causing uncleanliness on the trail!"

Autumn advanced, but Nathan's hand across her chest stopped her. "He's unstable. He'll kill her. Don't get closer." The words were spoken quietly under his breath. "He wants his ritual and we will have our chance to save her."

"What do you think will happen if he drags her into the woods and disappears?" Autumn asked.

Her uncle was moving with her mother farther away. The FBI would swarm at any moment. They would capture her uncle and rescue her mother. Were they circling around waiting to close in?

"Someone do something. Please," Autumn said.

"They won't stop him until they can safely secure the hostage and be sure he doesn't kill her."

"She's not a hostage, she's my mother," Autumn said.

"Uncle Ryan, it's me. Autumn," she said, trying to break into whatever train of thought her uncle was on and stop him. How had he eluded the FBI? Was he so driven by his anger he didn't care this had been a trap?

He stopped moving for a few beats. He said nothing. Out of the corner of her eye, she saw Blaine step down the stairs of his cabin.

"This is my land," her uncle shouted. "I am duty bound to protect it."

"Please stop. Let's talk about this. We're family," Autumn said.

"Uncle Ryan, please don't run away," Blaine said.

Her uncle looked between the two of them and his posture relaxed. They'd gotten through to him. But just as fast, he tensed and pulled their mother away. After a few seconds, they had disappeared from view.

Autumn pushed past Nathan and scanned the tree line for them. Thor came to her side, whimpering as if sensing her devastation.

Roger Ford jogged over to them, speaking into a walkie-talkie. "All units respond. The suspect has broken the perimeter with a hostage. Proceed with extreme caution."

"Why didn't you stop him?" Autumn asked, grabbing the front of Roger Ford's jacket. He had promised her mother would be safe. Being taken by a madman did not seem safe.

"He had a hostage. We couldn't easily stop him. We were afraid he would shoot," Ford said.

How did her uncle get close enough to her mother to grab her? No time for questions or excuses. She had to get her mother back.

"Blaine, I need you," she called. Her brother ran over, regarding Ford warily.

"Blaine, we've got to track him. Get your pack. Let's go," Autumn said. If they had to track her uncle and her mother all night, that's what they would do. They had to bring their mother home safely. Her mother had recently become a part of their lives and Autumn wanted to see if they could rebuild their relationship.

Ford grabbed her hand to stop her. "You cannot go on the trail. We have this covered."

Anger tore through her. "You do not have this covered. You allowed a murderer to kidnap my mother. You're not going to find them. No one knows these trails as well as Blaine and I do. No one knows our uncle how we do. We're going and we're not coming back until my mom is safe."

Ford let out a heavy sigh. "I'll gather my team to escort you."

"Escort me?" Autumn was already heading in the direction of her cabin for her pack. Ford followed her. "I don't need an escort. The more people who attempt to come with me, the more likely my uncle will keep running or outright kill my mother if he feels trapped." Thor ran to her side and trotted beside her.

Autumn grabbed her pack and put it on her shoulders. Nathan did the same with his. It was as if they were acting as one team, together. She hadn't needed to tell him her plan.

Ford raised his eyebrows. "What are you planning to do if you find him? Ask him nicely to stop?"

Autumn snorted. "I've had a preview of what I'm dealing with. I'll have Nathan with me. You had a chance to handle this situation and you failed. It's my turn." They left her cabin and she closed the door behind her.

"I'll come with you," Ford said.

Nathan ignored him. "If we don't hurry, he'll disappear."

Ford wouldn't last thirty minutes at the pace she'd set. "I'm not slowing down for anyone." She was already jogging in the direction she had seen her uncle and mother disappear. Blaine and Nathan were with her, Ford behind them.

The ground was too frozen, the snow too slicked over, for her uncle to have left a good set of tracks.

"The earth is solid," Blaine said, echoing her thoughts.

"Branches, broken brush," she said, thinking aloud. Every footstep into the backcountry left a visible albeit temporary indicator that someone had been there.

"Rock Valley?" Nathan asked.

"Where the bears were living? If he's taken her there, he has a death wish," Autumn said.

Nathan said nothing, but his look spoke volumes. Her uncle had a death wish and he had the person he hated most with him. Death was exactly what he wanted.

Autumn took the lead on their pursuit. She wouldn't let her mother die. Her mother had just returned to her life. While they didn't have much of a relationship, Autumn had hope of something for the future. Phone calls. Emails. Maybe a visit now and then.

For the first time in a long time, Autumn didn't feel alone. Despite her immediate fear, Nathan being at her side helped manage that feeling and made it possible to do what she did best: hike the trail.

Thor stayed at her side. He wasn't a tracking dog, but she trusted his instincts. He knew to remain quiet and not alert her uncle that they were closing in.

They were following the markings, the depressed leaves, the broken underbrush and then nothing. It seemed as if her uncle's and her mother's tracks had disappeared. Autumn looked up slowly, half-scared she would see her mother swinging from a tree.

Blaine, Nathan and Ford followed her gaze. They breathed a silent sigh of relief that the tree line was bare of bodies.

Autumn pointed to the last place where she'd seen evidence someone was on the trail. She pointed left and Blaine pointed right. Ford followed Blaine and Nathan and Thor followed her. If they split up, they could cover more ground. She moved slowly, looking for anything to give her an idea of the direction.

A crow caw, one that Autumn recognized as Blaine's bird whistle, sounded in the air. She scanned for Blaine and saw him gesture toward him. He'd found something. She, Nathan and Thor closed the distance.

Blaine pointed to some broken branches on a sapling. At her nod, they continued in that direction.

As children, she and Blaine had been outside with her uncle dozens, if not hundreds of times. He had favorite hunting areas, bird-watching posts, fishing holes and climbing sites. He could have taken their mother to any of those.

Autumn heard the distinct sounds of fire. She sniffed the air, turning, getting a sense of direction. She mouthed the word *fire* to Nathan.

Was her uncle starting his ritual or were they already too late?

Watching Autumn and Blaine was fascinating. They were one with nature, moving purposefully and carefully, and finding signs to help them track their mother and their uncle.

They were close enough to see movement in the trees, but from this distance, it was difficult to make out what was happening. Ryan Reed had built a fire and he was moving around in a small clearing.

Where was Autumn's mother? Had she been scared into silence? Or was she dead?

Nathan hadn't heard a gunshot, but despite the gun he had threatened Blythe Reed with, bullets weren't the Huntsman's preferred method of killing. He could have cut her throat, stabbed her or shot her with an arrow.

Nathan stayed close to Autumn as they approached, wanting to protect her. He gestured to Ford to circle around counterclockwise. He and Autumn would travel the other way. When they were closer, they would decide how to proceed.

Autumn stopped behind a downed tree. It was the nearest to the clearing and provided a good view of Ryan Reed. Nathan couldn't see Blaine or Ford and assumed they had also found a place to hide and watch.

Autumn gestured for Thor to be quiet and still. He obeyed her and lay on the ground.

Autumn moved closer and Nathan grabbed her hand and shook his head. *No*, he mouthed.

She wasn't walking into the Huntsman's campground unattended. They didn't know how many weapons they were dealing with or where Autumn's mother was.

A noise came from the camp, a low song, rising in a melodic tempo. He and Autumn exchanged looks. The Huntsman was beginning his ritual.

Autumn motioned that she was moving closer. She ignored his gesture to stay where she was.

Nathan followed her. The leaves seemed to crunch more loudly and it seemed harder to remain unseen. The birds were silent in the trees and only the rustling of leaves and Ryan Reed's eerie song filled his ears.

Autumn clamped her hand over her mouth. She turned to him, her eyes wild with fear, and pointed. From this vantage point, he could see Blythe tied to a tree by vines. He didn't see arrows protruding from her chest, but she wasn't moving, either.

Were Ford and Blaine seeing this?

Should he step in? Before he could think, Ryan Reed did something that didn't give him a choice.

He picked up a bow from the ground and slid an arrow into it.

Ryan Reed pivoted, still singing, and aimed the arrow at Blythe.

"Uncle Ryan!" Autumn called.

The arrow was released from the bow. Autumn ran forward, the sound of leaves against her feet and the ground causing her uncle to turn in her direction.

Nathan ducked out of view. He was a threat Ryan Reed may not respond well to. Nathan saw the arrow in a tree behind Blythe. Thanks to Autumn's interruption, the arrow had missed its mark.

Ryan Reed seemed fixated on Autumn. Nathan moved closer, knowing he couldn't reveal himself, but needing to be in range to protect Autumn. He would open fire on Ryan Reed when he had a clear shot. He had his gun at his hip and firing would protect Autumn and Blythe, and claim justice for Colleen.

Revenge tasted sweet and Nathan imagined unholstering his gun, aiming and firing his weapon at Ryan Reed and killing him. The finality of that action swept relief over him. He never aimed his gun unless he was prepared to use it.

He pictured his sister when she was younger, a free spirit, full of dreams and happiness. The memories of her with her family, at picnics and pool parties, merged into an emotional haze that clouded his vision. His throat grew tight with anger and grief. Colleen should have had a good life. The alcohol had robbed her of happiness and then Ryan Reed had robbed her of her life.

Nathan reached for his gun and withdrew it. As he

leveled it at Ryan Reed, he caught sight of Autumn. She had her hands in the air and was saying something to her uncle. Nathan lowered his weapon, thinking of how she would feel if he killed her uncle. Not relieved or happy. She would be devastated. He had seen her face when she'd realized her uncle was the Huntsman. This was a nightmare for her.

It had been his intention to keep Autumn safe. She had been let down too many times in the past and he would be a man who kept his promises, who did as he said and who cherished and loved her.

Love. A word he didn't use freely, but in this moment, he knew without a doubt that he loved Autumn. He kept his gun in his hand and moved to where he could hear.

"You're not Autumn. She's just a little girl." Ryan Reed's voice echoed confusion.

He didn't resume singing and he sounded more lucid than he had at the Trail's Edge campground. He reached for another arrow and slid it into the bow.

"It is me. Look," Autumn said and knelt. She rolled up her pant leg and pivoted, showing him the back of her calf. "See? I have the scar from when I fell off Pike's Cliff that summer we went hiking. It still twinges sometimes in the winter."

Her uncle blinked at her. He did not lower his arrow.

"Why don't we get something hot to drink? It's freezing out here," Autumn said.

Her technique was good. She wasn't demanding he put down his weapon. Nathan didn't like that she was so close to the Huntsman. Uncle or not, he was a killer, he was unpredictable and he was irrational. If he shot Ryan Reed in the leg or arm, would he release the arrow? It could hit Autumn or Blythe.

"Something to drink? Should you be out here now? Your father will want you home."

Autumn's shoulders slumped. "No, Uncle Ryan. We're okay. Let's go home together." Her voice cracked.

Nathan could see her struggling. Her uncle was a man she cared for deeply. He was also a sick man who needed help. Resolving those two things in her mind had to be hard for her.

A groan sounded from the tree. Blythe was waking up. Her head lolled back and forth. When she lifted her head, she started screaming.

Her scream jolted through Ryan Reed. His body tensed and he swung his arrow in her direction. "Shut up! Shut up!"

"Autumn, run. Get out of here. He'll kill us both," Blythe shouted.

Ryan Reed began singing again, the same low song. A crackling of leaves from the other side of the clearing.

"Who's there?" Ryan Reed called in the direction of Blaine and Roger Ford. "Show yourself." His arms were shaking under the weight of the bow and arrow. Could the arrow slip through his fingers?

Blaine stepped out and raised his hands. "Uncle Ryan, it's me."

Though Nathan mentally chided Ford for letting Blaine show himself, it might have been the better option. Ford was a stranger to Ryan Reed.

"Blaine? What are you doing out here? Did you follow Autumn? She doesn't stay on the campground when she's supposed to. Always running out here and getting lost." He laughed.

"I came out to bring you two home," Blaine said.

Autumn and Blaine moved closer. Ryan Reed watched them, a dazed expression on his face. When they were close, Autumn slipped her arm around her uncle's shoulder and pressed lightly on his arms. Blaine was blocking the sight of Blythe.

Ryan Reed lowered his bow and dropped the arrow.

"Hands on your head, now!" Roger Ford's voice broke the moment.

Autumn and Blaine had had it under control! Why was Ford interrupting?

Ryan Reed grabbed Autumn and held her in front of him. He pulled a knife and pressed it against her throat. "Get away from us. I'll kill her. Don't make me kill a child, but I will to protect her. You can't take us alive."

Autumn was walking with her uncle as he re-treated, her legs scrambling beneath her. If she slipped, the knife would slice her throat.

Ford charged forward and Nathan read disaster. Autumn would be killed because of a mistake in timing.

Nathan stepped out. He didn't have a plan. He was only acting on the woman he loved being in trouble. Ryan Reed was a war vet. He'd spent time in a war zone. He'd witnessed violent, terrible things. If he was somehow back in that time, his brain caught somewhere between the present and the past, Nathan needed to play into his fantasy world and by his rules.

"Blaine, I got you covered!" he said.

Everyone looked in Nathan's direction, confusion on their faces.

"Autumn, Ryan, Blaine, get out of here," Nathan said, waving his gun and pointing it in Ford's direction.

"Uncle Ryan, come on, we have to run!" Autumn said.

"Who is that?" Ryan Reed asked.

"A friend," Autumn said. "We can trust him. He'll cover us while we escape."

"No, he's with the enemy."

Though it went against his training, Nathan turned his back on Autumn and Ryan and held his gun on Ford. "Go! Go! Get out of here!" he said.

"Now's our chance," Autumn said. "Run!"

Nathan turned to see Ryan Reed holding Autumn's hand as they fled. Nathan pursued him, standing in Ford's line of fire. Ford was a good shot, but he wouldn't attempt it if he couldn't get one clean.

Nathan tackled Ryan Reed from behind, pulling him down. Autumn tumbled to the ground next to him.

"Autumn, are you okay?" Nathan asked.

"I'm fine."

Her uncle moaned. Nathan climbed off him and Ford rolled him over and secured his hands with a pair of cuffs.

Nathan looked at the man who'd killed his sister. He didn't feel anger. He felt unabated sadness and grief for his loved one who had died. Grief at losing her and contentment that his family would have closure. He wasn't sure how he would explain why Colleen had died. He wasn't sure there was any way to explain it. But he could call his mother and tell her that no more families would suffer at the hands of the man who had killed Colleen.

Autumn touched his shoulder. "Thank you for not letting Ford shoot him. Thank you for knowing that helping my uncle is important to me."

Nathan hadn't been sure how he would react when he found Colleen's killer. But in the moment, with the woman he loved near, anger had not been his primary emotion. "I didn't want revenge. I wanted to find Colleen's killer." Looking at Autumn, the love he felt for her surged inside him and warmed him as nothing else could.

Ford called his team to the scene to collect evidence. Blaine untied their mother and they embraced. Autumn joined them, wrapping her arms around her brother and her mother. They were silent on the walk back to the Trail's Edge.

Ryan Reed was put in the back of a squad car.

"I guess this is when we say goodbye?" Autumn asked.

Knowing what she meant, Nathan shook his head. "I will say goodbye to my sister and let my family heal, but I won't say goodbye to you. I need you, Autumn. I need you in my life."

Autumn smiled. "In what way do you want me? As your trail guide?"

"I love you, Autumn. I want you in every way I can have you. Trail guide, lover and best friend. You'll be there for me when I get lost and I promise to do the same for you."

"I'm very good at getting lost. It might take up a lot of your time," Autumn said.

"That's fine with me because I plan to spend as much of it as I can with you."

He lowered his mouth to hers. He had never felt more at home.

* * * * *

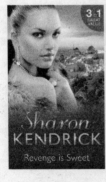  

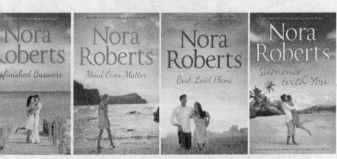
_ST_11

MILLS & BOON®

It's Got to be Perfect

IT'S GOT TO BE *Perfect*

UNCORRECTED PROOF COPY

HALEY HILL

* cover in development

When Ellie Rigby throws her three-carat engagement ring into the gutter, she is certain of only one thing. She has yet to know true love!

Fed up with disastrous internet dates and conflicting advice from her friends, Ellie decides to take matters into her own hands. Starting a dating agency, Ellie becomes an expert in love. Well, that is until a match with one of her clients, charming, infuriating Nick, has her questioning everything she's ever thought about love…

Order yours today at
www.millsandboon.co.uk

MILLS & BOON®

The Thirty List

* cover in development

At thirty, Rachel has slid down every ladder she has ever climbed. Jobless, broke and ditched by her husband, she has to move in with grumpy Patrick and his four-year-old son.

Patrick is also getting divorced, so to cheer themselves up the two decide to draw up bucket lists. Soon they are learning to tango, abseiling, trying stand-up comedy and more. But, as she gets closer to Patrick, Rachel wonders if their relationship is too good to be true…

Order yours today at
www.millsandboon.co.uk/Thethirtylist